Joseph Rogers, James E. T. Rogers

Joseph Rogers, M. D.

Reminiscences of a workhouse medical officer

Joseph Rogers, James E. T. Rogers

Joseph Rogers, M. D.
Reminiscences of a workhouse medical officer

ISBN/EAN: 9783337426781

Printed in Europe, USA, Canada, Australia, Japan

Cover: Foto ©Andreas Hilbeck / pixelio.de

More available books at **www.hansebooks.com**

REMINISCENCES OF A
WORKHOUSE MEDICAL OFFICER.

JOSEPH ROGERS, M.D.

REMINISCENCES OF A WORKHOUSE

MEDICAL OFFICER

EDITED, WITH A PREFACE

BY

PROF. THOROLD ROGERS

London

T. FISHER UNWIN

26 PATERNOSTER SQUARE

MDCCCLXXXIX

PREFACE.

THE author of the brief narrative which I have
edited, and have seen through the Press, passed
away before the printing of his work was completed. What he wrote was composed under the
presence of a mortal disease, the issue of which he
clearly foresaw. But he was unwilling to quit life
without leaving behind him some record of the evils
with which he grappled, of the obstacles which he
had to encounter, and of the changes which he strove
to effect. He might indeed, and with the acquiescence
of the profession which he honoured, have claimed
the credit of those great reforms in the treatment of
the sick poor, and in the status of his professional
brethren, to which the labours of his life were directed;
but he has preferred to give a narrative of his experiences, and to leave his reputation to the members
of the great and beneficent calling which he followed,

and to those among the public who were cognizant of his zeal and perseverance.

My late brother was the descendant of three gene-rations of medical practitioners, who, from the first quarter of the eighteenth century, plied the art of tending and healing the sick down to the last quarter of the nineteenth, for his elder brother relinquished his practice only about ten or a dozen years ago. And this was in the same locality. But soon after my brother Joseph was qualified he went to London ; and very speedily after he came to London he began the labour of his life—the reform, namely, of the medical relief accorded to the indigent poor. To this he surrendered the prospects of professional success and fortune—prospects which his professional abilities might have made certainties ; for this he sacrificed popularity, health, and all that a vigorous constitution might have assured to him. He literally wore him-self out by his labours.

It is infinitely more difficult for a medical practi-tioner to urge necessary but unpopular reforms than it is for any other professional person to do so. The physician believes that he can succeed only by raising no prejudice against himself. He is always tempted to be neutral, when partizanship may seem likely to imperil his interests. There are no safe prizes to be

won in the one profession which every one allows to
be beneficent, whatever may be thought of other
professions. By a code of honour which is rigidly
adhered to, the process of a physician's treatment
cannot be kept to himself. By an equally rigid rule,
the confidences reposed in him are as sacred as the
secrets of the confessional. It is no easy matter to
win position and fortune in a calling which is regulated
by the strictest rules of professional honour. It seems
easy to imperil the most carefully acquired reputation
by running counter to obstinacy and prejudice. A
medical man has every motive to avoid hostile
criticism. If he determines on doing that which is
unpopular, the risks which he runs are far greater
than those of any other person. Now all this was
encountered by my brother's action, and he never was
allowed to forget that he had to encounter it. He
had to reckon with sordid London vestrymen, perhaps the worst class of men with whom honest people
have to deal, and with the officials of the Poor Law
Board, who were determined, as far as possible, with
rare exceptions, to shirk all responsibility. In the
pages of this volume he shows plainly what were the
obstacles to his endeavours. As might be expected
from an honest man, who never counted the odds
against him when he was convinced that he was in

the right, his original manuscript commented, with
no little indignation, on the persons who thwarted
his efforts, and would have baffled his ends. But it
is entirely superfluous to stigmatize such people;
and I have excised these just but unnecessary judg-
ments. It is sufficient that the reappearance of such
persons has been made improbable, if not impossible.

The new Poor Law of 1834 was probably a necessary measure ; but it was suddenly and frightfully
harsh. The Whigs carried it, in deference to a
particular school of economists, now happily, I
trust, extinct. It was exceedingly and reasonably
unpopular. The working classes had been im-
poverished in the country by the enclosure of the
common lands, and in both town and country by
restraints on the right of combination with the object
of raising wages. But they had always been assured
that the maintenance of the poor was a first charge
on the land, and that it must be satisfied, and should
be, before the profit of the enclosure should accrue to
the landlord. When the plunder was completed the
other side of the bargain was repudiated, and the
easy-going system of the old method of parochial
relief was abandoned for the new and severe provisions of the new departure. I am old enough to

remember the indignation which the change aroused. I am sure that indignation and resentment against the new Poor Law had a good deal to do with the political reverses of 1841, and the entire destruction of the popularity which the Whigs had achieved by the Reform Act of 1832.

It is true that the Act established a central authority which should control the action of the new Boards of Guardians. But these persons were by no means willing to check the machinery which they had erected. If the legislation of 1834 was distasteful to the country, they were resolved to limit their responsibility to the change which they had themselves made in the law, and to avoid further odium. The case of the permanent officials, who are really the departments of state, was much simpler. They wished to earn their salaries with as little trouble as possible, just as they wish now, and always will wish. To importunately call attention to the cruelties practised under the new system was to diminish their ease, to give them trouble, and such action must be resented and discouraged. In my personal experience of the permanent staff of the Poor Law Board I have met with officials who were persistently resolved not to give themselves, if they could help it, the trouble to rectify evils which were brought before their notice

by the Board of Guardians to which I belonged, if
they could in any way find a dilatory plea.

Of course a reformer is always odious to a large
number of persons. There are people who profit by
the abuse or malpractice which he tries to remove,
and such persons are naturally indignant at his
meddlesomeness. There are others who acquiesce in
the existing state of things from sheer indolence, and
are impatient only at being disturbed. There are
others who hold that all reforms cost money, and are
alarmed at the expense which they may incur; while
the fact is that all reforms which are wise and true
save money in the end and diminish cost. To build
a proper hospital for the sick poor, to supply it with
properly qualified nurses, and sufficiently paid medical
officers, one must incur initial expense, which is in
the end constantly overpaid by eventual economies.
My late brother constantly predicted that the changes
which he counselled would relieve the rates in the
end, and his prediction was constantly verified. The
reader will find these facts illustrated in the pages
which follow. A genuine reform is a sensible saving.
But even if this result did not follow, the system
which he found and attacked was a scandal to
humanity and a dishonour to civilization. The
London vestrymen did not see this; but Londoners

have found out at last that the average vestryman is
unteachable and incurable.

The courage which will attack abuses such as were
found in those workhouses near forty years ago is
rare indeed. The person who undertakes the unpopular task has to come to close quarters with such
Guardians of the Poor as are described below, and
such government officials as are resolved to wink at
abuses. Not but that, even in the worst days, the
Poor Law Board and the Local Government Board
were of great public service. They could be squeezed
in Parliament. A judicious and temperate question
has often discomfited the most corrupt official, and
stirred the most lethargic. I am pretty sure that
nearly all the reforms which have been achieved in the
administration of the law for the relief of the poor,
have been derived from persistent questioning in the
House of Commons. Much indeed remains to be
done, but much has been done ; and my brother was
exceedingly fortunate during his lifelong efforts in
the advocates which he obtained among Members of
the House.

It must not be forgotten that a medical reformer is
apt at first to be unpopular with his brethren, or at
least to be discouraged by them. The more fortunate
members of the profession are apt to feel a serene

indifference to the purposes which he avows. I do
not think that the reform of those evils with which
my brother concerned himself has had much assistance from the more wealthy and influential among the
physicians. As Arnold said, contemptuously and justly,
of Isaac Walton, that "he fished through the civil
wars," so these good people held, as a rule, severely
aloof from the struggle. To the poorer members of
the profession, who had to make every effort for a
livelihood, and were constrained to give their services
for nominal sums in order to get a status in their
calling, it seemed more practical to get them better
pay and not to give offence. In the end this was
part of the result of my brother's labours. He was
able to assert, towards the close of his active career,
that he had added £18,000 a year to the incomes of
the Poor Law medical officers in the Metropolis, and
to allege that the change, with others, had saved ten
times that amount in the Metropolitan rates. I am
convinced—having once been a Guardian of the Poor
in the city where I live—that the adoption of the
policy which he recommended has effected a still
greater saving.

   The first reform which my brother undertook, per-
severed in, and speedily saw achieved, was the prohibition of intramural interment. He had good reason

to make efforts in this direction, for he had abundant
evidence of what came from the old practice in the
experience of his profession. Most of the Metropolitan clergy were very hostile to this reform, and
for obvious reasons. But it came gradually, finally,
and thoroughly. The present generation in London
has a very inadequate conception of the abominations, in the midst of which their fathers and
mothers lived, and not a few of them were born.
The abandonment of intramural interment, and the
drainage of London, imperfect as the latter is, have
turned one of the unhealthiest cities in the civilized
world into one of the healthiest. One of the first
churchyards closed was that of St. Anne's, Soho, the
parish in which my brother lived for many years.

His next efforts were directed towards obtaining
a mortuary in the parish. Every one admits how
serious are the evils of overcrowding, and how
difficult a problem it is to supply the London poor
with decent homes at moderate rents. A century
ago, as I know very well, house-rent, even in London,
took a small part of the workman's scanty earnings;
now his earnings are sometimes very little better
than they were a century ago, and his rent absorbs
from a fourth to a half of what he earns in poorly
paid labour. At best his home is crowded and un-

healthy enough, but when death occurs in the
family the condition of things is intolerable. It
cost my brother three or four years of incessant
effort and pleading to obtain this concession from
the Vestry of St. Anne, and for a long time this was
the only London parish which made this necessary
provision.

The next mischief which he attacked was the
window tax. His experience as a physician proved
to him that lack of light and air intensified disease
and rendered recovery difficult. There was a plea
for the window tax. It seemed to bring a fair charge
on large houses, which an assessed tax notoriously
does not. In assailing the tax his principal helper
was Lord Duncan, at that time one of the Metropolitan Members. The tax went at last in 1851.
The repeal of this tax took nearly twenty years'
agitation, the first physician who attacked it on
sanitary grounds having been Dr. Southwood Smith.

My brother commenced his practice in London
in 1844. In 1855 there was a serious visitation of
cholera in St. Anne's, Soho, and he became a super-
numerary medical officer in the district. Cholera
had a very serious effect on his private practice, as
he states himself, and nearly twelve years after he
had taken up his abode in London, he concluded to

become a candidate for the function of medical officer
to the Strand Workhouse. He was to receive a
stipend of £50 a year, and find all medicines for the
sick. It may be doubted whether he knew what he
was undertaking : certainly they who appointed him
and the officials who confirmed his appointment at
the Poor Law Board had no conception of what they
were doing. The character of his duties, and a
description of the place in which he had to perform
these duties is to be found at the commencement of
his narrative. For its condition it is hard to decide
whether the Guardians of the time, or the central
authority were most to blame.

The Strand appointment was the beginning of those
systematic labours on behalf of the sick poor and
the medical profession which thenceforward became
the principal business of his life, to which he sacrificed such leisure as he had, health, and money
which he could ill spare. He gave also what was
more important—undaunted courage, and accurate
information. Thus in 1861 he gave evidence before
a Select Committee of the House of Commons, on
the subject of the supply of drugs in Workhouse
infirmaries, such a supply being as essentially part
of the Guardians' duty as the purchase of food
and clothing are. His views were adopted by the

Committee and pressed on the Department. What he advocated was the germ of the Workhouse infirmary.

During the last few months of his life he lived at Hampstead, in the hope that the air might help him. At the back of his new home there was built one of those great hospitals for the sick poor which it was the principal aim of his labours to render general, and to see constructed in such a way as would give the fairest prospect of recovery for the patients who were treated in them.

The practice of the Poor Law Board at this time was to assert on paper the supremacy of the medical officer in his own department, to give him no personal support when he did his duty, to visit on his head all the consequences of their own negligence or dilatoriness, and, right or wrong, to support the Guardians when they took offence at conscientiousness and zeal. Now, in 1865, a scandalous case of neglect led to an inquest, to an exposure of the facts, and to very severe comments by the Press. Shortly afterwards the proprietors of *The Lancet* newspaper —a medical journal which has, during a very long career, been distinguished alike for its zeal in maintaining the honour of the medical profession and for its advocacy of humanity in dealing with the sick and destitute poor—resolved on investigating the condition of the London workhouses and their hospitals. Among other places, Dr. Anstie visited the Strand Workhouse, in Cleveland Street, and made his own report on what he saw in the columns of the paper which he represented. The report was candid, graphic, and by no means flattering to the Guardians, to their management, and to their officials. But it was entirely accurate, for the Strand Union and its Guardians at that time were probably the worst examples of a thoroughly bad and vicious system. Of course the Guardians were as angry as they could have been if they had been known for the best of characters and motives and had been grossly defamed.

The time was plainly come for concerted action, and one of the Strand Guardians, a Mr. Storr, a gentleman of very different character from most of his colleagues, convened a meeting at his own offices, in order to discuss the situation. It was at first suggested to call a public meeting; but my brother pointed out that even if the meeting were a success its effect would be ephemeral. It was determined, therefore, to create an association under the title of the Workhouse Infirmaries' Association, Mr. Storr offering to find £100 towards its preliminary ex-

1*

penses. But his generous offer was not needed. As soon as it was known that the Association was in process of formation, names and money poured in upon the scheme. New evidence about the Strand Union came out, and was forwarded to Mr. Charles Villiers, then President of the Board. An inquiry was held, and, as usual, the permanent officials strove to throw the blame on the medical officers, and to exonerate the Guardians. Now, to counteract this, my brother called a meeting of all the Workhouse medical officers in London. The object of this meeting was the formation of an Association for the protection of the character and interests of these officials, and for supplying information to the public as to the manner in which their best efforts were hampered and thwarted. This was the nucleus of the Poor Law Medical Officers' Association, an organization which has extended itself to the three kingdoms. Of this my brother was, as long as his health allowed, the president and principal administrator.

In 1867 Mr. Gathorne Hardy, now Lord Cranbrook, was President of the Poor Law Board, and in this capacity introduced the Metropolitan Poor Bill, some of the provisions of which were the establishment of Workhouse hospitals and dispensaries, and the supply of all medicines and medical appliances at the charge of the Guardians. The President frankly acknowledged that he owed much of the information which he had acquired from my brother. It was unfortunate that the provisions of the Act were not made general, throughout England at least. But London at last got an instalment of Poor Law Reform, and on rational lines. The administration of the Poor Law is far from perfect ; but the best part of it is that of the sick poor. Even here officials for a long time obstructed the will of the legislature and the objects of the law, but, on paper at least, the ancient abominations described in the earlier part of my brother's reminiscences were swept away.

In the eyes of the Strand Guardians, or rather of a majority among them, his offences on behalf of justice and humanity were unpardonable. He had to be got rid of. In this the officials of the Poor Law Board, then under Lord Devon, agreed with the Guardians. The Guardians picked a quarrel with him, the Poor Law Board instituted an inquiry, and apparently instructed their Inspector as to what he should report, and the President gave solemnity to the farce by removing him from his office. The ground on which he was dismissed was that " he could not get on with the Board of Guardians." Of

course he could not. No man of sense, honour,
humanity, decency, and conscientiousness, could get
on with them, or, in those evil days, with the Poor
Law Board either ; for the President and his
officials, perhaps unconsciously, leagued with the
Guardians in the maltreatment and oppression of
the poor.

It is a common trait in mean and malignant
natures to think, if they can injure in fortune or
character an advocate of justice and right dealing,
that they can arrest his efforts and discourage those
of others. Many experiences will occur to those
who have any knowledge of public affairs which will
illustrate this policy and its failure. It always fails
with such men as have any character at all. They
disregard the loss or the insult, and redouble their
efforts after the object which they have put before
them. I do not remember that my brother ever
dwelt with any peculiar acerbity on the circumstances
of his dismissal; but he gave himself more than
ever to the self-imposed task which became the
business, and eventually the success, of his life. He
spoke, indeed, with bitterness, and wrote with
bitterness of the crew who had sought to injure
him, but for the reason that they were prolonging
the miseries of the poor, and for that reason only.

Of course my brother had the sympathy of his profession and the support of the medical papers. But he resolved to perfect and extend the organization which he had founded. The result was the formation of the Poor Law Medical Officers' Association. In order to give strength and stability to this agency he visited most of the principal towns in England. He made several journeys to Ireland, the infirmary system of which he highly commended, and went once at least to Scotland, where indeed reform was greatly needed. And in these places he inculcated the important truth, that where medical relief was abundantly and generously accorded by the Guardians, pauperism decreased and rates were lessened. In my frequent communications with him, I urged him to insist on this as a matter of principle and a matter of fact. Generous relief to the poor, if it be discriminating and founded on a few intelligible rules, is the truest economy in the end. Owing to his efforts, many towns voluntarily adopted the principle of the Metropolitan Act, and with the best results. In the earlier years of his campaign he obtained great assistance in Parliament from the late Dr. Brady, Member for Leitrim, and from Dr. Lush, Member for Salisbury.

Four years after his expulsion from office in the

Strand Union, he was elected to a similar office in the Westminster Union. His career here was not one of incessant and unavailing remonstrance. The Poor Law Board, subsequently the Local Government Board, began to awake to a sense of its duties, and to see, though reluctantly and haltingly, that Boards of Guardians sometimes need supervision. But soon his troubles recommenced. The inferior officials were harsh, violent, and dishonest, and they were abetted by a majority of the Guardians. The inevitable consequences followed. My brother undertook the cause of the poor, and the Guardians and their tools or accomplices turned on him. They tried their old trick of suspending him, in hopes that the Poor Law or Local Government Board would endorse their ruling. My brother employed his enforced leisure in extending the organization which he had founded. In due course he was reinstated by the Department, and his enemies were baffled.

The mismanagement of the Workhouse by these Guardians, and the outrageous misconduct of the master, at length roused the wrath of the ratepayers. An influential committee was formed, which recommended a new list of Guardians to the electors, and the whole of the old gang were ejected from

office by overwhelming majorities. I have reason
to know that the atrocities perpetrated by the master
roused the anger, and secured the unobtrusive but effective co-operation of a very exalted personage. The
resentment which affected this total change was not the
act of one section of society or of one party only, and
it is just to say that my brother had the assistance of
eminent persons in both political parties. I mention
this the rather, because my brother made no secret
of his political opinions, and never omitted any
opportunity of inculcating them. He belonged, as
all his brothers did, to the advanced Liberal party.

During the remainder of his active life he was in
perfect accord with the Board of Guardians. He
had the good fortune to see that what he had
laboured for, and had been persecuted for, was now
acknowledged to be humane, politic, and economical.
He even had the opportunity of checking reckless
and unwise expenditure. He had done great services
to the poor, though his clients were unable to express
more than their personal gratitude to him. He had recognized and secured the co-operation of some among
those excellent women who have worked so ener-
getically and unobtrusively on behalf of the poor
destitute. He had done great services to his own
profession, and had secured them a little of their

due; for, I repeat, there is no class of persons who
do so much, from whom so much is expected, and
who are more scantily remunerated than medical
practitioners among the poor. Some of these
practitioners in 1884 determined to offer him some
recognition of his lifelong services. There was
nothing in his whole career which he dwelt on
with more satisfaction than on the rout of the
Westminster Guardians, in 1883, and on the testimonial of 1884.

Two years afterwards he was attacked by heart
disease, and became conscious of the organic mischief against which his naturally strong constitution
struggled for nearly three years. His incessant
labours had literally worn him out. His disease
rapidly increased on him, and with great pain
and effort he wrote out, in the intervals of his
trying disorder, the reminiscences which follow.
Had he been in better physical health, they would
have no doubt been fuller, for his memory was exact
and tenacious. That which is printed will show
what manner of man he was. But it will be seen
that he dwells but little on his own unwearied labours.
During his sickness he was attended by many
physicians who knew him and valued him : chief
and most untiring among them was Dr. Bristow.

I can say, without consciousness of partiality, that my brother's life was one of incessant devotion to a noble object. They for whom he laboured were the poor and helpless ; who could make him no recompense, could, perhaps, hardly understand his purposes. He was met by obstacles which would have daunted a less resolute man ; but he was sustained by the rectitude of his aims, and by a firm belief in their wisdom. Such men change the face of the world, as far as their own sphere goes. Their reward is generally the approval of their own consciences, and sometimes evidence accorded in their lifetime as to what has been the fruit of their labours. Thousands of our fellow-countrymen have been saved from suffering and misery by the life-work of Joseph Rogers.

JAMES E. THOROLD ROGERS.

Oxford,
April 10.

CONTENTS.

REMINISCENCES OF A WORKHOUSE MEDICAL OFFICER.

CHAPTER I.

THE STRAND.

IN the latter part of the summer of 1854 I was living in Soho, where I had been engaged in general practice for some ten years, and where, by dint of laborious attention to my profession, I had secured a sufficiency on which to live, when I became aware that an outbreak of Asiatic cholera might be looked for. Some suspicious cases had appeared, when, towards the end of the month of August, there was suddenly developed an epidemic outbreak of such virulence and extent that it became necessary for immediate action to be taken, if this fell disease was to be effectually dealt with. Having taken an active part for some years previously in sundry sanitary mea-

2

sures, I was requested by the parochial authorities
of St. Anne's, Soho, to take charge of one of the
districts into which the parish was at once divided.
During the busiest of those very busy days, a medical
friend and neighbour called on me, and in answer
to my remark that I was too busy to talk to him,
replied, " You are busy now, but you will live to
regret this outbreak in Soho. It will ruin the
neighbourhood and your practice for many years to
come, for the public will believe that it is too un-
healthy to live in, and ere long you will have nothing
to do."

This casual prediction was amply verified in the
following year by the death of many inhabitants, and
by the removal of others. As was the case with
others in other callings, I had to commence the
world afresh. When casting about for the best
course to follow, the medical officership of the
Strand Workhouse, Cleveland Street, and of the
parish of St. Anne's, Soho, fell vacant. The person
who held the appointment proposed to resign in
favour of his son, and I was strongly urged to compete for it. I elected to try my chance, and, after a
severe contest, was selected. Here I began my
experiences of the sick poor, which lasted, with a
very brief interval, for thirty years. My first im-

pressions were not very exhilarating, and could I
have foreseen all that was in store for me, I question
whether I should have applied for the appointment
at all, but, having been appointed, I resolved to try
it for a time at least. The Strand Workhouse in
the year 1856 was a square four-storied building
fronting the street, with two wings of similar eleva-
tion projecting eastwards from each corner. Across
the irregularly-paved yard in the rear was a two-
storied lean-to building, with windows in the front
only, used as a day and night ward for infirm women.
There were sheds on each side for the reception of
so-called male and female able-bodied people, whilst
in the yard, on each side of the entrance gate, was a
two-storied building, with an underground apartment
lighted by a single window, and with a door for the
reception of male and female casual paupers; the
wards above being for those of both sexes admitted to
the house.

The necessary laundry work of the establishment,
which never in my time fell below five hundred
inmates, was carried on in the cellar beneath the
entrance hall and the general dining-room, whence
it came to pass that the said hall, &c., was for four
days in each week filled with steam and the odours
from washing the paupers' linen. A chapel was con-

trived out of one of the male infirm wards on the ground floor on the Sunday, and utilized on that occasion for both sexes. On the left of the entrance hall was the Board-room ; the corresponding apart- ment on the right, and the room above on the first floor, being the apartments of the master and matron. On the right side of the main building was a badly paved yard, which led down to the back entrance from Charlotte Street ; on each side of this back entrance there was—first, a carpenter's shop and a dead-house, and secondly, opposite to it, a tinker's shop with a forge and unceiled roof. This latter communicated with a ward with two beds in it, used for fever and foul cases, only a lath and plaster partition about eight feet high separating it from the tinker's shop.

There were no paid nurses. Such nursing as we had, and continued to have for the first nine years I was there, was performed by more or less infirm paupers, with the occasional aid of some strong young woman who had been admitted temporarily and was on pass. Unfortunately it frequently happened that just as she was becoming useful she left, and there was nothing for it but to fall back upon the ordinary broken-down inmates, the selection of whom did not rest with me, but with the master or the matron, or both.

Just outside the male wards of the House, at the

upper end of the yard, there were two upright posts
and a cross-bar. On this bar were suspended the
carpets taken in to beat by the so-called able-bodied
inmates, from whose labour the Guardians derived a
clear income of £400 a year. In despite of the continued noise and dust caused by this beating, the
Guardians persisted in carrying it on for ten of the
twelve years that I was there. The noise was so
great that it effectually deprived the sick of all chance
of sleep, whilst the dust was so thick that to open
the windows was entirely out of the question until
the day's work was over. I attempted repeatedly to
get this nuisance done away with, but so fierce was
the antagonism of the majority of the Board that I
had to abandon it.

The male insane ward, used also for epileptics
and imbeciles, was on the right wing above the male
casual and reception ward. To reach it you had to
go up some four steps; it was absurdly unsuitable
for such cases, and when I had lunatic and imbecile
there together I was always in dread lest some horrid
catastrophe might happen. One case of an epileptic
was to me the cause of much anxiety, for he was
wholly unaware when his fits were coming on. When
a seizure occurred he always sprang up and then
dashed himself to the ground on his forehead and

face. He contrived by these means to smash his nose, make dreadfully disfiguring wounds on his forehead and face, and from a good-looking, became a perfectly repulsive-looking person. Poor fellow! I tried all sorts of expedients to prevent his doing himself any further injury, but though he constantly wore a stuffed helmet, he sometimes managed to injure himself. I got him away at last, but I had two or three years of him, during which time I had a very extensive surgical experience from his case alone. I was constantly stitching up his wounds.

The female insane ward was a rather large room, and was situated over the Board-room. As we always had the place full the space was desirable or necessary. It was immediately beneath the lying-in ward. When we had a troublesome or noisy lunatic in the ward, it must have been anything but a comfort to the lying-in women above, but then neither their interests, nor the feelings of any of the other inmates, were at that time officially considered by the Guardians, by the Poor Law Inspectors, nor by any one else. To be allowed to remain in the House and get waited on somehow was all that was looked for by these truly wretched women.

The master of the House, a certain George Catch, since deceased, had been a common policeman in

Clare Market, where he had made himself useful to the Chairman of the Board, who was the proprietor of an *à-la-mode* beef shop in that locality. Through this Chairman's influence he became the porter of the Workhouse, and the master falling sick, he had performed his duty for him. The illness ending fatally, through the same influence Catch was promoted to the vacant office, though, at the time I first knew him, he was so ignorant that he could only write his name with difficulty. He was single on his appointment, but an alliance with the late master's niece, who had acted as matron for some time, was talked about on my taking office. As this official, Mr. G. Catch, appointed with the sanction of Mr. H. Fleming, some time Permanent Secretary of the Poor Law Board, played an important part in bringing the Department into deserved contempt, I must hereafter again refer to him.

On the morning of my entering on my duties I went over the sick ward with the son of my predecessor. My curiosity was excited by sundry ill-shaped bottles, all of which contained the same description of so-called medicine. The salary did not admit of an extensive variety of medical necessaries, as it was only fifty pounds a year, out of which all drugs were to be found. It is true that

this stipend was supplemented by an occasional fee
from attendance on parturient women, in cases
where difficulty or danger arose, or in any illness
which took place prior to the ninth day after the confinement. That fee was limited to twenty shillings
only. The decision as to the necessity for such
attendance was vested in the midwife or matron, and
until that was given the medical officer was inter-
dicted from entering the lying-in wards. This
regulation was in direct contravention of the Poor
Law Regulations, but then the Department were very
unwilling at that time to interfere with the so-called
discretion of the Guardians, however much their
regulations were disregarded.

I have stated that the Chairman of the Board was
the proprietor of an *à-la-mode* beef shop. During
my first year of office this dignitary would often
come to the House on Sunday morning dressed in
the dirty, greasy jacket in which he had been serving
à-la-mode beef the night before, and unshaven and
unshorn, he would go into the chapel with the pauper
inmates, and afterwards go to the Board-room, and
have breakfast with the master and matron. Of
course, between the three, there was an excellent
understanding, and during this Chairman's reign all
alterations for the better were resisted.

I have before stated that all my nurses were pauper inmates. The responsible duties they had to perform were remunerated by an amended dietary and a pint of beer. Occasionally for laying out the dead, and for other specially repulsive duties, they had a glass of gin. This was given by the master or matron, but I was expected to sanction the supply.

I have referred to the ward used for foul cases, which was in immediate proximity to the tinker's shop. It was altogether unsuitable for the reception of any human being, however degraded he might be ; but it had to be used. I remember a poor wretch being admitted with frost-bitten feet, which speedily mortified, rendering the atmosphere of the ward and shop frightfully offensive. At first I was at a loss to know whom to get to go through the offensive duty of waiting on him. At last a little fellow, called Wiseman, undertook the task, the bribe being two pints of beer and some gin daily, with steaks or chops for dinner. Presently the patient was seized with tetanus, and after the most fearful sufferings died. He was followed almost immediately afterwards by poor Wiseman, who had contracted from his patient one of the most malignant forms of blood poisoning that I ever saw.

These two successive deaths took place whilst the
tinker was plying his business on the other side of
the partition which separated this ward from his
smithy. This place was an utter disgrace to the
Board, but they never attempted to alter it whilst I
was there.

I have referred also to the nursery ward. This
place was situated on the third floor, opposite to the
lying-in ward. It was a wretchedly damp and
miserable room, nearly always overcrowded with
young mothers and their infant children. That
death relieved these young women of their illegiti-
mate offspring was only what was to be expected, and
that frequently the mothers followed in the same
direction was only too true.

I used to dread to go into this ward, it was so
depressing. Scores and scores of distinctly preven-
tible deaths of both mothers and children took place
during my continuance in office through their being
located in this horrible den.

It frequently happened that some casual was admitted with her child, or children, to the room below
the female receiving ward. On my visiting the
House next day I would find that her child had got
an attack of measles and could not go out ; and in
spite of my sending the mother and child to the

children's infectious ward above, measles always
broke out in the nursery some eleven days after, and
I have had as many as twenty down with it at a
time. I will not horrify my readers by stating the
proportion of deaths to recoveries, but content myself
with stating that the latter were very few.

What made these continuous outbreaks so vexatious was this, that I had laid down the most
stringent regulations as regards isolation and disin-
fection ; but unfortunately my orders could only be
given to pauper women. I had no other persons to
act with, and with that habitual carelessness which
had led to their becoming paupers, they only in
exceptional instances paid any attention to what I
said.

Now and then a decent widow with an infant came
in, and became an inmate of the nursery ward,
there being no other place for her to go to. What
her feelings must have been when forced into day
and night companionship with some of the most
abandoned of her own sex in this miserable Gehenna,
I will not attempt to portray, and yet the majority of
the Board looked upon this den as a perfect paradise,
and looked on me as an irreconcilable fellow for
troubling them with my complaints respecting it.

I had not been the medical officer for many

months before I found that my pauper nurses were
frequently under the influence of drink, and that, too,
in the forenoon. On inquiring, I heard to my surprise that the master was in the habit of giving out
the stimulants at 7 a.m., and, as many of the
inmates sold their allowance, the nurses had become
partly or wholly intoxicated when I reached the
House in the morning.

My first request to the master was that some other
time should be selected for the issue of stimulants.
Such request was angrily refused, and it was not
until I had appealed to the Board that I succeeded
in effecting an alteration, but my success made the
master, henceforward, my determined foe.

As I have stated, the medical officer's salary was
intended to cover the provision of medicine. The
Guardians, however, had supplied my predecessor
with linseed-meal and mustard, but finding that I
had a great many consumptive and bronchitic
patients, I was induced to apply to the Guardians for
some linseed, to enable me to give the patients some
linseed tea. Now there was one nurse in the female
sick ward, by name Charlotte Massingham, who had
been in supreme authority there some years. She
was nearly always muddled; to work with her was
impossible; Charlotte invariably treated me with

supreme indifference, not unmingled with undis-
guised contempt. I had introduced new-fangled
notions, would have my medicines correctly given,
and the patients well attended to. On hearing that
my application for the linseed had met with success,
I went up to the Workhouse. On going into the
female sick ward I told Charlotte of my having
gained the assent of the Board, when, suddenly
springing up at least a foot, she came down slapping
both sides, with her arms on to the ground, with the
startling observation, "My God! linseed tea in a
workhouse!" Charlotte's reign, however, was not of
long continuance after this; she died, worn out by
the effects of habitual intemperance. I heard, after
she was dead, and the inmates were free to speak,
that she systematically stole the wine and brandy
from the sick.

It was obvious that one of the first points to secure
was the removal of the laundry before referred to,
situated in the cellar beneath the dining hall. The
Guardians having assented to my suggestions, a
contract was entered into with the builder to put up
a laundry in the back yard. The structure was to
cost some £400. On proceeding to dig out the
foundation, the workmen came on a number of
skeletons, the yard having been originally the poor

burial ground of St. Paul's, Covent Garden, for which parish the Workhouse, &c., had been built, and had been rented by the Guardians from that parish when the Strand Union was formed. So full was this yard of human remains, that the contractor was compelled to go down twenty feet all round, before a foundation for the laundry could be obtained. In making this huge trench, they disinterred the remains of the poor Italian boy, murdered by Bishop and Williams, whose murder was discovered by the late Mr. Partridge of King's College Hospital, to whom Bishop and Williams had sold their victim for anatomical purposes. Similar murders of the same kind in Edinburgh, led to the passing of the Anatomy Act, and to the suppression of the practice of body-snatching by the abandoned wretches who formerly supplied Schools of Anatomy with subjects.

My next endeavour was an enlargement of the cellar at each wing so as to secure better accommodation for the reception of casual poor, and increased space for sick children and others. This was accomplished by nearly re-building the wings. Unfortunately these suggestions rendered me extremely unpopular with many of the Guardians, and delayed for some two years any increase of my wretched stipend, which would otherwise have been granted, if I could have remained a passive observer of that which I saw around me. But worse was in store.

My first serious quarrel with the Board happened thus. Many of the young women who came in to be confined, came under treatment afterwards, suffering from extreme exhaustion, and some were hopelessly consumptive. On making inquiry, I found that the practice in the lying-in ward was to keep the single women on a dietary of gruel for nine days, and then, at the end of a fortnight, to dismiss them to the nursery ward on House diet, with their children. Assuming, as I had a perfect right to do, that this dietary had emanated from an order of the Poor Law Board, I wrote to the Department telling what I had observed, and asking that Board's permission to introduce a more generous system. My communication was sent to the Guardians, and I was informed in a letter from the Board at White-hall that it rested with me exclusively to order whatever form of dietary I chose, a power which I did not hesitate to use. The Board of Guardians condemned my conduct in writing to the Poor Law Board, in the strongest possible terms, and the use I had made of the power vested in me. The course taken by me was held to be in the highest degree

reprehensible, as it traversed the deliberate action of
the Guardians, who had established the starvation
dietary for single parturient women, as a deterrent
against the use of the Workhouse as a place in which
to be confined. As the number of fresh admissions
went on increasing, and I had not sufficient accommodation, I recommended that the side wings should be
enlarged by carrying the building up a storey higher.
This was done, and the pressure put on the accommodation was met for a time, but all these suggestions
increased my unpopularity with certain of the Board,
who condemned me for the expense I was putting
them to. About this time the annoyance and obstruction I met with from the master and matron compelled me to apply to the Inspector for support. He
came to the House to make inquiry, but so large a
number of the Guardians attended to support the
master, that after a few questions had been put, he
closed the inquiry. Some years after he expressed
to me his regret that at that time he could not see
his way to aid me.

At the end of the first year some business took me
to Scotland. The Board sanctioned my absence, and
gave their approval of the gentleman who was to act
as my substitute. On my return journey by the
night train, on getting out at Peterborough at 6 a.m.

to get some coffee, I was surprised to see the master
of the Workhouse and the clerk of the Board
standing on the platform. On reaching King's
Cross I remained in the carriage till all the
passengers had alighted and had passed me. I
was in doubt whether I had been deceived, but I had
not been, for presently the pair passed the carriage,
each carrying a small bag. About ten days after, a
letter was sent from the Board, asking for an explanation of an alleged neglect of a sick person in
the House. I forthwith called on my substitute
and showed him the letter. He denied in the most
positive terms the allegation of neglect. On visiting
the House, no information could be gained from any
one, but it occurred to me on leaving to ask the
porter whether he could throw any light on the
matter. After reading the clerk's letter he made
the remark, "Why, Catch was not in the House at
the time he alleges the neglect took place, for he and
the clerk went down to Peterborough from the
Thursday to the Monday morning, to be entertained
by the contractor who put up the laundry boiler."
In my defence, I stated this to the Board, when
great was the indignation expressed by some of the
Guardians; first, at his false charge of neglect, and
secondly, that he and the clerk should have gone

away without leave, and for their being entertained
by the contractor.

The exposure of course intensified this master's
hostility, in which his friend the clerk cordially co-
operated. The consequence to me was that I was
continually sent for on most frivolous pretences.
The messenger would come to my house and say,
"You are wanted at Cleveland Street;" if I asked
for what, he was studiously ignorant. If I went, or
if I sent my assistant, Catch would keep us waiting
in the hall until it suited his humour to come out to
me, when in a loud voice he would say, "You are
wanted in such and such a ward." Hard as this
was to bear with from this ignorant and incompetent
official, I put up with it for a time, but at last I
again called on the Poor Law Inspector, and asked
him his advice, when he informed me that the
master was bound to send a written order, stating
the name of the sick person, &c. On my having
intimated to him that I should not again notice his
calls unless this requirement was complied with,
the annoyance was stopped—nearly all of these
second visits having been wholly unnecessary, and
arranged with the view of wearing me out.

I have stated that, unless called on, either by the
midwife, matron, or master, to visit a woman recently

confined, I was debarred from attendance on her, and could not claim any fee. The master and clerk arranged that no order should be given until nine days had elapsed, when it was held that I was bound to take charge of the woman as in an ordinary case of illness. This calling one in on the morning of the tenth day was so frequently done that I saw that the thing was arranged, especially as I learned on inquiry that the woman had been ill for some days, and had asked that I should be sent for. I thereupon took on myself to visit the ward daily, and to judge for myself as to the necessity for my attendance. Some half-dozen of these cases occurred within three months. On sending notice to the clerk that I had visited such and such a case, I received the reply: "I have made inquiries and find that you attended without getting the necessary authority." This I afterwards learned was done without any authority from the Board. I therefore decided that I would give up going into this ward for the future.

Some time after, and in pursuance of this man's policy of annoyance, a case occurred just as I expected, which enabled me to get rid of him. On going to the House one morning, the porter told me there was a woman ill in the lying-in ward. On going into my room the pauper attendant came and asked me to go to this ward. To the inquiry, "Who sent you?" "No one," she replied. I then said, "Go to the matron, or if you cannot find her, to the master, state that the woman is very ill, and bring me the authority to visit her." She went away. Some half-hour after, I went by the ward door, and heard this poor wretch's cries for assistance, but I did not visit her. Again the attendant came to me and implored me to go up. I asked, "Have you seen the master or matron?" "Yes," she said. "What did they say to you?" "Why, they only laughed." I again declined to visit the ward. Shortly after I left the House. I had hardly passed the gate when the master rushed into the hall and inquired whether I had left; on hearing I had done so, he said in a loud voice, "I have caught that damned doctor at last," and directed the porter to go for the nearest medical man. Some gentleman came and attended to her, and the bill, and a garbled statement of the facts, was sent by Catch to the Board. I was ordered to attend their next meeting and explain my conduct. I requested the attendance of the porter and of the pauper nurse at the Board's meeting. Catch gave his version of the story. When called on for my explanation, I narrated the course adopted by the master, the matron, and the clerk, and pointed out to the Guardians the evident intention of all three to prevent me being paid any fee ; that in the case in question I had asked for an authority to visit the woman ; that, although both of these officers knew of the poor woman's condition, they had maliciously allowed her to remain without proper attendance, and would not give any order, so that I should not be paid a fee. The defence was so complete, and so completely turned the tables on all three, that a severe censure was passed on the master and matron for their inhumanity, and a hint was given that they had better look out for some other appointment. This they did, and a vacancy for a master and matron having taken place at Newington Workhouse, Mr. and Mrs. Catch applied for the post, and, to the delight of all the inmates and officers of the Strand Workhouse, were selected. So intensely tyrannical and cruel had been the rule of this man, that the day he resigned the keys, and was leaving the House, the whole establishment—at least, all those who could leave their beds—rose in open rebellion, and with old kettles, shovels, penny trumpets, celebrated their departure from the premises. The incoming master subsequently told me that he had never witnessed

anything like it in his life, and that the row was so
general and spontaneous, that he was powerless to
check it. Mr. Catch's subsequent career did not
disappoint the expectations of those who were
cognizant of his utter unfitness for so responsible a
post. I shall refer to him again in a subsequent part
of this narrative.

Before I had been long in office, I became aware
that there was a benevolent agency at work, conducted by some Christian ladies, whose mission it
was to visit the wards, read to the sick and infirm,
and generally to help them in the effort they might
make in re-establishing themselves. At the head of
this movement was Miss Louisa Twining, who has
devoted years of her busy life to the amelioration of
the lot of the workhouse sick ; Lady Alderson, the
widow of the late judge, her daughter, Miss Louisa ;
and, though last, by no means the least, Miss
Augusta Clifford, were associated in this good work.
It was to Miss Twining's initiative that the abolition
of the system of entrusting the care of the sick poor
to the numberless Sairey Gamps and Betsy Prigs
was mainly due ; but she did not succeed in her
laudable efforts until after several years of incessant
appeal to the Guardians of the Poor and the Poor
Law Board. Ultimately her demand was conceded
in deference to outraged public opinion.

The efforts of Miss Clifford demand a special reference here. Very early in my official life she called on me and volunteered to help any deserving case brought to her notice. Over and over again did she put her hand in her pocket, and give money to inmates of her own sex, whose cases I called attention to. At last her good doing attracted the notice of the Board, who passed a very eulogistic resolution, in which they thanked her for her great kindness to their sick.

Here let me remark that, although the majority of the Strand Board were wholly unfitted for any administrative duties, yet it would be ungrateful not to state that there were several kindly-disposed persons among them. They were generally, however, outvoted, though occasionally their suggestions for a milder and more generous *régime* prevailed. Catch had hardly left the house when it was proposed to increase my stipend, at first to £75, ultimately to £100 a year ; and I was also entrusted by the Board with the duty of certifying as to the lunacy of the inmates who were admittedly insane.

This office had been filled for many years by a Dr. Beaman, of Henrietta Street, Covent Garden, in deference to a view recently revived by the present Lord Chancellor, in his hitherto abortive attempts

to amend the Lunacy Laws, and was to the effect
that it would be hazardous to entrust such a duty to
the Workhouse medical officer, as he might be
tempted to eke out his salary by certifying that
healthy persons were mentally affected, so as to
secure a fee. The injustice implied in this gratuitous imputation, having been brought before one of
the Presidents of the Poor Law Board, he was
induced to get the prohibition removed, and one of
the results was that my friends at the Board carried
a resolution that in future I should be the examining
official, as I had all the trouble of the case, whilst a
stranger pocketed the fee. Dr. Beaman was much
annoyed at this ; and as the relieving officer, who was
a friend of Beaman's, persisted in sending all cases to
Dr. Beaman, a collision was inevitable. A short while
after, a lad was brought by the police, found wandering
at large. I diagnosed that he was a homicidal
lunatic, and that it was necessary that he should
be sent away. The relieving officer having called
in Dr. Beaman, he visited the House, examined the
lad, and took him down to Bow Street, and
deposed before the magistrate that he was of sound
mind. He would have been discharged, but the
police having testified to the very questionable
condition in which he was on coming into their

hands, the presiding magistrate directed that he should go back to the House for further observation. This was done, and I again saw and examined him, and gave a fresh certificate of his insanity. Dr. Beaman was again requested to attend; he, however, sent his partner, who also decided that the lad was not insane. He was again taken before a magistrate, with the result that he was ordered to be discharged. Thereupon Dr. Beaman wrote to the Poor Law Board complaining of the action of the Guardians in appointing an inexperienced young man as the examining medical officer, and stating that neither he nor his partner could discover any evidence of insanity in the case in question. A copy of this letter was sent to the Guardians, who directed the clerk to write to me for an explanation of my conduct. I was satisfied that I was right, but I had a great deal of trouble in tracing what had become of the boy. Ultimately I found his father, who informed me that the day he was discharged he came home and sat down to his dinner; after the meal was over, the father resumed his work, that of shoe mending, when his son, without saying a word, struck him a severe blow on the head with a hammer. The aid of the neighbours and of the police was invoked, and after a desperate struggle he

was overpowered, handcuffed, taken before a magistrate, who sent him to Marylebone Workhouse, from
which establishment he had been sent to Hanwell,
where he had been some days.

I sent a copy of my reply to the Guardians to the
Poor Law Board. My judgment was never again
called in question in cases of lunacy. I found this
part of my duty an agreeable episode in my daily
routine of all but thankless work. I also made the
acquaintance of Sir Thomas Henry, Mr. Flowers,
and Mr. Vaughan, and from all these magistrates
received the greatest courtesy.

Before I had long held office my attention was
drawn to the marvellous zeal displayed by the
Catholic priests, who, although unpaid, were untiring
in their attendance on the sick poor of their persua-
sion, a large number of whom were always in the
House. A somewhat ludicrous incident occurred
about this time. There was a very old woman in
the infirm ward, across the yard. She was stated
to be ninety-five; she had been blind from
childhood, and the balls of both eyes were gone,
leaving nearly empty sockets. Although life under
such circumstances was not very attractive, I never
met with any one who so strongly objected to dying.
She was constantly sending for me to prescribe for

her imaginary ailments. One very cold night, when
the snow was on the ground, and it was blowing
strongly from the north-east, at about 11.30 my
night-bell was rung violently. I had not gone to
bed, and therefore answered the door, when I found
a young Irishwoman, cowering in the recess of the
doorway. On asking what she wanted, she replied,
" Oh, if you please, sir, the Father has sent me over
to ask whether Bridget Gaines is dying, as a
messenger has just come from the House saying
Bridget is going, and requesting the Father to go
there at once. Now the Father has a bad cold, and
his feet are in hot water, and he has a poultice on
his chest, and he is afraid to go out as the night is
so cold." I laughingly told her to go back and tell
the Father that I thought Bridget was not near her
end yet. On the following morning the priest called
on me. He was very anxious about Bridget, and
earnestly asked whether I had heard from the House.
I told him there was no need for anxiety, when, in
a deprecatory tone of voice, he said, " I should have
gone after all, but Bridget has been very tiresome.
Do you know," he said, "Bridget has had extreme
unction administered nineteen times." I saw
Bridget that morning, she was much in her usual
condition ; she lived a long time afterwards, and

probably was anointed on a great many subsequent
occasions.

I was constantly encountering odd stories and odd
people—many of them profligates who had seen
better days. One person in particular attracted my
attention, as he had evidently been a gentleman;
indeed, he assured me that he had once a large
estate in Yorkshire, and was Master of the Hounds.
I had no reason to doubt him. He did not live very
long after his admission to the sick ward. After his
death I received from five different solicitors written
requests for a copy of my death certificate. It was
accompanied in each case by a fee of a guinea. This
poor fellow had insured his life in five different
offices, and had sold the policies. It will be seen
that I shared in the pecuniary advantages that sprang
from his death.

The immediate successor of Mr. and Mrs. Catch
did not stay very long. The matron's health broke
down, and she had to resign. They were followed
by Mr. and Mrs. Thorne, who remained master and
matron until the death of the former some years
afterwards. Mr. Thorne was a kind-hearted person,
who had filled a position of responsibility in the
parish of Marylebone; whilst Mrs. Thorne was a
well-educated, ladylike woman. They managed the

House well, and treated the inmates with kindness
and consideration, but do as they would they could
not alter the structural deficiencies of the building,
make it larger, nor prevent the fearful over-crowding
with its disastrous results, nor improve upon the
wretched system of pauper nursing, which was the
curse of that and all similar institutions, and which
the powers that were in those days at Whitehall
made no genuine effort to change.

Shortly after the collapse of his friend Catch, the
proprietor of the à-la-mode beef shop ceased to be a
Guardian, and a wholesale fruit-dealer in Covent
Garden reigned in his stead. He was a far less
satisfactory Chairman than his predecessor, as all
thoughts, words, and deeds were actuated by the
consideration of his personal and private interests,
as will be shown by the following, among other
instances that could be related. One of the earliest
things very properly done by the new master was to
find out the previous occupation of those who had
come in sick, and to utilize them, when recovered, in
the trade they had followed, for the improvement of
the House. One day a middle-aged man came in
very ill. He had evidently seen better days; in
fact, he turned out to have been a highly-skilled
decorator, especially in the representation of marble

and in graining.   As soon as he was well enough the
master set him to work to decorate the entrance hall.
This he did most admirably, and his work was much
admired by the Guardians, and by visitors to the
House.   This employment coming to an end he was
allowed, as a reward for his industry, to go in and out,
ostensibly to look for work.   I used frequently to
meet this man on my daily visits.   As he continued
to go out in this manner, I one day stopped him and
asked whether he had been successful in finding a
job.   His reply, in the negative, was accompanied by
a look so significant, that I was induced to push
my inquiries, when he told me that he was occupied
in decorating the Chairman's house, and he had
been engaged at it for some three weeks.   To the
further inquiry, " What have you got there ? "
pointing to a bag he was carrying, he replied,
" That is my dinner, which I always take with me,
from   the   House."   " Oh,   then,"   I said, " the
Chairman does not find you your dinner even ; does
he give you any beer or any money ? " He replied,
" I have been working there all day long for the
last three weeks, and he has never given me anything."   As he shortly after disappeared, I made
an inquiry as to what had become of him, when
I learned that he had suddenly left the work he was

doing for the Chairman, and gone off and drowned himself. This Chairman did not long continue to act as such, as some months after this he died suddenly of heart disease, the only evidence he had ever afforded that he possessed one. Having occasion just at that time to go to the Poor Law Board, I was waiting in an office for the gentleman I went to see, when one of the junior officials said to me, " You have lost your Chairman." "Yes," I replied, "but I do not feel his loss very acutely;" on which he said, "It is customary for the clerk of the Board to write and apprise us of the death of the Chairman, and we always send a sympathetic letter in reply. On the clerk's letter being read the question was asked, 'Should the usual reply be sent?' The official reply was grim enough: 'Write and say that we are delighted to hear it.'"

The successor in the Chair was very friendly disposed towards me, and remained so until after the official inquiry in 1866, when, having attended to hear the evidence that was given, and having made himself conspicuous by some irrelevant interruptions, he brought down on himself the criticism of the Press, which he most absurdly attributed to me, and resented by becoming a most determined opponent ever afterwards.

About this time a Select Committee of the House
of Commons was appointed to take into consideration
the administration of the Poor Laws, and to decide
as to the desirability or otherwise of the maintenance
of the Central Department. In conjunction with my
friend, the late R. Griffin, of Weymouth, who
distinguished himself so much by an advocacy of
an amended system of medical relief, and the late
Dr. R. Fowler, of Bishopsgate Street, I volunteered
to give evidence before the Committee. Some time
after, being asked by the late Metropolitan Inspector,
H. B. Farnall, Esq., C.B., to call upon him at the
Poor Law Board, I did so. "I hear," said he,
"that you have asked to give evidence before the
Select Committee; pray, what are you going to
state?" "Nothing," I replied, "that bears on my
personal position as a Poor Law medical officer, except
so far as I may support my views by reference to
my personal knowledge. I shall give evidence for
the purpose of urging on the Committee the desirability of abolishing the system, whereby Boards of
Guardians for a stipulated sum, often wholly
inadequate, bargain with medical men to find all
medicines and appliances, because the inevitable
outcome of the system is this—that the poor do not
get the medicines they require. I feel that the sick

of the Strand Union got very little in the way of medicine before I was appointed, and the provision of such medicines was to me in every sense a pecuniary loss, until the Guardians quite recently increased my stipend so as to make the strain less felt."

He at once assured me that he would do his best to put my views before the Chairman, C. P. Villiers, M.P. for Wolverhampton. I did not at that time know Mr. Villiers personally, except by repute, but I came to know him some years later. Mr. Farnall then proposed to put some questions to me and take down the answers. This he did, and as each question was put I replied briefly, giving my reasons for my suggestion. I had to be guarded in my answers, as I was not desirous of bringing the charge against my medical brethren that they systematically failed to supply medicines for the sick, though very many have with more or less questionable candour said to me, "Why do you bother about the supply of medicines? Go in and get for us an increase of our pay."

After Mr. Farnall had put me to the question, he shook me very warmly by the hand, promising that as far as I was concerned the views I held should be brought prominently forward.

4

Some time after I received a notice to attend, when I found Mr. Richard Griffin and Dr. Fowler in the room. Griffin had come there with evidence that would have taken a month to take down. Fowler was not so diffuse, a couple of days would have got through what he had to say. Appalled by the vast body of evidence offered by these two, the Committee ordered the room to be cleared ; on our re-admission we learned that the Committee had decided that Mr. Griffin and Dr. Fowler should put in their evidence, which should be taken as if delivered. I was then called on. I had neither note nor paper, as I relied on Mr. Farnall's promise. The questions were mainly put by Mr. Villiers. I amplified briefly the views I had expressed to Mr. Farnall. This led to my being asked for some additional explanations, which I supplied. Ultimately I was dismissed, but not before I had convinced myself that my day's work had not been thrown away. Poor Richard Griffin had worked for many years with wonderful industry to call attention to the grievances of Poor Law medical officers, and thought he should succeed. But he was destined to fail, for although the Committee had allowed him to put in his evidence, yet the facts he had collected with so much pains were successfully traversed by

Mr. R. B. Caine, Poor Law Inspector, who by
certain statistics made out to the Committee's
satisfaction that medical men had no great cause for
complaint. Poor Fowler's evidence was similarly
snuffed out; as regards mine, the Committee reported in its favour, but not as to the whole of it.
They probably dreaded the cost to the various
Union Boards of the provision of all medicines,
but they suggested a compromise, to wit, that Boards
of Guardians should be required to supply expensive
medicines, such as cod liver oil, quinine, opium,
&c. Small as the concession was, Mr. H. Fleming
delayed the issue of the Committee's recommendation for fifteen months after it had been made, and
then sent out a letter couched in such official
language that a great many Boards contented
themselves with ordering the letter to lie on the
table. Some years after, I asked Dr. Lush, M.P.
for Salisbury, to move for a copy of the Board's
letter and a return of what had been done. I found
from that return that about half of those bodies had
not noticed the letter at all. Subsequently, twenty
years after the issue of the letter, my brother, Thorold
Rogers, moved for a similar return, only to show that
there were still several Boards where nothing whatever was supplied.

When the letter was read at the Strand Board, a suggestion was made that I should be offered an increase of my stipend and be required to purchase the medicines myself. This I declined. Ultimately it was arranged that I should be allowed to order drugs of a wholesale chemist, but only to the extent of £27 a year : anything beyond that I was expected to pay for myself.

About this time (1862) the matron informed me that on the previous day a very aged woman had been admitted, and that she had sent her to the infirm ward across the yard. On looking at the order I found it was stated that she was 104. I went to see her. She was undeniably of great age, but she still retained her faculties and conversed with me for some time. She told me that she had lived in Chancery Lane between fifty and sixty years, and was forty-five years old when she went there to live. She also told me that she went down the Lane to see Nelson's funeral procession go by, that her children and her grandchildren were dead, and that she had been looked after lately by her great grand-children, who had grown tired of waiting on her, and that was why she had come into the House. Her eyes were blue and complexion fair. She did not live long after her admission, the change from her

own airy room to the close and at times fetid atmosphere of this overcrowded ward was too much for her
aged frame. She passed away quietly, and I remember filling up a death certificate for 105 years.

One day, I was informed that a very distressing
case had been passed from Canterbury. It was a
young woman about twenty-four. She had one
child, and was about to be confined again. It would
appear that she had married a coach-builder, who
was born in St. Paul's, Covent Garden. She told
me that he was a very good, quiet man, when sober,
and had been very kind and good to her, but that
when he took anything to drink he became as one
insane, and in one of his drunken fits he had
knocked a man down and killed him ; that he had
been tried and found guilty of murder, and was then
lying under sentence of death. I also learned that
the Guardians of Canterbury had passed her on to
us, away from all her friends. The poor creature
was simply broken-hearted. She had a very bad
confinement, and remained long sick and ill. When
she got better she made an application to the Strand
Board for outdoor relief. She was told to come
before the Board at the next meeting in Bow Street.
It was unfortunately a very wet night, and being
thinly clad, she got wet through, and sat in her wet

clothes two hours. She also got wet on her return
journey. That night she was seized with inflam-
mation of the lungs, and remained for many weeks
in the greatest jeopardy. Ultimately, she got better,
when I sent her to a Convalescent Home in Hert-
fordshire. She was so patient and grateful that
I wrote an account of her sad story, which was
published in *The Morning Star*. It evoked dona-
tions amounting to £25. After buying her some
additional clothing, I paid her journey for self and
child to Canterbury (the baby had died), handing
her as she went away some £20. The Board, at my
request, allowed her outdoor relief for a twelvemonth. Some years after, I happened to be in
Canterbury, when I found her out. She had been
in the same situation some seven years. She had
supported herself and child, and had no occasion to
spend the money I had collected for her; altogether
she fully bore out the opinion I had formed of her.
The reason why the Guardian Board had acted so
harshly to this young woman was this : If they had
allowed her to remain in their workhouse until after
the execution of her husband, as a widow they could
not have removed her for a twelvemonth ; they
therefore sent her away at once to avoid this dilemma.

About two years after Mr. Catch's departure, I

was surprised by a visit from the medical officer of
the Newington Workhouse. He told me that he
had called to ask me whether I could advise him
what he was to do; that Catch obstructed him in
his duty, swore at him, and refused to obey his
orders. I told him to go down to the Poor Law
Board, but that they might or might not assist him.
Unfortunately, at that time, Mr. Farnall was away
in Manchester, superintending the special relief
arrangements in Lancashire with regard to the
Cotton Famine, and there was no one at the Board
who could or would advise him. He called on me
on several occasions subsequently to tell me of the
misery he daily underwent. On one occasion I told
him to write down in a journal all instances of
obstruction, and if possible get every case verified
by a witness. Sooner or later you will catch him,
I said. He followed my advice. One day he came
to me and told me he thought he had got together
sufficient evidence, and should now ask for an
official inquiry. Mr. Farnall, one of the most
honourable Poor Law Inspectors the Board ever had,
had just then come back to town. I got some influence to bear on the Board, and an inquiry was
granted. It lasted some time, and Mr. Simmonds
proved the obstruction, &c., so completely, that on the

last day, and when it was evident how the case would
go, Catch followed the doctor and paid nurse out of
the Board-room. They stopped in one of the day
wards to discuss the case and its probable results,
when Catch went to his office and wrote in his
journal that he had surprised the pair holding improper relations. This charge coming to the knowledge of the nurse, who was a respectable young
woman, she went at once to the physician accoucheur
of Guy's Hospital and requested that he would
examine her. This he did, when he gave her a
certificate that Catch's allegation was untrue. A
special meeting of the Board having been called to
investigate this charge, it was made absolutely clear
that Catch had hatched this foul accusation. The
Board immediately suspended him. The circumstances were reported to the Poor Law Board, who
called on him to resign. It will hardly be believed
that after this, Catch, mainly through the influence
of his friends at the Strand Board and the aid of the
clerk, got appointed to the Lambeth Workhouse,
where for some time he tyrannized over the subordinate officers and inmates, until at last, his cup
being full, he lost that appointment also. Hereafter I will give the particulars of this episode, and
of the notable trial in the Court of Queen's Bench,

where he attempted to clear his character and to get reinstated.

For five or six years after the departure of Mr. Catch my life was a fairly pleasant one. There was no obstruction from the master or the matron, and as there was nothing to ask of the Board things went on quietly, and therefore the daily duty ceased to be onerous added to which I had several pupils whose instruction in the wards was to me a very agreeable pastime. Here let me remark how melancholy it is that the vast field for clinical observation and study which the sick, nursery, and lying-in wards of large urban workhouses afford, should be utterly thrown away. There are certain diseases which can hardly be seen anywhere else, such as of those of young children and of aged persons, and yet they are completely ignored.

I have said that for a time everything went on peacefully, but a rude awakening was in store, for about the years 1862–1865, in consequence of widespread distress in the metropolis, persons were admitted beyond the capacity of the House to hold them. This necessitated a representation to the Board, and, as a consequence, a revival of the antagonism from the so-called economical members of the Board, who charged me with being too squeamish,

and with having brought the influx on myself by
being too indulgent to the sick. The hostility went
so far with one Guardian who considered me so very
troublesome that he put a notice on the agenda to
reduce my salary. This was renewed by him from
time to time, indeed, whenever I made a representation to the Board on this subject.

That there was abundant cause for such representations will be understood when it is stated that, in
consequence of the overcrowding and the heated and
vitiated atmosphere caused thereby, cases of fever
induced therefrom were constantly cropping up, and
it was one of my perplexities how to deal with them.
In those days there were no such facilities as now
exist for sending fever cases away to separate
asylums, and we had to do the best we could.

Having, in 1863, had a succession of boys affected
with fever sent in from St. Anne's, Soho, I inquired
of the relieving officer from where they came, whereupon he informed me that a Mr. Williams, a clergyman in Porter Street, Soho, had opened a home for
friendless boys. On interviewing this clergyman,
I told him that I had called to protest against his
sending these fever cases to the Workhouse, there
being no room for them. He replied by asking me
what he was to do with them, as at that time he had

some four or five boys down with fever; and then he
took me into an old, disused slaughter-house, where,
on some straw, I saw these lads lying ill. Before
leaving him I arranged that he should go over the
House and see for himself that there were no vacant
beds. On the morning appointed he came, bringing
with him a person whom he represented to be his
secretary, and who he asked to be allowed to take
with him. No objection being made, he accompanied
us. I was somewhat surprised at the bearing of this
so-called secretary, and still more so at his conduct
in the House, when we went through the wards. I
thought he was a very intelligent gentleman, and
wondered at him occupying the position of secretary
to Mr. Williams, at say, £1 a week. I satisfied Mr.
Williams that I could not continue to take in his
numerous waifs and strays, and on leaving, his companion parted from me with many expressions of
thanks for my courtesy in allowing him to accompany
me. I had not the least idea who he was, or his
name, but I felt pretty sure that he must be a gentleman. It transpired subsequently that he was no
other than Mr. J. Alexander Shaw Stewart, and my
chance acquaintance became in after years one of my
kindest and truest friends. As a result of this
interview with Mr. Williams a school was opened,

called afterwards the Newport Market Refuge Industrial School, and for several years it was under my medical charge. During the years I was connected with that establishment I never had a case of fever of any kind, although the school was located in a densely crowded and repulsively degraded neighbourhood. It was a striking instance of what could be done in keeping schools free from epidemic disease, if only the persons having control of them adopt, and strictly carry out, judicious sanitary arrangements. During my period of office I made the acquaintance of the Duke of Westminster, Mr. and Mrs. Gladstone, the latter of whom was a frequent visitor there, as well as many ladies of rank, &c.

About this time there came an urgent request to go to the House. On my arrival I found a young German woman near her confinement who was in a state of great mental distress. On asking for an explanation, I was informed that the day before a gentlemanly-looking person had called at the house and asked to see the matron. To her he stated that he was a medical man, and had been commissioned by the friends of one of his patients to look out for some healthy young woman near her confinement who might be engaged as a wet nurse by a lady under his care. The master brought down to him this girl, when he instructed her to send her next day to his consulting-room, where the lady's friends might see her. She accordingly went. Shortly after her arrival there she rushed out of the house, stating that she had been insulted by the doctor. Police aid coming to her assistance, the doctor's residence was visited, with the result that he was taken into custody, and brought before the magistrate, who remanded him without bail for inquiries to be made. The publicity of the case led to the bringing of other charges of a similar character, and he was ultimately committed for trial. Having been called upon to attend the German girl, I was naturally called as a witness, and was subsequently subpœnaed to attend at the Old Bailey. I found four other young women there in a similar predicament, all in charge of a police constable, and for three days I spent my whole time in their company, for whenever I got up to walk anywhere the women and the constable got up also and followed me. The situation was suggestive, but by no means pleasant. On the Thursday morning I was informed by the prosecution that I might go away, as the prisoner, who turned out to be a man of good family and an officer in the army, had pleaded guilty to a common assault, &c., &c. As the girl's history was somewhat interesting I sent an

account of it to *The Times* newspaper. It was as
follows : She had been living at Chicago with her
two brothers, when they received a letter stating that
their mother in Germany was very ill, and begged
that her daughter would come home. She started
immediately, but on arriving at her native town
found that her mother was dead. She thereupon
sold all the effects, and with upwards of £100 started
back again for Chicago. She passed through London
to Liverpool to take passage for New York, but the
machinery of the steamer breaking down when two
days out, the captain returned for repairs. She had
made the acquaintance of a young Frenchman on
board, who finding she had money, made love to her,
and induced her to go back to London and become
his wife. After living with her until all the money
was gone, he deserted her, and being without friends,
she had to come into the House. My letter appearing in *The Times*, some £45 was sent me, which
sufficed to enable me to send her and her child to
her brother in Chicago. I provided her with an out-
fit, and arranged with the captain of the steamer to
take charge of her, and send one of his trustworthy
officers to see her to the station in New York for
Chicago, and parting with her to put into her hands
the balance remaining. Some months afterwards

I had a letter from the captain, stating that he had carried out my request, and had finally given her the £25 or thereabouts. There was every reason to believe that one of the subscribers was Her Majesty the Queen, though it was not so distinctly stated in a letter I received from a gentleman connected with the Court.

In the early part of 1865 the Guardians appointed a superintendent nurse. She was a young, and very respectable-looking woman. The Guardians had been moved to do this by the evidence of Miss Twining before the Select Committee, and by the general feeling excited by the revelations made in Gibson's case in St. Giles's, and that of Timothy Daley in the Holborn, Union. In the winter of 1863 and 1864, and again in 1864 and 1865, as also in 1865 and 1866 the admissions had been so many, and the crowding so great, as to tax the resources of the establishment to the utmost, notwithstanding that I had moved the sick ward to the top of the building, and gained additional cubic space by removing the ceiling and re-ceiling the rafters ; but I could not by any contrivance increase the area. The beds therefore were placed so close together that the patients had to get out at the end of their beds, there being no possibility of getting out at the side. It was a task

beyond this young woman's strength to effectually
supervise the numerous patients, but she could check
some of the graver abuses connected with pauper
nursing. This she did to the best of her ability.
In the same spring that she was appointed—that of
1865—the late Dr. Francis Anstie called on me.
He said he was deputed by the late Dr. Wakley to
call and state that he had decided to appoint a
commission for the purpose of investigating the state
of London workhouses, and he thought I could
suggest the best course to follow to obtain admission
to them. I told him I would introduce him to the
Chairman of the Board, who alone had the power to
grant permission to a stranger to enter the Workhouse, unless special application had been made to
Board, and leave given. He called on the Chairman,
who gave him a letter to the master, authorizing his
admission. Before he left, I told Dr. Anstie that
when he went over the House I would accompany
him. Some short time after, he wrote, making an
appointment. I showed him through the whole House,
pointing out the defects and shortcomings, and told
him of my continued efforts to get the place improved,
and of the determined hostility of the majority of the
Board to any efforts I had made. I also showed him
a list of the fever cases I had attended, and how

constantly fever was developed when the numbers increased and the overcrowding was greatest. Dr. Anstie took careful notes of what I showed him, as the sequel proved. Some month or so after, I had a note from him, asking me to look in that week's *Lancet* for the report of his visit. I did so; when I found that he had exposed the rotten condition of things with marvellous clearness and fidelity, but as he had referred to me and my efforts to clear out this Augean stable, I was perfectly convinced that the least intelligent element of the Board would be incited by their clerk to charge me with having written the article in question. As I anticipated, this came to pass, for I heard that so it had been said at the Board meeting, and in consequence, a most insulting resolution was adopted, in which I was directly charged with trying to bring the Guardians—'who were my masters'—into contempt. So angry was their language and so bitter their hostility, that Dr. Anstie wrote to the Board, stating that he had been permitted by their Chairman to go over the House, and that the observations he had made were his own, and that I had not seen a line of his manuscript, or knew of his report, until it appeared in print; he further challenged the Board to show where, in his description, he had departed from the

truth. The storm he had raised was, after a while,
allayed. Dr. Anstie continued to visit other workhouses, the condition of which he similarly described.
These reports, which appeared in *The Lancet*, were
copied into, and commented upon, in sundry daily
and weekly journals, and gradually produced a feeling
of intense public indignation. Dr. Anstie had acted
so generously towards me in screening me from the
hostility of the worst elements of the Board, that I
arranged a dinner-party, to meet and discuss workhouse abuses. Among the guests was Mr. John
Storr, of King Street, Covent Garden, who was one
of the wealthiest, as he was one of the most respectable, members of the Strand Board, and who, since
his election two years before this, had proved to be
my most able advocate and friend. When Dr. Anstie
arrived, he brought with him Mr. Ernest Hart, whom
he introduced as one of the staff of *The Lancet*, and as
one interested in the question of workhouse administration. After dinner a discussion took place as
regards the general condition of these establishments.

Ultimately it was arranged that a conference should
be held at Mr. Storr's offices, King Street, Covent
Garden, at a time hereafter to be named. Our
dinner-party was held in December, 1865. In the
early part of January, Dr. Anstie, Mr. Hart, and I,

met by appointment at Mr. Storr's, when our discussion was resumed. At first it was proposed that
we should call a public meeting and denounce the
system, when I pointed out that if we only did that
the agitation would soon come to an end, and therefore it would be better to form an Association for the
purpose of more thoroughly enlightening the public.
My suggestion was adopted. Mr. John Storr generously offered to put down £100 to float the Association.
He also offered to become its treasurer, and to give
us the free use of one of his offices, in which the
meetings of the Association could be held. This
meeting took place on a Thursday evening, and as
The Lancet came out next day, Mr. Hart left us and
went down to *The Lancet* office, to announce in the
paper the formation of the society. At our meeting
it was also arranged that we should respectively write
to those we knew and ask them to join our Association.
I wrote, among others, to Mr. Shaw Stewart, who at
once joined us, and to Miss Twining, and to many
other ladies and gentlemen who had been engaged in
works of benevolence. The Association prospered
beyond our wildest anticipations, and we were speedily
joined by Earl Carnarvon, Earl Grosvenor, the Archbishop of York, &c.; whilst money came in freely.
Shortly after the formation of the Association, of

which, in conjunction with Dr. Anstie and Mr. Hart,
I was one of the honorary secretaries; Mr. Farnall,
the Metropolitan Poor Law Inspector, wrote to me,
stating that he had been deputed by Mr. Charles P.
Villiers, the President of the Poor Law Board, to offer
his services in giving information to the youthful
Association, and that he had written to me, as I was
the only honorary secretary he knew. Mr. Farnall
subsequently attended the meetings of the committee,
and afforded us much valuable information. No use
was ever made of Mr. John Storr's office, as all subsequent meetings of the Association were held in Mr.
Hart's house, in Wimpole Street.

In the month of May, 1866, Miss Beaton, the
superintendent nurse, informed me that she intended
to resign her situation, and apply for another as a
nurse at a general hospital; at the same time asking
me whether I would give her a reference. Whilst
expressing my regret that she was going, I readily
promised to do all I could for her, and with that object
gave her a letter of introduction to Dr. Anstie, assistant
physician to the Westminster Hospital, and to Mr.
Hart, who was then connected with St. Mary's Hospital. Dr. Anstie took her name and address, and
promised to do what he could for her; Mr. Hart
asked her to sit down, and proceeded to question her

on the various matters connected with the Strand
Workhouse I had mentioned at the committee
meetings, &c. Ultimately he dismissed her, but not
until he had a promise from her that she would
write down all her experience of the wrong-doing
she had witnessed at the Strand. She did this. On
getting her manuscript statement he sent it to Earl
Carnarvon, one of the committee, and asked him to
apply to Mr. Villiers for an official inquiry. I had not
the remotest knowledge that anything of the kind had
been done, nor had my other colleague, Dr. Anstie.
In the early part of June Mr. Hart told me that there
was to be an official inquiry into the management and
the condition of the Strand Workhouse, and that I
should be called as a witness, but he did not tell me
how it had been brought about. A few days after I
received an official intimation that such inquiry
would be held, and that my attendance would be
required. I had hoped that the inquiry would
be conducted by the Metropolitan Inspector, Mr.
Farnall; but it was not so. Mr. Fleming sent
another member of the staff. The inquiry was held,
the first witness called being Miss Beaton. She
astonished me by the extent and character of her
revelations, of some part of which I was an eye-
witness, and therefore knew to be true. Her exam-

ination lasted all day. Next morning, the evidence
she had given appeared in all the papers, which commented thereon. On the second day I was called.
On taking my seat Mr. Caine said, " Oh ! we have
met before ; " I did not know where. I had not long
been under examination before Dr. Anstie, who was
in the room, came behind my chair, and said, " Take
care how you answer questions; this inspector does
not mean fairly by you ; he is trying to put you in
a false position." Forewarned by this, I simply
answered his questions, and parried those which were
irrelevant and misleading. The next day my evidence,
in full appeared in every paper, and all the leading
journals denounced the Board of Guardians for their
management of the House. It was unfortunate that
my Board should have been selected, inasmuch as
nearly all the workhouses in the metropolis were in
very much the same condition. After the close of
the inquiry Mr. R. B. Caine returned to Whitehall,
and made the remarkable statement in his official
report that the condition of the House was due to my
not having made proper representations to the Guardians. I subsequently heard that on his report being
submitted to the President of the Board, it was altogether set aside by him, and that he wrote the report
himself. It had, however, come to my knowledge

that Mr. Caine had delivered himself of this view;
when I wrote to the Poor Law Board complaining of
his injustice, and pointed out that for some three
years he had, as Metropolitan Inspector during
the time Mr. Farnall was away in Manchester, visited
the Strand, and that he had always entered in the
visitors' book that he was completely satisfied with
the state of the House. I am happy to say that Mr.
R. B. Caine got very little credit out of the whole
transaction, for his report was severely criticized by
the press for its transparent bias. Just at this time
a circular letter was sent by the Poor Law Board to
all the workhouse medical officers—some forty in
number—in the metropolis. It was issued evidently
with the view of entrapping these gentlemen into
contradictory answers to the questions which were
submitted to them. It was clearly necessary to take
immediate action. I therefore sent a letter to each
of them, asking them to meet me at the Freemasons'
Tavern, Great Queen's Street, Lincoln's Inn Fields.
The majority of them came. Having been voted into
the chair, I pointed out to them what was the object of
the letter, and earnestly urged that we should agree
as to the form of reply. This view was adopted, and
the answers as agreed upon were sent by all present to
the Poor Law Board. On the same occasion it was

arranged that an Association should be established of metropolitan workhouse medical officers, so that we might be prepared to deal promptly with any similar departmental trickery. This was done, and I was elected as the first president, an office which through various changes I have occupied to this day. The Association was, during the two following years, enabled to play an important part in the settlement of many vexed questions in the administration of workhouse medical relief, which, without the practical knowledge of medical men, would have been wholly left in the hands of the officials at the Poor Law Board, who at this time exhibited a singular unwillingness to face the facts. My official life after this was a particularly unpleasant one, inasmuch as I was credited with having asked for the inquiry, and having resolved to state that which would bring " my masters " into contempt. I should have survived all this misrepresentation, but unfortunately just at this juncture the Liberal Government was overthrown, and the Derby-Disraeli premiership was established. Earl Derby speedily pointed out that he intended to deal effectually with the scandal that had been brought to light in connection with workhouse infirmary administration, and with that view he had selected Mr. Gathorne Hardy—now Lord Cranborne—

as the President of the Poor Law Board, he being in
Lord Derby's judgment one of the fittest men in Her
Majesty's dominions to put things straight. Mr.
Hardy up to that date had been principally known as
a Chairman at Quarter Sessions, and an *ex-officio*
Guardian of a Kentish Board of Guardians. One of
the first official acts of this gentleman was to punish
Mr. Henry Farnall for his conduct in aiding the
Workhouse Infirmary Association. He was banished
from London and sent to the northern counties.
As Mr. Farnall's residence was at Blackheath, where
his wife and children were living, this act of Mr.
Hardy's was a serious inconvenience to him. The next
thing done was to appoint Dr. Markham as a Poor
Law Inspector and so-called medical adviser. Dr.
Markham up to this date had been the editor of what
was at that time an obscure journal. He was not
known to have ever been associated with any sanitary
work, nor to have seen the inside of a workhouse in
his life, and yet out of all the able physicians at the
time in the metropolis he was selected. The popular
explanation given for this appointment was that he
spent the larger portion of the day in looking out of
the windows of the Carlton, Pall Mall, and that Mr.
Hardy, making his acquaintance, gave him something
to do. He fully justified the selection thus made,

as will be shown hereafter, as he became in every
sense one of the most difficult officials of the Board.

At this time the permanent officials, notably Dr.
Edward Smith, promulgated the heresy that the area
and cubic space suggested by our Association for the
housing of the sick was excessive ; indeed, that the
area did not so much matter if the roof of the sick
ward was carried up high enough. These and other
statements having been promulgated by the staff, a
meeting of the Workhouse Medical Officers Association was called, to take the subject into consideration.
We had the aid of the late Dr. Parkes, the eminent
Professor of Hygiene, at Netley Hospital, as well as of
my two colleagues in the secretaryship of our Association. Conjointly, we drew up a paper stating what
was in our view the minimum area and the minimum
cubic space that should be sanctioned. This action
forced the hand of Mr. Hardy, and caused him to
issue a cubic space commission to determine this
question.

Shortly after the formation of the Conservative
Government a numerous and influential deputation,
consisting of Earl Shaftesbury, the Archbishop of
York, Earl Grosvenor, and many others, waited on
Mr. Hardy, when representations were made to him
urging extensive alterations on the then system. I

was so hurt at the intrigues going on at the Poor
Law Board and the attempt of Mr. R. B. Caine to
make me solely responsible for the condition of the
Strand Workhouse, that I availed myself of the
opportunity to tell the President that in any scheme
he might lay down for an alteration, I hoped that he
would be guided by his own judgment, and not by
that of the permanent officials, who would most
assuredly lead him astray. This plain speaking was
not particularly relished by those against whom it
was mainly directed; it doubtless intensified ill
feeling against me. I also handed to him a series
of Resolutions drawn up by the Council of our Poor
Law Medical Officers' Association protesting against
the misstatements that had been propagated by Dr.
E. Smith, Poor Law Inspector, against the Metropolitan Workhouse medical officers.

Immediately subsequent to this our Workhouse
Association engaged itself in drawing up a scheme
for a general dietary for all London workhouses,
which differed in every establishment; in some
being, as at the Strand, when I first went there,
niggardly in the extreme, while in others it was
absurdly liberal. This question had engaged my
attention many years before, and when I introduced
an amended dietary at the Strand I was often twitted

by the economical element of the Board to the effect that my liberality in the way of dietary was the reason why the House had filled so much, paupers being attracted to the Union by the prospect of being better fed by the liberality I had evinced. This allegation was absurdly unjust. Years before, in 1863, I had, at the time I amended the dietary at the Strand, addressed a letter to the Department urging that they should issue a general order to the London Boards of Guardians enclosing a copy of a uniform dietary to be used in all Metropolitan workhouses (acute cases of sickness alone excepted). Although this suggestion had the approval of Mr. Farnall, who invited me down to the Board to talk the matter over with him, it was set aside. Mr. Fleming, the secretary, objected to everything of a controversial character. About this time, understanding that Mr. Hardy was engaged in drafting his Metropolitan Poor Bill, I wrote to him on several occasions ; one of the subjects I urged on him was the advisability of turning the vast field for clinical observations which our Workhouse infirmaries afforded to some practical purpose by throwing the wards open to medical students, pointing out what had been done at the Marylebone Workhouse Infirmary some thirty years before; I also urged that the hospitals he was about to establish should be officered by a resident medical man or resident medical men, but that in no instance should they be left alone in their control, but that their work should be superintended by an extern physician. I understood that my view was overruled through the opposition of certain physicians who thought that the educational opportunities thereby proposed would interfere with the voluntary hospitals they were connected with and the students attached to them.

I also pointed out how desirable it was that pauper schools should be consolidated, and that permanent young pauper children should be separated from those who were constantly going in and out of workhouses. Mr. Hardy always replied personally and with marked courtesy to the letters I sent him. In the session of 1867 Mr. Hardy brought in his Metropolitan Poor Bill. In his speech introducing it he referred to my evidence before the Select Committee, and said that he had resolved to adopt the views I had advocated, namely, the provision of all medicines and appliances at the cost of the rates ; but although the Bill passed with great facility and amidst general approval it was a very long time, in some cases four, five, and six years, before the dispensary clauses were carried out.

The Bill had hardly become law before Mr. Hardy
was transferred to the War Office and Earl Devon
became President. This nobleman when Lord
Courtenay, Poor Law Inspector, or Lord Courtenay,
Parliamentary Secretary, had entirely supported the
worst parts of the old system of administration and
control. He always yielded to Boards of Guardians, and, when President, entirely deferred to the
permanent staff. During the short time that he
held office—for the election of 1868 shortly afterwards occurred and with it a strong reaction—he
instituted a new order of officials at Gwydyr House—
to wit, *Assistant Inspectors.*

Of course it was not to be expected that the
evidence given by me at the official inquiry would
fail to intensify the bitter hostility of a section of
the Board towards me, especially as the clerk to the
Guardians never lost an opportunity of putting my
conduct before them in the worst light. Consequently, shortly after my evidence had been given
an attempt was made to displace me. The Guardian
who moved my resignation was a lodging-house
keeper in St. Clement's Danes. Having been told
that this Guardian contemplated this procedure, I
forwarded a letter to the Board in which I gave an
outline of all I had done and had attempted to do

during the ten years I had been the medical officer, the amount of antagonism I had provoked, and the various resolutions which had been adopted as the result of my endeavours. It was not very pleasant reading for some of them to hear, as there were several still there who had taken an active part in thwarting me at all times, and this letter thoroughly answered them. In spite of all that was alleged, when the resolution was submitted to the vote it was found that I had just as many friends as enemies, and therefore the motion was not carried. I do not know whether at that time the intrigue between the clerk and certain permanent officials of the Poor Law Board had commenced, but it took place not a very long time afterwards, as I found out some twenty months after.

One result of the evidence I had given as regards the over-crowding was this: I was empowered to send some of the acutely sick to the voluntary hospitals, and I did so to a limited degree, but my action here was again met by the hostility of a section of this Board. It was suggested that I had sent them away to get rid of the trouble of attending to them, and it was gravely proposed that I should have the cost of the cabs in which they were removed deducted from my salary.

As an illustration of the mode adopted by some Boards to annoy their medical officers I subjoin the following : In June, 1867, a person was sent into the Strand Workhouse by the district medical officer, insane. In conjunction with a Justice of the Peace, I examined him, and we certified as to his mental condition, whereupon he was sent to Hanwell. Three weeks after, he was discharged from the asylum, not because he had recovered, but through an informality in the certificate given by the justice. As this latter gentleman was out of town, I took the lunatic before Mr. Vaughan, at Bow Street, who, after examining him for a minute or so, threw up the certificate, and said he would not sign it, the man was not mad. I again implored him to fill up the certificate, as the man had been only sent back to the House through an informality in the certificate. As he again refused, I said, " Then I have to re-quest that Sir Thomas Henry be apprised of the case." This was done, and Sir Thomas advised that he should go back to the House for another week. That afternoon the lunatic was interviewed by three of the Board, who pronounced the opinion that he was of sound mind. Hearing of this irregu-larity, I wrote to the Commissioners in Lunacy, and asked them to see the man. They attended at the

House and examined him, and directed his removal
to Hanwell without delay. That night he escaped
by scaling a high wall, and was not captured for
three days, when the police caught him. In the
following September he was discharged cured, when
I received a letter from the clerk, informing me
thereof, and stating that the Board was of opinion
that I had been too hasty in sending the man away,
and that too by an unusual course. I immediately
wrote to the Commissioners in Lunacy, enclosing
the clerk's letter, and asked their opinion, when the
secretary, Mr. C. P. Phillips, wrote to me stating
that at the time the Commissioners saw him he was
clearly insane, and that the Commissioners approved
of my action under the exceptional circumstances
of the case. I sent their reply to the Board. The
evening the clerk read my letter to the Board, the
man's wife made an application for his re-admission
to the House, as he had a relapse of his insanity.
This man went into and out of the asylum on several
occasions subsequently. Whenever he was at liberty he
made me aware of it by coming to my house between
1 and 2 a.m., and ringing my night-bell violently.
Of course I had to put up with the infliction, as the
man was not in his right mind. This annoyance
went on for years, and only ceased when I left Soho.

6

The Guardians also authorized my sending some of the infirm women to Edmonton, where the school for the pauper children was situated. This school was a favourite place of resort for the worst members of the Board, and very comfortable parties were kept up there at the expense of the ratepayers. A certain portion of the Guardians went down fortnightly in carriages to inspect the schools, and every scheme was adopted by those not on the School Committee to be asked to go out of their turn by those who were entitled to go. It meant an outing in the country, and a splendid dinner with wine, &c., and tea, free of cost, to all who went there.

Of course the resident officers were always in high favour with the majority of the Board, and to arraign them or their conduct was a hopeless affair, as the least competent element immediately stood forward to shield them.

In the September of 1867 a young girl was admitted, suffering with rheumatic fever; she remained ill some time, but towards the end of the month she recovered sufficiently to be sent to a Convalescent Home, but as the autumn was a cold one I decided that she should be sent to Edmonton, and to secure her considerate treatment I wrote a special certificate, which was addressed to

the matron, in which I stated what had been the
matter with her, and begged that she should be
kept warm and not employed in scrubbing or any
damp occupation.

About a month afterwards I found this girl again
in the women's sick ward in Cleveland Street with
a severe relapse of her rheumatic attack. On inquiry
I was told by the girl that shortly after she had
gone to Edmonton the matron came into her ward
and told her to go to the laundry. On her reminding her that she was still weak, and that the London
doctor had directed that she was to be kept warm,
the matron abused her and again ordered her there.
She went. In a very short time she broke down;
the matron, however, persisted in keeping her at
work, but at last she became so ill that she was
compelled to put her to bed. On the school doctor
seeing her it was decided to send her back to town,
some eight miles distant. She was sent in a tilted
cart and very imperfectly clad—that, too, on a very
cold day. It was altogether so improper a proceeding
that I complained to the Board, who made inquiries
of the matron, &c., who of course denied the facts
in toto. This false answer was sent to me. I was
so enraged that I drew up another complaint and
sent it to the Poor Law Board and asked for an

inquiry. Dr. Markham was deputed to go through
the form of an investigation, which he interpreted
by going, unknown to me, to the sick ward, asking
one or two questions of the girl, and sending for
the matron at Edmonton to come to his private
house in Harley Street. I did not know this at the
time. He then reported that I had made a " frivolous and vexatious complaint." I will leave my
readers to determine whether this procedure was
not a mockery of a Departmental inquiry. This
report, thus obtained, was sent to the Guardians,
whereupon a man, who had misconducted himself at
the official inquiry by coarsely asking " whether
mesenteric disease was not something to eat," moved
that I be suspended from my office. This was
adopted by the Board, only four of the members
supporting me, the fact being that the Board had
changed very considerably at the preceding election,
some of the Board ejected from office two years
before having unfortunately returned again. Of
course it was necessary for the Board to report this
suspension to the Poor Law Board. The clerk asked
permission to absent himself from duty for a time.
He took with him the minutes of the Board for the
preceding twelve years, and busied himself with
extracting all the hostile resolutions which the

Board had adopted against me, frequently at his suggestion, in return for my continuous efforts to cleanse their augean stable. I do not know who had distinctly intimated to the clerk that it was desirable to get rid of me, but the mover of my suspension stated that he knew the Poor Law Board wanted to get me discharged. That was admitted some time after by Sir Michael Hicks Beach in a conversation he had with a medical gentleman living near him in Gloucestershire.

Some month after my suspension a copy of the clerk's extracts was sent me by the Poor Law Board, and I was asked what I had to say to it. I acknowledged its receipt, and asked for an official inquiry. This request was ignored, although it was suggested by a minority of the Board, by the Vestry of St. Anne's, Soho, who unanimously supported me, and by many influential inhabitants of the parish in which I had lived and worked. That my suspension would have been followed by the Poor Law Board calling on me to resign my office, without delay, would have been certain, but the President, Earl Devon, was away, although the most terrible distress prevailed that winter in East London. He had gone off to the South of France, and there he remained some three months. On his return, he at once put me out of doubt by removing me from my office. It is very curious, but true, that when I turned on this Department and stated my own case, he made the remark to a friend, who repeated it to me, that he was surprised at my hostility to the Board, as in calling for my resignation no reflection had been made by the Department on my character. At this time a general order was issued by the Department, imposing, without payment, additional and onerous obligations upon Workhouse medical officers. It was to the effect that they should make, from time to time, a return of all that was amiss in their respective workhouses to the Board of Guardians, the doing of which, on my own account, had led to my differences with the Strand Board. It had always been understood that this was one of the duties of the Inspectors, but it was attempted to throw the obligation on the doctors. After Earl Devon resigned, our Council had an interview with Mr. Goschen at the House of Commons, who promised an important modification of this unjust order.

When my compulsory resignation was called for, it was decided by the Rev. Harry Jones, the late Dr. Anstie and others, to call a meeting of the all but moribund Infirmaries Association at Mr. Hart's house, to discuss the matter, and arrange for action. The meeting was addressed by both of these gentlemen, and by several others, and the action of the Department was severely censured by all who were present, except one person. Sir John Simeon, M. P., undertook to put a question in the House, and to move for papers. In due course the question was asked, when Sir Michael Hicks Beach made reply that the Board did not desire to make any reflection on my character, but that I had been called on to resign as I could not get on with the Board of Guardians.

The insufficiency of this answer will be understood when I state that it had been already decided to break up the Strand Board by taking away St. Anne's and joining it to St. James's, in order to make the Westminster Union, and by adding St. Martin to the remnant of the Strand—thereby making it a perfectly new Union.

I have stated that it was arranged at the meeting of the Workhouse Infirmaries Association, called to consider the action of the Department in requesting me to send in my resignation, that the papers connected with the subject should be moved for in the House. This was done, and in due course they were presented. On their appearance, *The Lancet* commented as follows thereon—

"At last, after months of delay, the Parliamentary

Papers concerning the enforced resignation by Dr.
Rogers of his post as medical officer of the Strand
Union have been published. They amply justify
everything we have said as to the unwarrantable cha-
racter of the action of the Poor Law Board and of the
Strand Board of Guardians in the whole affair.

" It is impossible for us to afford space for a
detailed analysis of these papers, but we beg to draw
attention to the following damning facts. 1. The
evidence upon the whole case consists (*a*) of a series
of quotations by the Guardians, or rather by a party
among the Guardians, hostile to Dr. Rogers, from
minutes and other documents extending over many
years, these extracts being selected without any
reference to contemporary facts which would throw
light upon them, and (*b*) of utterly gratuitous and un-
founded insinuations that the various leading articles
in the general press which were written apropos of
the notorious scandals at the Strand were written
by Dr. Rogers and his friends. 2. That although
Dr. Rogers (backed by a most respectable minority of
the Guardians and by the Vestry of St. Anne's,
Soho) protested that it was impossible to deal with
these charges without an open inquiry, such inquiry
was refused by the Poor Law Board. 3. As regards
the Edmonton scandal which was the cause of the dis-

pute which led immediately to the suspension of Dr.
Rogers, the printed evidence distinctly bears out the
justice of Dr. Rogers' allegations. 4. Nevertheless
Dr. Markham reported to the Poor Law Board that
his inquiries had proved these charges to be false.
He does not, however, venture to specify the nature of
the inquiry by which he disproved charges which, with
unblushing effrontery, Mr. Fleming says were made
on the unsupported testimony of a pauper, but which
are now seen to be absolutely corroborated by two
respectable witnesses (one of them a medical man),
besides the direct observation of Dr. Rogers; and
either Dr. Markham did not take, or the Poor Law
Board has suppressed, the evidence of at least one
other impartial witness, the master of the Strand
Workhouse, which we have reason to believe would
have absolutely settled the matter in Dr. Rogers'
favour.

"It is well-nigh incredible, but we have heard it on
authority which we cannot discredit, that although
the so-called inquiry on which the Medical Inspector
of the Poor Law Board based the unfavourable report,
which gave the Strand Guardians courage to make
their onslaught upon Dr. Rogers, included an
examination at Dr. Markham's private house of the
Edmonton officials chiefly inculpated by Dr. Rogers'

charges.   Dr. Markham never asked Dr. Rogers one
single question.   Volumes of comment could not add
anything to the ugly emphasis of this fact."

Sir Michael Hicks Beach has been recently afflicted.
I would ask him if he does not consider that his sufferings would have been intensified if his sleep had been
disturbed by the noise of carpet-beating—if he had
been waited on by infirm and drunken women, and
broken-down potmen—if the air he breathed had been
poisoned by the dust from the beating of carpets, and
utterly vitiated by over-crowding? And yet, because I
had protested against this hideous wrong-doing, and
had done my best to get it altered, he had to get up
in the House of Commons and do his best to justify
the action of the Board.

The Department thought I was disposed of; it
was not long before I showed them the contrary,
as some of them did not subsequently hesitate to
admit.

I have stated that it had been decided, owing to the
all but unanimous application of the ratepayers of
St. Anne's, Soho, to the Poor Law Board, to take that
parish out of the Strand Union and join it to St.
James's, so as to constitute the Westminster Union,
and within a very brief space of time after my compulsory resignation this was done.   As there was no

returning officer for the Union, the Poor Law Board
directed that the Vestry clerks of each parish should
act as such for this time, consequently all books and
papers relating to St. Anne's had to be handed over by
the clerk, of Peterborough notoriety, who was the
friend of Catch, when a notable discovery was made,
to wit, that the proxy book, as it was called, was altogether illegal, and had been so for years, as by the
efflux of time the power to vote by proxy in most instances had expired, and yet this clerk had gone on
year after year issuing voting papers to persons,
though he must have known that they had no right
to vote. We had often wondered how it happened
that we could not oust the Guardians who sat for St.
Anne's : they had been returned by illegal proxy
votes for years. Although the Guardians who had
recently represented St. Anne's in the old Strand
Union had lost the kindly aid of the clerk, it was so
necessary to some of them that they should still be
Guardians, that they again got themselves nominated,
only to meet with a unanimous rejection on the part
of the ratepayers, as the following letter from an
ex-Guardian for St. Anne's, Soho, who was a supporter
of Dr. Rogers, but precluded from again standing
through serious illness, of which he subsequently died,
will show—

" To the Editor of *The Daily News.*

" THE STRAND UNION AND THEIR LATE MEDICAL

OFFICER.

" Sir,—It will be gratifying to the friends of Dr. Rogers, who was suspended by the Board for his continued advocacy of the rights of the sick poor, to know that at the election of Guardians of St. Anne's, Soho, which took place on Saturday last, the whole of those who voted for his suspension, &c., were rejected by an overwhelming majority of ratepayers.

" I am, Sir,

" Yours obediently,

" Joseph George.

"81. Dean Street,

" *April* 11, 1868."

The story of two of these men I will here relate. The first had been appointed Assessed Tax Collector for St. Anne's, Soho, but two or three years after my resignation of the Strand he was discovered to be a defaulter to some hundreds of pounds, which his sureties had to make up. He was one of the most active of my opponents. The second had commenced life as a milkman. Very shortly afterwards he began to take tenement houses in the worst part of St. Anne's, Soho, which he let out from garret to cellar to the very poor. His lodgers lived under the most insanitary conditions, and my local knowledge induced me always to protest against this man as a Guardian of the poor. He was always the most energetic of my opponents at the Strand Board. At last retribution came upon him. It was in this wise : he was a freemason, and, though very illiterate, he had managed to obtain a high position in the masonic brotherhood, so much so that he was deputed to preside as the returning officer in an important election. There were two candidates, one a Guardian of the Strand Union, who was his personal friend—in fact, that very person who had recommended the broken-down potman as one of my nurses—the other was to him a comparative stranger.

After the ballot had been taken, this returning officer gave the election to his friend by such a majority of voting papers that the unsuccessful candidate, who had been promised support to a large extent, suspected foul play, and made an application to the Prince of Wales, as Grand Master, to order a scrutiny. His Royal Highness assented, and directed the Earl of Carnarvon to hold it, when it came out clearly that this ex-Guardian of St. Anne's, Soho, had knowingly made a false return, and he was sentenced to a deprivation of all his offices in the brotherhood, and exclusion from his Lodge for three years. He was at this time holding various offices in St. Giles, also in St. Pancras, but the different

parochial Boards' requested him to send in his resignation forthwith, as they refused any longer to
associate with him or allow him to remain a member
of their respective Boards.

Here let me remark that there is no occupation
that can be followed at which so much money can
be made as by the system adopted by some specu-
lators of taking houses in poor localities and letting
them out in single rooms to the humbler classes.
To get therefrom all the benefit possible you must
be absolutely heartless and unprincipled. If the
wretched tenants do not pay their rent weekly, they
must go out—and do go ! Having, after their weekly
collections, much spare time on their hands, these
men often get on to Boards of Guardians and
frequently on to the District Boards as well : at
the first they are always present when outdoor relief
is given, which they strongly advocate as a means
whereby the rent may be more readily secured;
secondly, on the District Boards, where they are
always at hand when the Inspector of Nuisances
and of insanitary tenement houses makes his report.
They generally try to be on the best of terms with
this latter official, their scheme being to minimize
the character of their reports, and to minimize what
is required to be done, as it saves their pockets.

One of these persons, who had some three hundred
of these houses, was fined by the magistrate for neg-
lecting to keep his houses in a sanitary condition.
I had the honour of his permanent hostility.
He was, at the time of being fined, not only a
member of the Board, but of the Health Committee
also. When I was a member of the Strand Board
of Works I carried a resolution that the name of
the owner of these tenements should be always
included in the Inspector's Report. In my deliberate judgment, all persons of this class should be
disqualified from sitting on a Board of Guardians,
or on any District Board. The same class of middle-
men are to be found in all large towns ; they are
the most dangerous members of the body politic, and
should be rigorously treated as such. The person
I have before referred to, was not only a member
of the Strand Board of Guardians but a member of
the District Board also. He was also on that of
St. Giles, and St. Pancras. In all these places, and
districts, he had tenement houses.

It having been my habit to go to the Workhouse
infirmary for twelve years early each morning, I
found my time at first hang somewhat heavily on
my hands, but after a short while I made up my
mind what to do. I resolved to watch the action

of the Department, and to do my best to make the permanent officials do their duty, so far as my observation could aid me. With that object in view, I arranged for an aggregate meeting of the profession, at the Freemason's Tavern, to discuss the composition of the so-called Board at Whitehall, and the grievances of the Poor Law medical officers. Among other things, I told them that the nominal Board never met, and that documents requiring the various members' official signature, were taken round to the residences of the Ministers, and, it was alleged, frequently signed without reading the contents.

This statement had been made in the House by an ex-President.

This meeting was an immense success, for not only was there a very large attendance of medical men, but they came from all parts of the country, and the Department had an opportunity of learning how their permanent officials were watched and criticized throughout the country as permanent officials always should be. Mr. Griffin having retired from further vindicating the claims of his professional brethren owing to an attack of paralysis, to which, unhappily, he ultimately succumbed, the balance of the money in his possession was handed over to me in trust for carrying on the objects of the Association. It was also decided that the Provincial Poor Law Medical Officers Association, of which he was the Chairman, should be merged in the Metropolitan Association, which had been started by me two years before, and I was elected the President, a position I held for some years, and which I resigned only when I recognized that the objects of our Association would be more readily advanced by selecting some medical member of the House of Commons to act in that capacity. So I contented myself with the humbler position of Chairman of Council.

At this representative meeting of the profession, I alluded, *inter alia,* to my evidence before the Select Committee, and to my advocacy of the supply of all medicines. I also mentioned the action of one of the Inspectors, a Mr. Gulson, when Mr. Fleming's letter containing the recommendation of that committee was read out by the clerk of the Weymouth Board of Guardians at their weekly meeting. The Chairman having appealed to this official, who was present, as to what should be done, he stated that the resolution was only carried in committee by one vote, and that the Chairman of the Committee, had voted against it. Thereupon the Guardians of the Weymouth Union directed that the official letter

7

should lie on the table, and no expensive medicines
were found. I took care that a report of this meeting should be sent to every Poor Law medical
officer, and to the Department, as well as to every
influential Member of Parliament I could reach.
One of the reports having fallen into the hands
of Mr. C. P. Villiers, the ex-President and Chairman
of the Select Committee on Poor Relief, that gentleman wrote to me protesting against the statement
which had been made, and assuring me that it was
in direct opposition to what had really taken place,
as he had warmly supported my suggestion, and that
he should at once call on Mr. Gulson for an explanation of his statement. He also stated that he
had been much annoyed at the long delay that had
occurred ere the Chief Secretary, Mr. H. Fleming,
had drawn up and forwarded to the various Boards
of Guardians the letter containing the recommendation of the Select Committee. From other sources,
I subsequently learned that for a very long period
of time prior to the resignation of Mr. Villiers as
President of the Board, he held hardly any communication with his Permanent Secretary. It will
be well understood, that if it took some fifteen
months for the Permanent Secretary to draw up
and issue the letter containing the Committee's

suggestion as regards expensive medicines, that no hurry would occur in the establishment of Poor Law dispensaries in the Metropolis, which was only an amplification of my original suggestion. And that actually happened; and it was only by our constantly pegging away, that at last the Board commenced to establish them. But whilst no *bonâ fide* effort was made to carry out this portion of the Metropolitan Poor Act, an absolute epidemic took place as regards the building of asylum hospitals, district hospitals for fever and infectious diseases, asylums for epileptics, idiots and imbeciles, district schools, &c. This arose partly from indifference on the part of the permanent officials, but to a greater degree from their complete ignorance of the necessary details required for economic building. It was never my desire, in striving to amend the system—that is, to substitute for the absence of all system of medical relief to the poorer classes the reverse policy —that architects, surveyors, and builders, should be at liberty to extract all the money they could get from the pockets of the metropolitan ratepayers. As it was, finding that the absence of all efficient control was leading to an enormous outlay, and that the public was naturally getting not only alarmed, but indignant, at the profligate expenditure of their money, I put myself in communication with Mr. Torrens, then M.P. for Finsbury, and asked him to question the President of the Poor Law Board on the subject, and to move for a return of what had been already spent and what was proposed to be spent in such buildings. I also requested him to inquire to what cause the delay in establishing Poor Law dispensaries under Mr. Hardy's Act was due. This action considerably alarmed the permanent officials. More important still, it led to a very considerable curtailment in the amount of contemplated expenditure on buildings, and, with this, an approximation to some control. Soon afterwards the establishment of Poor Law dispensaries was commenced, which was an important feature of the Act.

I cannot but relate the close of Mr. George Catch's career.

I have already stated that after the enforced resignation of his appointment at Newington, this model master was selected by the Guardians of Lambeth, as the master of their Workhouse, notwithstanding that he had as opponents some respectable persons who had creditably filled similar appointments elsewhere. His election was due to the assistance he received from the clerk of the Strand Union, and his old friends at that Board.

His appointment was challenged at the time, but in spite of the serious evidence afforded by the Newington inquiry, it was confirmed by the Department, but with this proviso—that a special report as to his conduct should be sent by the Guardians to the Poor Law Board at the end of six months.

It was not very long before the opponents of this man's appointment were fully justified in the course they took, as he speedily renewed his old course of cruelty to the inmates, and of quarrelling with the other officers. One of these acts was inquired into, and reported on by Dr. Markham. Although it was clear that the master was in the wrong, yet Dr. Markham, in his official report, managed to throw a doubt on the evidence of the medical officer, evidently to screen the master; but he was not saved for long, for shortly afterwards a young woman, who had been subjected to much harshness by Catch, ran away and hid herself, as it was supposed, in the chimney of one of the women's infirm wards, when the master, with the view of forcing her to come down, induced the junior resident medical officer, to bring from the surgery some substance, on which he poured some hydrochloric acid, whereby some extremely pungent gases were evolved, thinking thereby to compel her to come down; but as the young woman was not there (fortunately for Catch, for if she had been she would have been suffocated), the only effect was that all the old women in the ward, were set sneezing and coughing. This atrocious proceeding, having been reported to the Poor Law Board, Catch was called upon to resign. It will hardly be believed that certain of the Guardians memorialized the Poor Law Board to let him retain his office, when Mr. Shaen, the eminent solicitor, on the urgent repre-sentation of his wife, who was a lady visitor at the Workhouse, and knew a great deal of Catch's doings, took the matter up. Mr. Shaen saw me, and asked me whether I could tell him anything about Catch. I narrated the incident of the false charge which he, in connection with the clerk, had made against me when I was away in Scotland, and also told him the story of his behaviour in reference to the sick woman in the lying-in ward of the Strand Union which had led to his leaving that Workhouse. Mr. Shaen took down my statement, and subsequently he sent me a pamphlet of some two hundred pages, in which I found not only my own statement, but sundry others of a highly damaging character, but unfortunately these were so recklessly drawn, that it gave Catch the opportunity of bringing an action

for libel. Its publication had induced Mr. Goschen
to peremptorily call upon him to resign his office.
Catch sent out an appeal to all the masters of
workhouses to support him in his action, and a
sufficient sum having been collected, the Attorney-
General of the day, now Lord Chief Justice Coleridge,
acted as his counsel. Having been asked by Mr.
Shaen to support my statement in the Court of
Queen's Bench, I attended. When called on, I went
into the witness-box, and after giving my evidence-
in-chief, was cross-examined by the Attorney-General
in such a manner that three times during the cross-
examination Lord Chief Justice Cockburn interfered
to stop it, giving as his opinion that the Attorney-
General was pressing me unfairly. As I was leaving
the witness-box I turned round and thanked the
Lord Chief Justice for his kindness in screening
me. I was followed by the late porter of the Strand
Workhouse, who was there to substantiate my
evidence. A similar attempt to browbeat this
witness afforded fine fun. The witness was an
Irishman, and at every effort made by the counsel
to confuse him, Pat was too much for the Attorney,
and feeling that he could make nothing of him, he
told him peremptorily to stand down, which he did
in such a comical way as convulsed the court with

laughter. Unfortunately Mr. Shaen failed to justify
several of the libels, and the jury, after twelve days'
trial, gave a verdict in favour of Catch for £600—an
amount which the judge said was excessive, and for
which he refused to certify, thereby affording Mr.
Shaen the opportunity for asking for a fresh trial.
Subsequently a compromise was effected at the
instance of the Lord Chief Justice. In summing
up the case to the jury, the judge said that my
evidence, if it stood alone, was sufficient to stamp
Catch as an improper person to hold the office of
a Workhouse master. Mr. Goschen would not allow
Catch to resume his office, and, having no resources
whatever, he drifted downwards until ultimately,
being without means and having tired out all his
friends, he in a fit of despair threw himself in front
of a Great Western train and was cut to pieces.

I was so much annoyed by the action of the
Attorney-General in cross-examining me that on
my return home I wrote to the Lord Chief Justice
again thanking him, and enclosing for his perusal a
pamphlet I had just written on the administration of
the Poor Laws. To my great surprise he sent me
by hand the next morning a letter, in which he
acknowledged its receipt, and informed me that he
should read my pamphlet with the greatest pleasure.

There is no doubt that my labours up to that time were very well known to his Lordship, as, when at the Bar, he was the standing counsel of *The Lancet* newspaper, in which my name had frequently appeared. When he became a judge he kept up his interest in that journal. This was told me by the late Dr. Wakley, to whom I related Catch's story and the account of my cross-examination and of the courtesy and support afforded to me by Lord Chief Justice Cockburn whilst under cross-examination. The Lord Chief Justice was a man of scrupulous integrity and honour. I remember a solicitor of good position in Soho, whose brother was then the Treasurer of the County of Middlesex, and whose son now holds the position, saying to me, "Although I am opposed to him politically, yet I have the highest opinion of his conscientiousness, and of his extraordinary ability—we are all proud of him." I esteem it a high honour to have received a letter from such a man written under such circumstances. I have this letter still.

An illustration of profligate expenditure, and the absence of all efficient control at the Poor Law Board, was at this time supplied by my old friends, the Strand Union Board. Shortly after I resigned the Board decided to build a new Workhouse at

Edmonton, and plans of the contemplated building
were issued to builders, &c. Tenders from sundry
large firms for its erection were sent to the
Guardians, the lowest tender being from an eminent
firm that had acquired a great reputation for the
buildings it had put up in various parts of town,
as well as in the country. Their tender was rejected,
and the contract given to a small builder, resident in
St. Paul's, Covent Garden, whose estimate was some
£2,000 higher. It was stated at the time that after
the contract had been signed the members of the
Board were invited to a dinner given by the lucky
contractor. The large firm that competed for it,
feeling that they had been improperly treated, got the
question raised, and the new President, Mr. Goschen,
investigated the transaction, but it was too late, as
the builder had already set to work, and had a
considerable amount of his plant on the ground.
Although Mr. Goschen felt that he could not
interfere to stop this disreputable transaction, he
did not fail to give this party of jobbers a most
severe lecture, probably the most severe that ever
emanated from the Poor Law Board, in connection
with the doings of a Board of Guardians. The issue
of it to this Board must have brought about a change
of policy among the permanent officials who had not

remonstrated against it. I know not whether it was
this transaction, or Mr. Goschen's general knowledge
of the laxity of the staff, certain it is that during his
Presidentship he kept the Secretary in his place, and
did not permit him or Sir John Lambert (then plain
Mr. Lambert) to obtrude themselves upon him when
he received deputations from public bodies and from
societies. But I am anticipating.

In the autumn of 1868 a general election took
place, with the result of replacing the Liberal party
in power. With the concurrence of the Council of
the Poor Law Medical Officers Association, I had
issued a circular letter to the various candidates for
Parliamentary honours, in which I drew attention to
the imperfect character of the Poor Law Board, and
the usurpation by the permanent officials of powers
they were not entitled to, and asked whether the
candidate would assist us in our efforts to reconstruct
the Board, and to improve the system of medical
relief. The replies I obtained were not only very
numerous, but they held out the prospect of an
alteration for the better. Looking back at the
various changes that were made subsequently, I
have no hesitation in asserting that many of these
improvements were brought about by the action our
Council took at this general election. These will be
briefly referred to.

I will here relate an incident that gave me the cue as to the line to be taken in the introduction and establishment of a Public Health Act. I was desirous of visiting an aged relative who lived in a village in Hampshire. The local medical gentleman kindly volunteered to fetch me from the station, some seven miles distant, and to put me up for the night, &c. As I neared his house my sense of smell was assailed by one of the most awful odours I had ever encountered. To my inquiry from whence it originated, my host said, "That is from the farmyard over there. Young Green, the son of the corn dealer, has taken Miss Smith's farm, and has commenced to breed pigs. He has at least 300." "Well," I replied, "if I lived here I should make short work of Mr. Green and his pigs; I would at once indict him." "Ah," he said, "you can afford to be independent, you live in London. I dare not; for if I complained, or took any action in the matter, old Green would go to all the markets round about, and would denounce me for attempting to interfere with his son's business, and I should make enemies by the score." Some three or four years after Mr. Stansfeld brought in his Public Health Bill, one of the essential features of which was that every district medical officer should be the health officer in his district. I opposed the proposition with all my might. I knew the Act would be absolutely abortive if Poor Law medical officers were placed in this utterly false position which Mr. Stansfeld proposed. In taking this course I encountered much opposition, and became for a time very unpopular, though at last my views prevailed, and gentlemen wholly independent of local influences were appointed to large areas. Among the remonstrants was the medical man who was the neighbour of the pig breeder, when I silenced him by reminding him of Mr. Green and his pigs, and of the fear that he had that if he complained that his business as a country medical gentleman might be damaged. He said no more.

Having come to the conclusion that the course followed by my poor friend, Richard Griffin, of Weymouth, in continually calling attention to the grievances of Poor Law medical officers, would never eventuate in an improvement of their position, for the general public have never cared for our class in any way, I cast about to ascertain whether there could be any course adopted by which the attention of the public could be drawn to the shortcomings of the system, and decided that the only chance that existed, whereby an improvement could be effected, was by proving that an

amended system of medical relief would eventuate in
the diminution of the duration of sickness, and
consequently of its cost to the ratepayers; and
having at this time a copy of the annual report of
the Irish Poor Law Commissioners placed in my
hands, I studied its pages, and saw that under the
Irish Medical Charities Acts the poorer classes of
that country had secured to them the most complete
system of Poor Law medical relief. I resolved to go
over to Ireland, and study its administration on the
spot. I carried out my intention, and during my
stay in Ireland obtained a complete insight into the
way in which the Irish dispensary system was carried
out. I also brought back with me all the papers and
documents that enabled me to popularize the subject
here. I also spent much time in examining the
annual returns of the English Poor Law Board, with
the result that I was enabled to prove conclusively
that efficient medical relief was followed by diminished poor relief expenditure, not only by shortening
the duration of sickness, but by the actual saving of
human life : this latter was shown also by a return I
got Mr. W. H. Smith to move for, which was as
follows—

" A return of the population at the last census in
England and Wales, in Scotland and in Ireland.

"A return of the mortality from general causes in the three portions of the United Kingdom, and of preventable mortality."

That return exhibited the following: That whilst one in every 43 died yearly in England, one in 44 in Scotland, only one in every 60 died in Ireland; and whilst in England zymotic, or preventable diseases, constituted one-fourth of the total mortality, or one in 190 of the population, Scotland one-fourth, or one in 194 of the population, in Ireland it was one-fifth of the total mortality, and one in 308 of the population; the fact being this, that in England and Scotland there existed the same miserable system of medical relief, whilst in Ireland, after the potato famine and the fever which followed it, calamities which swept away a large portion of the inhabitants, the Medical Charities Act was introduced, and led, by its efficient working, to the beneficial changes which had taken place in the health of the country.

The views I advanced met with much favour, and were commented on and approved by many general, as well as by all the medical journals. Having sent a copy of the paper I read at a meeting of our Association to Mr. C. P. Villiers, that gentleman wrote to me stating that he had derived much

pleasure from its perusal, and that I had thrown
more light on the causes of pauperism, and devised
better measures for its diminution, than any previous
writer on the subject. Subsequently, through the
influence of Mr. Corrance, then M.P. for East
Suffolk, I was invited to address the Central
Chamber of Agriculture, which I did, when a
resolution, couched in very flattering terms, was
adopted, and further it was moved that a copy of
the Chamber's approval of my address, and the
principles contained in it, should be sent to the
Poor Law Board, coupled with the request that
the attention of all the provincial Chambers should
be called to the subject. Subsequently I was invited
to address the Worcester Chamber on the same
subject, as well as that of Suffolk.

At a very early period of the presidency of Mr.
Goschen, several of the provincial Poor Law Inspectors were directed to make inquiry into the
question of medical relief to the poor, and the
desirability, or otherwise, of establishing dispensaries,
modelled on the principles contained in the Irish
Medical Charities Act. One of the most able and
exhaustive reports was sent in, as might have been
expected, by Mr. Farnall, who thus proved true to
the views he held in his interview with me some ten

years before; whilst the very feeblest of these was
that preferred by Mr. R. B. Caine, who manifested
the same lack of heartiness here as he exhibited
earnestness some years before in upsetting poor
Richard Griffin's statistics, of which he boasted to
me during his conduct of the inquiry at the Strand
Union in 1866.

One of the results that sprang from my visit to
Ireland was the establishment of a good understanding between our Association and that of the
Irish Dispensary Medical Officers, of which the late
Dr. Toler Maunsall was the honorary secretary. Dr.
Maunsall was the most indefatigable secretary I ever
knew. His appetite for work, and his skill in
getting up statistics was remarkable. He was most
valuable to me, as he assisted in getting out dry
figures for my use, which would have given me
infinite trouble. Poor fellow! like many others of
my fellow-workers, he was destined to die early, and
I sustained a great loss by his premature death.
Unfortunately, too, he died badly off. I started a
subscription in England for the benefit of his widow
and children, which helped to swell the sum that
his friends got together in Ireland.

During my stay in Ireland it was arranged between
us that we should mutually help each other, and

consequent on that, when the Irish Association
strove, under the leadership of the late Dr. Brady,
M.P. for Leitrim, to obtain superannuation allowance
for dispensary and workhouse medical officers, I
called attention to the subject in the medical
journals, and induced the members of our Association not only to petition, but to interview members
in their respective localities, in favour of the Bill.
Dr. Brady, having succeeded in carrying this
measure, essayed the next year to do the same for
England and Wales. The success of the appeal we
had made to members in the general election of
1868, facilitated the passing of the measure most
materially, as we had promises of support from
upwards of eighty gentlemen who were subsequently
elected. Prior to the second reading of our Bill, I
interviewed several members, and got promises to
attend the second reading and vote for the measure.
Some of these gentlemen, having intimated their
desire to speak in its support, and having asked to
be supplied with information on the subject, I
coached them up. To one of the ablest of our supporters, who asked me to provide him with facts, I
said that I was opposed to superannuation on principle, as I held that every one should be able during
the working days of his life to provide for the

exigencies of his old age—but then it was necessary if he held an office that the pay should be such as would enable him to do so. Now it was notorious that the pay of the medical officer was based on such a starvation principle as to render it impossible for him to save anything. This argument, reproduced very much as I have written it, in the House assisted a great deal in the success of the Bill. At the time this occurred I was out of office, and had not the most distant idea I should ever again be a workhouse medical officer. I did not know what was again in store for me, nor that I was destined to have another fourteen years of it ; that I should be again suspended, restored to office, and eventually, through broken health, compelled peaceably to resign and to be myself a pensioner.

After the Bill had become law Dr. Brady most generously bore tribute to my efforts, and stated that he never could have carried the Bill without my help. *The Lancet* published this statement of Dr. Brady's, and I for the time gained from my Poor Law medical brethren credit for what was, at that period, absolutely disinterested labour.

About this time I was invited by a leading physician in Edinburgh to visit that city and address a meeting at the College of Physicians on the subject of Poor Law medical relief in Scotland. Although I was aware that the condition of things in that country was worse even than it was in England, yet I had not studied the subject so completely as to justify me in asserting it. Consequently I declined what was a very great compliment. Some years afterwards I went and delivered an address. It took place at the time when the annual meeting of the British Medical Association was last held there, when a highly complimentary resolution was adopted at that meeting in reference to that visit and address of mine. After occupying the position of president for a brief period only, during which time the Department was administered most vigorously and successfully, Mr. Goschen was transferred to another office in the Government, and Mr. Stansfeld was appointed President, the effect of which became immediately apparent, for the leading permanent officials, whose influence had been checked during Mr. Goschen's presidency, came directly to the front again.

One of the first measures introduced by Mr. Stansfeld was the conversion of the Poor Law into the Local Government Board. This was carried out by the absorption of the Public Health Department of the Privy Council in the destitution element of the Poor Law Board—a most disastrous act of policy, as it subordinated the Health Department, which had done its work so well to the discredited section of the Poor Law Board as exhibited in the permanent officials of the Board, who had always been obstructive, and had neither carried out, nor permitted any one else to carry out, any reform whatever.

This was early made apparent, for at the first deputation to the President, at which I was present, after his appointment, I saw Mr. H. Fleming and Mr. Lambert sitting together with the President, whilst Mr. (only just recently made Sir), John Simon and his staff, who were the only intellectual element of the new Board, were relegated to distant seats in the corner of the room.

That a Public Health Bill started under such circumstances should be framed absurdly, seeing that those who understood the subject were ignored, and those were consulted who had never done anything well, was nothing but what might have been expected.

One of the provisions of the Bill was, as I have before stated, that every district Poor Law medical officer should be the health officer of his district, and that his reports of insanitary conditions should be sent to the Board of Guardians, many members of which Board would be found to be the principal offenders against sanitary requirements.

This scheme speedily evoked an opposition, and a deputation, representing the British Medical Association, the Social Science Association, and the Poor Law Medical Officers Association, had an interview with Mr. Stansfeld at the Local Government Board. The speakers from the two first Associations having addressed the President, Mr. Stansfeld announced that he had just received a summons to attend a meeting of the Cabinet, but he would leave Mr. Fleming to hear any further remarks that might be made, which would in due course be communicated to him and meet with attention. Being the sole remaining speaker, I said to Mr. Fleming that when I first heard of the proposed utilization of the Poor Law medical officers in the Public Health measures of the Government, I hailed it as a tardy recognition of the valuable services that class of official might render. But when I came to look into the details I saw it would not work, as medical officers would hesitate in affronting their Board of Guardians, many members of which would be found to be the principal offenders against the contemplated Act, and that in the few cases where the parish officers would faithfully carry out the requirements, and thereby offend their respective Boards, they would be sacrificed to the resentment of their mem-

bers, and if appeal was made for support to the
Central Department, such honest men would be
called on to resign for not exhibiting sufficient courtesy, &c., and working with their Boards. It was
very evident that my observations went home to this
Permanent Secretary, but whether they were ever
communicated to Mr. Stansfeld is open to much
doubt, for his Bill was eventually brought in on the
lines he had originally indicated, only to turn out on
trial a disastrous and ludicrous failure.

CHAPTER II.

ABOUT a twelvemonth after the Act was in operation
I appealed, through the medical journals, to my
brethren in the provinces as to the arrangements
that had been made in their respective localities. A
large number of letters from all parts of England
and Wales were sent to me, and with the information
thus furnished I prepared a paper which I called
" Chaos," in which I turned into ridicule the arrangements that had been made, showing that the Department, faithful to its traditions, had made a complete
mess of the administrative arrangements. This
paper, read at the meeting of the British Medical
Association at Sheffield, attracted a good deal of
attention both in the medical and general Press. It
materially acted in evolving order out of the chaos
into which the subject had drifted, owing to the

indifference and incompetence of those who had
drafted the measure.

In the spring of 1872 I was informed that the
alterations and enlargement of the old Workhouse of
St. James's, commenced at the time when the Westminster Union was formed, were complete, and that
Mr. French, who had been the medical officer of the
workhouse and parish of St. James's for upwards of
forty years, was about to retire on a superannuation
allowance of £200 a year. I was told that the
Chairman of the Board, a Mr. Bonthron, a Scotch
baker living in Regent Street, had selected a fellow
Scotchman, one Dr. S., as Mr. French's successor,
and as Mr. Bonthron claimed to be omnipotent at
the Board, this gentleman's appointment to the
vacancy was considered to be certain. In the course
of a few days I heard that a formidable opponent to
Dr. S. had appeared in the person of Dr. M., who
was also a Scotchman. In due course the election
took place, when Dr. M. was elected. This resulted
from a protest on the part of certain members of the
Board who resented the predominance of Mr. Bonthron. When apprised of the result of the election, I
remarked that Dr. M. could not take the office as he
did not possess the necessary legal qualifications.
On the following Saturday morning a member of the

Board told me that a letter had been read at the
meeting of the Guardians, held the previous evening,
announcing that the election of Dr. M. was null and
void, as he held no surgical qualifications. As his
election had surprised all the Guardians, because it
proved that the Chairman had not the influence he
claimed, my informant advised me to apply for the
office. At first I hesitated, but upon being urged
again I assented. The same evening I called on Dr.
M., told him of my intention, and asked him for the
support of his friends. To my utter astonishment
he told me he had made up his mind to try again.
"Nonsense," I said; "how can you get a diploma
from the College of Surgeons?" "Oh," he replied,
"I have arranged all that; I have a splendid
memory, and I remember all my anatomy and
surgery." As I had every ground for the belief that
he had never attended lectures on surgery, nor
attended the surgical practice of an hospital, inasmuch as I had known him ever since he had come to
London, I saw that, without collusion with some one
in authority, it was impossible for it to be done; but,
as he appeared determined, I left him. As soon as it
was known that I seriously intended to compete for
the appointment, testimonials in my favour were
forwarded to me by several eminent physicians and

surgeons, by Members of Parliament, among them
one of a very flattering character from Mr. C. P.
Villiers, M.P., the ex-President of the Poor Law
Board, who strongly recommended me to the Board
of Guardians, those lady visitors who had known
me at the Strand, and others. Two days before the
election took place I was surprised by a visit from
Dr. M., who called to inform me that he had passed
his examination at the College of Surgeons the night
before, and now asked me to retire in his favour.
On my declining to do as he wished, he said it was
very hard I would not, as he had incurred an expense
of upwards of £60 to get the diploma. Prior to the
election my friends entered into a compact with his
supporters to the effect that if I was in a minority on
the show of hands my name was to be withdrawn,
when they would support him, but if I was in the
majority his friends would support me. This
occurring, I was elected, to the great surprise of the
Chairman, who looked on me as a dangerous person,
seeing that I had taken an active part in bringing
about the formation of the Union, whereby St.
Anne's had been joined to St. James's, which had
the effect of somewhat increasing his poor rate
assessment in St. James's—for St. Anne's, a poor
parish, had considerably improved its position by

being put into union with St. James's, which was comparatively a rich one.

Having at this time received an invitation from the Irish Dispensary Medical Officers Association to address them at the College of Physicians in Dublin, I did so, when Sir Dominic Corrigan, Bart., M.P., was in the chair; and I afterwards spent a very pleasant week there, visiting the North and South Dublin Workhouses, the latter having 4,000 inmates, with a large staff of visiting physicians and surgeons, besides resident medical officers. It is one of the finest hospitals in Dublin, and the arrangements for the efficient treatment of the sick poor were in the highest degree creditable to the Irish Poor Law, now the Local Government Board.

I also visited the Richmond Lunatic Asylum, situated on the outskirts of Dublin, at that date under the superintendence of Dr. Lalor, who, I understand, was the first physician who introduced vocal and instrumental music as a means of relieving the insane. There I witnessed one of the most extraordinary sights it was ever my lot to see. I will give a sketch of the tableau. In the foreground sat a young lady discoursing most eloquent music on a harmonium, immediately behind her there stood some young Irish women, three or four of them,

singularly beautiful, with music in their hands,
accompanying her; behind them were older women,
and then on to the old and weird, all joining most
heartily in the performance. The fringe of this
female gathering of nearly 100 performers were
harmless imbeciles and idiots. I stood and listened
some moments whilst this singular performance continued. I was so struck with the beauty of one of
the Irish girls that I asked her history, when I was
informed that her condition had been induced by a
disappointment in a love affair. It was the old story
of love followed by desertion, and she had been
admitted some six months before in a state of
maniacal excitement. She was too young and altogether too pretty to be an inmate of a lunatic asylum.
Dr. Lalor also showed me a typical case, exhibiting
the truth of the opinion I have long held, that of all
the forms of insanity, none are so uncertain of having
been really cured as those which have exhibited
symptoms of homicidal or suicidal violence. The
patient in question had been admitted when suffering
with a homicidal tendency but had steadily improved,
and his name was on the list of those to go before
the Visiting Committee for discharge on probation,
when a startling incident occurred. He had secreted
one of the knives used in the asylum about his person,

and he had, when unobserved, whittled away the
thick, blunt portion used in the asylum, until he had
given it a sharp cutting edge, from handle to point;
when, raising his right leg up, he cut through the
calf down to the bone, severing the muscle completely.
This patient, Dr. Lalor told me, had been employed
on various offices of trust, and that he was commonly
considered to be completely cured, and altogether
harmless. I obtained one of the old knives used in
this asylum, had it copied, and, having got the sanction
of the Board for getting several, used them all the
time I was at the Westminster Union, in the male
and female insane wards. The cutting edge was
about two inches in length, but the rest of the knife
was about the twelfth of an inch thick. It was impossible for lunatics to do any harm either to themselves or others with such knives.

On my return to London I was informed that my
appointment to the Westminster Union had been
confirmed by the Local Government Board.

A day or so before the 23rd of June an appointment was made by Mr. French for me to go over the
House with him, and to have the establishment
formally handed over to me. I went, accompanied by
a young Irish physician, recently one of the resident
surgeons of an Irish hospital, with whom I was in

treaty to be my assistant. I had never been in this
workhouse infirmary before. Shortly after my arrival
Mr. French joined us, and, in company with the head
nurse on the female side, we went through the female
part of the establishment. The nurse was most
elaborately " got up." We went on and examined
each patient, a large number of whom were in the
wards—in fact, although it was midsummer, the
place was full. I noticed bed-cards over each
patient's bed, but as I could not make out what was
given to the patients, I asked what was being done for
this and that case. To my astonishment Mr.
French said, " Nothing; I do not believe in physic,
and therefore do not give the people anything."
Presently we entered a large ward where a woman,
evidently in great pain, was lying in bed, writhing in
apparent agony. After ascertaining the nature of the
case, which was one of colicky diarrhœa, I asked,
" Well, what do you here ? " to which he replied,
" Nurse, give her a glass of Number Two." With that,
he pulled me into the centre of the ward, and giving
me a friendly nudge of the ribs, laughingly said,
" What do you imagine is Number Two ? Why it is
peppermint-water coloured ; I never give any physic."
Feeling by this time somewhat disgusted by these
remarkable confessions, seeing that his stipend was

£350 a year, out of which it was arranged by the
Board that he should supply these medicines. I
dropped his company, and went on examining the
people independently. Mr. French speedily button-
holed my young companion, and went on looking at
the patients with him. At last our visit came to an
end, and on coming out of the male sick wards he
shook me warmly by the hand and wished me the
same happy official life as he had had. He had
hardly got out of hearing when the young Irishman
commenced to reproach me with having transferred
Mr. French to him ; saying, " I take it, sir, as a
very unkind thing that you should have done so, as
I was shocked at his boasting that he never did anything at all for these poor sick people."

The next day I entered on my duties. On
taking my seat in the consulting-room the master
brought in and laid before me a large volume, the
Workhouse Medical Relief Book. I turned over the
pages for the week, and noticed the names and extras
ordered for the sick. I saw that ham, sausages,
tripe, fish, eggs, were entered rather frequently. At
last I said to the master, who was standing by, " You
surely have not all these people on the sick list in the
House ! I did not see a third of this number when I
went over the House yesterday." " Yes," he replied,

"they are here;" on which I said, "Let everything
remain as entered in the book until I can arrange to
go over the establishment and see them all, which I
will do this week." I then went through the sick
and infirm wards. On going through the wards I
ordered what in my judgment was necessary for the
sick in the way of medicines, much to the astonishment of the head nurse, who stared at me in a half-
dazed manner. There was one patient with a very
foul and offensive ulcer, for whom I ordered a charcoal
poultice : she came to me before I left the House to
ask me "what I meant." I replied, "A charcoal
poultice." She then said, "I never heard of such a
thing before." I then asked her how long she had
been there ; she said eight years. The next day I
had occasion to order a carrot poultice ; I met with
the same astonishment and ignorance of what was
meant. At last she frankly stated that she was about
to learn her duties, for nothing of the kind had ever
been used by her before ; and further, she said that
as she never had any medicine to give the people, she
had not troubled herself much about the patients ;
indeed, I learned on inquiry that she used to be in
waiting to see the doctor each morning, and so soon
as he was gone she considered her duties were over,
and she returned to her own sitting-room till next

9

day. I could never get her to give my medicines as
directed. Apart from this indifference as to medicines, she was kind to the patients and respectful to
me. On the male side I found a superintendent
nurse who really knew her duties. She confirmed
the statement voluntarily made by Mr. French, that
no medicines were ever provided for the sick. She
also said that the Guardians knew all about it, and
that they treated it as a great joke. This was not
correct as regards some of the Guardians, as I subsequently ascertained. It was known to the St.
James's section of the Board, but repudiated by those
of St. Anne's. Seeing that we had had a medical
inspector and self-called medical adviser for five years,
whose duty it was to visit this Workhouse infirmary,
his failure to discover these omissions was in the
highest degree remarkable ; but then the system
prevailed at the Local Government Board, and our
Workhouse Infirmaries Association had utterly failed
to alter it. The reason for all this was not far to
seek.

On the day after, in company with a pauper
inmate, told off to carry the Medical Relief Book, I
went through the wards for the purpose of seeing
the infirm men and women who were on extras. I
found on the women's side that, as it was leave-day,

many had gone out, and therefore drew the inference
that if they were well enough to go out they could
dispense with sausages, ham, tripe, eggs, &c., entered
against their names, and could eat the ordinary infirm
diet provided by Dr. Markham's diet table, which I
saw hung up in the wards, which diet table had been
drawn up from the form drafted by our Association
some years before. It is curious that he claimed it
to be his, without any reference to any one. Whilst
going through the female wards some of the inmates
returned drunk, one old woman very much so. She
at once proceeded to ask me who I was, and what I
was doing there. On my replying that I had come
into the ward to see why she was on a diet of daily
sausages, she tartly replied, pulling up her petticoats
and showing both her legs, which she struck with her
hands, " For these bad legs." I at once ran the pen
through her name. She lived in the House years
after that, but she ate no more sausages. I learned
on inquiry that this fat old woman, who could go out
and return drunk, had had sausages, nominally, as her
dinner for two years. I write nominally because I
learned afterwards that in the matter of diets an
extensive system of exchange obtained throughout
the House without any check or hindrance on the
part of the officials. It took me the greater part of

four days to see all the infirm people on extras, but
the result was satisfactory, as it enabled me to put
the establishment so far as the diets were concerned,
on an economic basis. The clerk of the Board assured
me at the time that I had caused a saving of some
hundreds of pounds, a statement which I honestly
believe was the truth.

It might be a matter of wonder how this could be,
but having regard to the very large amount of extras
purchased from day to day, none of which were
supplied under contract, it can be well understood
what an opportunity was given for large prices being
charged for such extras, as practically no check
existed on the cupidity of the tradesmen (selected
by the master) who supplied these things. I do not
state that such was the case here, but unless some
good understanding existed between those who
ordered and those who supplied, how is it possible
that masters of workhouses, with their limited
incomes, should succeed in leaving at their deaths so
much money, as many of them do ? I was informed
that the old master who preceded Catch at the Strand
Union had gone there after failing in business as a
tradesman in Covent Garden, that he held office as
master twelve years, and when he died that he left
some £2,000.

I found on inspection of the specially infirm,
paralytic, and wholly infirm, that the women were
located in wards 16, 17, and 18, and on inquiry discovered that there were no conveniences whatever for
the instantaneous removal of excreta, and yet this
condition of things had not been discovered by the
Government Inspectors or by the medical advisers,
or if it had been no steps had been taken to alter
it.

On my first visit to these wards I noticed some
black patches in the corners of the compartments,
which stood out very distinctly from the recently
whitewashed ceiling and walls. Noticing some days
after that these patches had increased in size, I asked
the nurse what it was due to, when she quietly said,
"Those are bugs." So soon as I could I saw the
master, and told him of it, and asked him to see to
it. He did not say he would or he would not, he
only laughed. Finding some days after that nothing
had been done, I again saw him in his office, when
I told him that I must insist on those bugs being
removed. The labour master was present, who
remarked, "Well, doctor, as you make such a fuss
about the bugs I will see to it for you" (evidently
regarding the matter in the light of a personal
favour) ; and the bugs were swept down into a dust-

pan by hundreds and put into the fire and burnt. This was told me by an eye-witness, who was present whilst it was being done.

I do not wish it supposed that the master was harsh or cruel; quite the reverse, he was very kind to the inmates. But he had lived long enough in the service of the Poor Law not to be fully aware that no good would accrue to him or his by too much zeal in the performance of his duty. He calmly let things slide; consequently there was more drunkenness on liberty days than could be possibly imagined, and was unchecked, and although I repeatedly begged that the names of all persons who were on my sick list who had been allowed to go out should be reported to me if they came home drunk, I never could get my wishes attended to, though occasionally it happened that I discovered the circumstance, especially when an accident occurred.

I was not wholly unprepared for this laxity of discipline, as some few days before entering on my duties I met the ex-chaplain of the Strand Workhouse, who, whilst congratulating me on my return to the Poor Law service, said, "You will have a great deal to meet with at St. James's. I have taken the duty there for the chaplain occasionally, and the scenes of drunkenness and quarrelling among the

inmates on their return home on liberty days, which
I have witnessed, exceeds anything you can imagine."
One of the most terrible exhibitions of this kind
I ever witnessed was on the first Christmas Day after
my appointment. The subject having previously
been brought under the attention of the Board, an
order was issued that for the future this indis-
criminate permission to the inmates to leave the
house on Christmas Day should be stopped. It will
hardly be believed that on the next Christmas Day
the Chairman took upon himself, most presump-
tuously, to go to the House and give permission for
them to again go out. The scene that occurred that
night was the most disgraceful that ever happened in
the history of a workhouse. Several of the drunken
inmates on their return home fought like demons.
I and my assistant were engaged for some time in
dealing with the injuries that were caused. I must
state that I never saw the master so justly indignant
as he was at the impertinent interference of this
Chairman, in setting his authority and that of the
Board at defiance in the way he had done.

Finding that no dietary for the sick and infirm
had been adopted at the House, I at once drew up a
form which continued in force until ill-health caused
my resignation. It was similar to that which I had

introduced at the Strand several years before. There was one diet for which I claim especial credit. It was framed with the view of dealing with capricious appetites or severe sickness. It was called Number Five, or *ad. lib.*, and consisted of either eggs, fish, a chop, beef-tea, or arrowroot, or anything else of the same value. It was enjoined that the nurse should at 8 a.m. ask what these special sick would take for dinner. When she had ascertained the wishes of the patient, a statement on a diet-sheet showing how many of each description of diet would be required was sent down to the kitchen. At the end of the week the cook handed to the master's clerk the number of each diets she had supplied, who then proceeded to distribute these among all those who were on *ad. lib.* diet. It might appear on the master's side of the Medical Relief Book that A or B had had a chop daily, whilst in reality the dinner might, by this arrangement, have been changed every day. This plan of dealing with capricious appetites has since been adopted in several workhouses.

Although five years had passed away since the Metropolitan Poor Law Act had become law, no attempt had been made to carry out the dispensary clauses until after my election, and one of the first things I had to do was to put the dispensary in order. I had been taught a lesson in economic prescribing whilst at the Strand, and therefore was enabled to speedily arrange for a pharmacopœia. I also drew up a formula for the supply of large bottles of simple medicines, which were placed in charge of the nurses, for administration in trivial ailments so common among the aged poor. I also introduced bed pulleys, to enable the sick to assist themselves in rising, or in getting in or out of bed. I also ordered small shawls for the aged women and woollen jackets for the men—a great comfort to those who were suffering from consumption or bronchitis, the principal affections I had to encounter.

I have stated that although it was midsummer the House was full of sick people, which arose partly on account of the sickness that prevailed in the worst part of St. Anne's and similarly in that of St. James's, and also to the fact that the Chairman had opposed the transfer of any of the sick to the Sick Asylum Hospital, at Highgate, to which the Westminster Union, in conjunction with the Strand, St. Giles's, and St. Pancras, was affiliated. He had opposed the junction of the two parishes on personal grounds, and being beaten, had, in conjunction with his party, obstructed the removal of the acutely sick.

As medical officer I did not object to this, for as

the sick wards were extremely good and were all
that I had desired to carry out when I initiated the
Workhouse infirmary movement, I simply complied
with the wishes of the majority of the Guardians not to
send any one away. I had held office some weeks when,
in the autumn of the year, I encountered Dr. Drydges
in Regent Street. This gentleman, who had acted
temporarily whilst Dr. Markham was ill, had about
this time been permanently appointed to be Metropolitan Inspector, Dr. Markham having resigned.
He came up to me and said, "I was coming to the
Westminster Union to learn why it was you did not
comply with the law, and send your acute sick away."
"Oh," I replied, "that is soon explained; it is
because the majority of the Board will not let me."
"Indeed," he said; "you must do your duty, even
if the Board object to it." To which I replied, "I
did that at the Strand, and your Secretary called on
me to resign because I was not sufficiently respectful
to the Guardians. I shall comply with the wishes
of the Guardians now, and not with that of the
Local Government Board, as they would throw me
over." To which he rather angrily replied, "You
speak to me like that, when I am an Inspector, and
you only a Workhouse medical officer?" To which
I answered, "And who, pray, made you a Poor Law

Inspector. Why, if it had not been for me and my initiation, neither you nor Dr. Markham would ever have been Inspectors." "Oh," he replied, "I did not know you had had anything to do with it." "I think," I said, "if you will trouble yourself to inquire you will find what I state to be correct." When I broke down in 1886, and he had to call and see me, he was then most kind and sympathetic, and I take this opportunity of stating as much.

This refusal on the part of the majority of the Board, led on by this Chairman, to allow me to send suitable cases of sickness to the Asylum Hospital, was in the highest degree absurd, seeing that the ratepayers of the Union had to pay their proportion of all expenses at the Asylum Hospital, and for the beds to which the Union were entitled; and although this Workhouse infirmary was a perfect paradise in comparison with the den at the Strand, still the House had not been arranged on the principle that all the sick should be retained in it. My nursing staff was insufficient to enable me effectually to deal with the great number of sick persons there at the time of my entrance on my duties. One illustration will suffice. There was a man in an infirm ward who had been under Mr. French some five or six years. He did not belong to Westminster, he was

kept there because he alleged he was so ill that he
could not bear the fatigue of journeying some sixty
miles in the country. He was a healthy-looking
man about forty years of age. He always lay in bed
with his knees drawn up, and constantly asserted
that he could not stand nor walk, nor put his legs
down. He complained piteously of his sufferings.
I exhausted every conceivable treatment, but all
without the least apparent benefit, as he never owned
to being any better for my attention to him. This
went on for two years, until I began to get suspicious
of him. One day an inmate of the ward, who had
recovered and left the House, called on me at my
private residence. On seeing me he said, "I have
called to thank you for your kindness to me, and
also to tell you that you have been deceived by that
man Webster, who you have done so much for. He
is an impostor. He can walk as well as I can, and,
what is more, does walk about." "Nonsense," I
replied; "he says he cannot get out of bed, and the
nurses confirm it." "Well," he continued, "he
takes very good care never to allow them to see him
get out of bed, he takes his constitutional walk about
the wards between 2 and 4 a.m., when the lights are
down, and most of the inmates asleep. "But,
surely," I said, "the night nurse must have seen

him, and if so she would report it to me!" "Oh,"
he replied, "she hardly ever comes into the ward
during the night, she is generally in her own room
fast asleep—she gets herself called when she is
wanted." I made some further inquiries, and finding that there was evidence of deception, I sent him
to the Asylum Hospital with a letter to the superintendent medical officer, giving his history, and telling him of my suspicions, and asking that he might
be carefully watched by reliable persons. He came
back in a fortnight, having been found out. He
was immediately transferred to his settlement, where
doubtless he recommenced the game of deception,
having found it answer so well.

It may be here said, If you had not confidence in
your nurses, why did you not get rid of them? For
the simple reason that I had no power to do so.
They were not selected by me, but by the Guardians,
and therefore were not my officers, but the Board's.
I once reported the night nurse on the male side
(the woman who had allowed the malingerer to
deceive me) for drunkenness, but I had so much
trouble to get rid of her that I was not induced to
repeat the experiment, added to which I was most
grossly insulted by the master for bringing this
woman's conduct before the Guardians.

In my opinion the medical officer should select and discharge all the nurses—of course, reason for this latter action being shown. I should have discharged several at the Westminster Union for neglect of duty and for general incompetence if I had had the power. Simple complaint would be attended by no beneficial result, as it would be a hundred to one that the nurse would be supported in her misconduct by some member of the Board, whose protege she might be. On mentioning this to an ex-workhouse medical officer, he told me that on having occasion to represent the conduct of the resident midwife, who claimed and exercised the right to go out on every Sunday for several hours, leaving the wards wholly unattended on every such occasion except by pauper helps, the only action taken by the Board as a return for it, at the instance of the midwife's friend, was the adoption of a resolution that a return should be prepared and laid on the Board-room table, showing the occasions when the medical officer went out and the length of time he was out, &c., &c. Of course he found out that he had achieved worse than nothing by his effort to check this abuse. This circumstance occurred in one of the largest of our metropolitan workhouse infirmaries.

When first I entered on my duties at the West-

minster Union the chaplain there was a very
energetic little man named Duval. I do not remember his Christian name, for the reason that he
was known and spoken of as Claude Duval, and for
a long while I supposed him to possess no other.
At last I discovered that the name had been given him
in joke, and that he was in no way connected with the
celebrated highwayman. He most asuredly did not
convey the idea that he had any brigand blood in
his veins. He was extremely attentive to his duties,
and deserved and had gained the respect of all the
inmates and officers.

Frequently he organized entertainments for the
aged and infirm. These were held in the dining-
hall, which on all such occasions was crowded to
excess. After I had held office about a year he
desired me to provide an entertainment, which I did
on several occasions, and my efforts met with much
success. In the carrying out of these entertainments, which were musical and recitative, I had the
assistance of my nephew, Mr. Julian Rogers, and his
wife, who brought with them vocalists of a high
order, who contributed much to the pleasure of the
inmates. These entertainments were highly appreciated by the inmates, and were frequently attended
by members of the Board, and by some of the rate-

payers living in the neighbourhood. Now and then I used to read extracts suitable for penny readings. On two occasions my efforts took a higher form, when I gave a lecture on the "Ear and Hearing," and on "Sight and the Eye." The preparation of these lectures and the diagrams to illustrate them was a work of considerable trouble and some anxiety, but the signal success achieved on both occasions amply repaid me for any trouble occasioned. To show the appreciation of my audience for a joke, I will relate an incident that occurred during the delivery of my lecture on "Sight and the Eye." I was describing the function of the iris, or coloured portion of the eye, as an involuntary movable veil, which regulated the amount of light which should be admitted to the eye, and said that in order to make the veil complete it was covered behind with a black pigment, so as to exclude all light except that which passed through the pupil. I then told them that in certain animals this pigment was wanting, and not only there but in the skin generally, and instanced the white mouse, ferret, &c., and showed that all these animals had red eyes and always blinked and winked when exposed to a strong light. I then passed on to state that this condition was sometimes found in man, where again the winking and blinking was noticeable as well as the whiteness of the skin and hair, from the absence of this dark pigment, hence the name of "albinos" applied to those thus afflicted. I then went on to state that recently we had a notable example of this in the Chancellor of the Exchequer, who suffered from this infirmity, and that his dread of light was so extreme that he had attempted actually to put a tax on matches. This joke was followed by a positive scream of delight from visitors and inmates—showing that Mr. Lowe's fiscal effort to increase the revenue was known to them all. At the conclusion of the night's proceedings, Miss Augusta Clifford, who was present, came up and said she should repeat my story of Mr. Lowe and the match tax wherever she went. At the next meeting of the Board, several of the Guardians having been present on the occasion referred to, it was moved and seconded and carried unanimously, that a vote of thanks should be given to Dr. Rogers for the entertainment provided by him, and for the highly interesting and instructive lecture which he had delivered.

I found in the sick and infirm wards several of my old acquaintances of the Strand, who were chargeable to St. Anne's, and had been transferred to this House when the Union was formed, among them

10

a woman by the name of Maria Hall. She had gone
into the Strand several years before I left ; her friends
at first paid for her maintenance. She was an
epileptic—and something beside. When I knew her
in the Strand she professed an inability to talk,
except unintelligible gibberish. She was very artful ;
she claimed to be a deeply religious character, and
contrived to take in the benevolent lady visitors to a
considerable extent. She continually showed me
letters she had received, and books that had been
given her by ladies, and would ask me to share with
her the grapes, cakes, and sweetmeats sent her by
her dupes. This went on for several years, altogether
about twenty. She always posed and was spoken of
as "poor Maria"—in fact, she was the pet of the
nurse and of the ward. At last it came to my
knowledge that she presumed on her condition to be
exacting and troublesome. Finding that remonstrance
was unavailing, I reluctantly ordered her removal to
the insane ward. It was attended with the best
result, for, finding that she was at last sternly dealt
with, she threw off the mask she had worn for
twenty years and talked as distinctly and clearly as
any healthy person. She had traded for years on
her alleged infirmity. It was true she was an
epileptic, and eventually died from that form of

disease; but she had been the most persistent cheat
I had ever met with.

On the male side I found a poor fellow who had
also been transferred from the Strand, where I had
known him when he was first admitted there. He
was paralyzed all down on one side. He was the
most patient, honest fellow I had ever seen. After
I had been in office some years Sir Charles
Trevelyan came to call on me respecting a public
movement that we were both engaged in. Finding
I was at the infirmary, he came round to the House
and was shown into my room. I asked him to go
over the wards with me. He did so. I introduced
the poor paralytic to him as an honest, patient, and
grateful poor man. Sir Charles asked him how long
he had been afflicted, and he answered, " Some twenty
years." Then I said, " This poor fellow cannot get
downstairs ; he has not seen the streets for all these
years, but he is always happy and cheerful." Sir
Charles kindly left with me £1 to pay his cab fare,
so that he might have the chance of seeing them
once again. As I had to send two people with him
each time the £1 soon went. His enjoyment of
this treat in his daily dull, routine life was, I was
informed, most pleasing to witness.

There were several other very interesting persons

I found on both sides of the ward. One was an old man who was said to be eighty-eight years old. On my morning visit he was always standing on the staircase smoking. He had lived many years in Australia, and his long white hair and beard, which reached to his waist, conjoined with a florid complexion and bright blue eyes, caused me to consider him one of the handsomest old men I had ever seen. One day I took two young ladies over the infirmary. We found the old man in his usual place. I jocularly introduced him to them as the Adonis of the House. The old man was terribly offended. As we walked away I heard him muttering aloud, " That's a pretty name to call a man—'Donis indeed ! " He did not forgive me for a long while. I wonder what he thought the epithet really was intended to signify.

I also found in the male infirm ward an old French physician whom I had known by sight for a great many years when he was practising his profession in Soho. He was a tall, fine man when I first knew him. He always used to wear a very singular-looking broad-brimmed hat. He was in all externals a very gentlemanly-looking person. I had missed him for a long time, and was surprised and hurt to think that he should have drifted to a workhouse infirmary. On inquiring into the cause of his becoming an inmate of the House, for I always thought he was well-to-do, as he dressed exceedingly well, I learned that he had lived with a lady who was an *employé* at a French milliner's in Regent Street, that she was much younger than he was, and that he had given to her all his money, which she, in preparation for possible consequences, had put in the Funds, but in her own name only. Unfortunately for him she was taken suddenly ill, and being ignorant of English courts made no disposition of the property, simply telling him, on her deathbed, where it was. When she was dead, he found to his dismay that the money could not be obtained, as he could not establish any legal claim of ownership. Grief at the loss of his mistress and of all his money caused the complete break-down of the poor fellow, and he had come into the House utterly crushed. He was a very interesting old man, being the only son of a French noble family. His mother and father were both executed during the Reign of Terror, and when the family property was confiscated he was but a youth. When he grew up he studied medicine, and in the year 1802 entered Napoleon's army as a regimental surgeon. After serving with his regiment in Germany, Italy,

and Austria, he was attached to the Army of England,
as it was called, which was stationed on the heights
of Boulogne. He was there some time. Suddenly
an announcement came that the encampment would
be broken up, and that the army would go to Russia.
He traversed the whole of Europe, taking part in the
various engagements on the road to Moscow, which
he saw in flames. He was in the memorable retreat,
and returned to France without a scratch. On the
return from Elba he rejoined his old regiment, and,
as its surgeon, fought against the English at
Waterloo. After the peace his regiment was dis-
banded, and as the old soldiers of the empire were
very much at a discount he elected to come to
England, where he lived since 1816. He died at the
age of ninety-five, retaining his faculties to the last.
After his death I raised a fund to bury him, by
writing a letter to *The Times*, in which I gave his
history, heading my letter, "A Relic of the Grand
Armée," and asking any friends of the first Napoleon
to help me in burying him in some other place than
a pauper's grave. My appeal having brought me
£25, the Empress Eugenie being one of the subscribers, he was buried at the Catholic Cemetery at
Kensal Green. There were two seamstresses who
lived in Gilbert Street, Oxford Street, who were his

countrywomen and his sole visitors, with the ex-
ception of the Catholic priest of the French chapel in
Leicester Square. I asked them and the priest to
accompany me to the funeral, which I attended as
chief mourner. On our arrival at the mortuary
chapel, the coffin was placed on a raised bier with
three others. Presently two lads, wearing long black
cloaks which reached to the ground, came from the
altar. When they arrived at the spot where the
coffin was resting, one lad suddenly produced from
under his cloak a censer containing fire and proceeded to incense the quartette. How he ever carried
the fiery thing without setting fire to himself was to
me a wonder. He was immediately followed by the
other lad, who, taking just as rapidly from under his
cloak a vessel like a whitewash-pot, proceeded with a
brush to throw holy water on the coffins. This
being completed, the coffin was put on a truck and
we hurried away as fast as we could go through the
miry ground for a long distance to the grave. On
reaching it, down went my two lady companions on
their knees in the clay. My respect for the deceased
did not carry me so far as that, especially as it was
raining hard and the ground was a mere bog.
Presently the acolyte produced his whitewash-pot
and brush, and I was courteously asked to sprinkle

the poor fellow's coffin with holy water, which I did. This having been also done by my companions, I was amused by a little girl about fourteen, who, suddenly taking the brush and pot from one of the young women, went to work sprinkling in grand style, and, what was rather alarming, let me in for more than I had expected. On our return journey the priest asked me to attend service in the Catholic Chapel, in Leicester Square, on the next Sunday. This I did. He was a very gentlemanly person. He thanked me very much for the little service I was enabled to render to the poor old French doctor, whom I missed very much, as it was my habit to sit beside the old man's bed and hear him fight his battles o'er again.

The opposition to the removal of the sick to the Asylum Hospital at Highgate continuing, and plausible ground for some action having been shown in the fact of that establishment being so far away, a move on the part of the Department became necessary. The old Workhouse in Cleveland Street being no longer wanted by the Strand Board (as they had built a new House at Edmonton), it was proposed to pull down and rebuild an additional Asylum Hospital upon the site. The vestry of St. James's, instigated by the Chairman of the Board, gave a determined opposition to the proposition. But for once the Department was firm and the hospital was built. At first the four Unions were associated in its use and management, but after a time its use for the reception of acute cases was limited to the St. Giles's, and St. George's, Bloomsbury, the Strand, and Westminster Unions. The Chairman having for a time retired from the Board, his place was filled by a fresh Chairman, and no obstacle being made to my utilization of Cleveland Street Asylum, suitable cases were transferred there, to the relief of the Westminster House, which, through the resistance of the Board, had become inconveniently full. The new Chairman was a very weak man, who was neither by his financial position or general intelligence justified in aspiring to hold such an office. It is possible that if he had devoted the time he spent at the Board and at the Sick Asylum to his private business he might have delayed, and possibly have staved off, his eventual bankruptcy and ultimate death in the Asylum Hospital in Cleveland Street, to the building of which he gave the most determined opposition. His successor as Chairman was a surgeon in Soho, who was a man of very fair attainments, and during the time he occupied the chair the business of the Board was carried on with remarkable success. I received from him the most generous support, and during his tenure of office my official life was hardly chequered by a single cloud.

I have spoken of the clerk of the Board as having expressed a favourable opinion of the economy I had effected on my first entrance on my duties. The clerk had occupied a similar position at St. Martin's prior to its amalgamation with the Strand Union. As I never went near the clerk of that Union after the discovery of his perfidy in making, in conjunction with Catch, a false charge against me, I was often at a loss to know to whom I could go when any difficulty cropped up. Having had an introduction to this clerk, I frequently called and consulted him ; consequently I was not surprised when, through the loss of his office, as the result of St. Martin's being joined to the remaining parishes of the old Strand Union, he was without employment, that he should call on me and invoke my good offices in favour of his being appointed to a similar position in the Westminster Union—the gentleman who had filled the office and that of vestry clerk for St. James's having elected to continue in the latter office only, and not to combine therewith any appointment under the Poor Law. Having some influence in St. Anne's at that time, and being also known in St. James's, I

gave him my support, with the result that he was
elected clerk to the Board. He never exhibited
gratitude for my doing this ; indeed, on the contrary, he was distinctly hostile to me during the first
few years after my appointment, more especially in
all matters relating to lunatics, the truth being that
he had a sympathy with all those who were alleged
to be of unsound mind, arising, I consider, from the
fact that he had a consciousness of not being quite
right himself. During the two-and-twenty years I
knew him I never saw him half-a-dozen times with a
shirt on. I do not state that he never wore one, it
was simply never visible ; what did duty for it was a
sheet of more or less crumpled whitey-brown paper.
His clothes were as torn and ragged as those of the
most poverty-stricken casual—his shoes down at heel,
and the legs of his seedy-looking black trousers
hanging in rags. He always complained of being so
very poor through the strain put upon him in having
to support some needy relatives. His condition and
poverty-stricken appearance were often the subject of
conversation and commiseration : " Poor fellow," it
used to be said, " he has had a great deal of trouble,
and is very poor." It was therefore a matter of
great astonishment to find, after his death, which
took place somewhat suddenly, that he was possessed

of several thousand pounds. He died without
making any will, and there was a legal struggle
among distant relations as to who should secure his
very considerable belongings. I have frequently
noticed on the part of eccentric people this disbelief
in and morbid sympathy with lunatics, and believe it
to arise from a species of innate consciousness of
mental deficiency, and a fear lest they also should be
incarcerated.

One morning, some time before his death, he came
to me in my room and showed me a letter he had
received from the military Commandant of Devonport
Barracks Hospital, which was to the effect that they
had a young soldier under treatment for lunacy, who,
in his attestation when enlisting, had stated that
he belonged to St. James's, London, and that the
authorities determined to send him up to us. The
clerk said to me, "That does not show that he belongs
here, as there are several St. James's in London; I
shall write and refuse to take him until his settlement has been determined." But he reckoned without
his host, for when did the military ever recognize the
civil power? The same evening I was requested to
go to the insane ward, where I found the young
soldier, and the attendant informed me that he had
been brought by a corporal and left in the ward, and

that the corporal said that he should call the next
day for the hospital clothes. The attendant also
stated that when brought in the man's hands were
tied together behind his back. I could make nothing
of the poor fellow, as no history was brought with
him, and he would not speak. As he appeared to be
very exhausted I ordered him some milk, beef-tea,
and wine, and desired that when the corporal called
the next day he should be detained, so that I might
learn something about the patient, but when asked
to stay and explain, the corporal would not stop.

On visiting the man on the next morning I found
that he had taken nothing, and as he would not open
his mouth, speak to me, nor do anything, I sent for
the stomach-pump and some of the strongest of the
pauper inmates, that he might be fed by artificial
means. It took four to take him out of bed, secure
him in a chair, and to assist me to get his mouth
open, when I made the dreadful discovery that all his
teeth had recently been broken away in the forcible
efforts that had been made to feed him. After a
most desperate struggle I administered some beef-tea,
arrowroot, and wine. This had to be repeated for
two or three days, until the necessary certificates
were ready, which enabled me to send him away to
Hanwell. I was so disgusted with the barbarous

manner in which the young man had been treated,
that I wrote an indignant letter to the military
authorities at Devonport, complaining of his treatment, and their neglect in sending the poor fellow to
the Workhouse without affording any history of his
case.   The reply was a cool denial of the truth of my
statement, and an assertion that he took his food
readily and without artificial feeding.   I sent this
letter to the medical superintendent of Hanwell, and
asked for his opinion, when he replied that the man
had been forcibly fed for some time, and that his teeth
had been destroyed in doing so.   I then wrote an
account of the case and sent it to Dr. Lush, M.P. for
Salisbury, and asked him to see the Minister for War
on the subject, and in the House to ask the question
I had drafted.

A few days after Dr. Lush replied, telling me that
he had seen the Minister, who read the statement,
and said he thought that it was a very shocking
story, but he hoped that I would not press for an
official inquiry, as it would ruin the officers inculpated, and promised that he would send out to
all military hospitals such an instructional letter as
would prevent the occurrence of such things in
future.   Dr. Lush also added, " I have promised not
to press the matter, especially as the Minister for

War did not hesitate to tell me that he entirely believed your statement," and continuing, said, "I know, Rogers, you do not want to ruin anybody, and if the matter is made public there will be a dreadful row, and the whole blame will be thrown on the doctor." I reluctantly assented to this view, and the matter dropped.

The poor fellow was afterwards proved not to belong to St. James's, Westminster, but to some parish in the East End. He did not remain chargeable to any parish very long, as he died soon after at Hanwell. Dr. Raynor, when I appealed to him for his opinion, stated that if I had not written at the time of his admission and explained how I had become possessed of the man, he should have felt it his duty to have made a special representation to the Commissioners in Lunacy as to the condition he was in on admission, and the barbarous usage he had received.

When at the Strand I was required to give the certificate in lunacy and attend before the magistrates in its support, and was paid a fee for my trouble ; when appointed to the Westminster Union it was arranged that my salary should include all extra fees, particularly because the magistrates at Great Marlborough Street, contrary to the statute, required two

certificates. The Guardians being unwilling to pay
the fees of two medical men, the medical man called
upon to give the second certificate was paid. As this
appointment was dependent on the caprice of the
Board, it frequently happened that the other medical
man, who was aware of the feeling of certain of the
Guardians, would refuse to endorse my opinion, but
I always succeeded in getting my way in the end.
One medical man who held this office for some time
was constantly striving to secure favour by giving the
most unaccountable certificates as to the condition of
the lunatic submitted to him. I had the satisfaction
of getting rid of him at last, but not until he had
given me and the officers of the House a great deal
of unnecessary trouble and annoyance. In addition
to this, the magistrates at Great Marlborough Street,
forgetting altogether that when two certificates were
presented their duty became simply a ministerial one,
would frequently decline to certify for removal of
undeniably insane persons, and direct the return to
the House for further observation. No magistrate
was more original in this way than Mr. Newton, of
Miss Cass notoriety. Over and over again Mr. Newton has set up his expression of opinion in opposition
to my certificate and that of the extern, but after
giving unnecessary trouble and delaying the removal

of the patient, thereby diminishing her or his chance of recovery, he would eventually be obliged to affix his signature to the certificate. To such an extent did this action prevail, and so much were the officers worried by this magistrate, that it became a custom on the part of the removal officer to send and inquire what magistrate would be on the bench, and if he found it was Mr. Newton, to take the case on the next day when he was not there.

As I am on the subject of lunacy, and as I believe that much mischief has ensued from the laity assuming that persons are improperly confined in asylums, I will relate one or two instances of ill results that have followed from treating insane persons as responsible for their conduct when a very small amount of consideration of their actions would show that they were of unsound mind. Upon one occasion, on going into the male insane ward, a tall, decent-looking man, turned round and looked at me. His aspect instantly told me that he was of unsound mind. To my inquiry where he came from the attendant replied, "I do not know, sir; all I do know is that his wife brought him here yesterday and left him. I spoke to the poor fellow, and was perfectly convinced that he was insane. I directed the attendant to go for the wife. On my return from the

11

wards to the consulting-room I found a decent-
looking little woman waiting my arrival. To my
inquiry what she wanted, she said, " You sent for
me." " Oh," I replied, "you are the wife of that
poor fellow over the way in the insane ward—how
long has he been out of his mind, and where have
you brought him from ? " To my astonishment she
burst into tears, at the same time saying, " He came
out of prison yesterday, sir." " Out of prison," I
replied ; " why, how could he have got into a prison ?
That poor man has, to my certain knowledge, been a
lunatic for a long while." She immediately said,
" Yes, sir, I have known it for nearly a twelvemonth,
but no one but you has ever said so before." I told
her to compose herself and tell me his history, when
she stated as follows : " We have been married about
five years, and a better husband no woman could
have had, but about a twelvemonth ago he complained
of his head, and could not sleep or work as he had
done. I did my best to cheer him up, and told him
to struggle against the feeling and all would come
right. His occupation was that of a coat-maker for
one of the best West End master tailors. One
afternoon, some months ago, he threw down a coat
he was making, saying he could not go on with it,
he must go out, which he did. About an hour after-

wards a policeman came to tell me my husband was in Vine Street Police Station, and that he had been taken up for stealing. I hurried there, when I heard that, walking along Little Pulteney Street, he came opposite a poulterer's shop, when, suddenly springing on the show-board, he clambered up by the hooks till he reached the top, and, taking off a hare, he put it over his shoulder, and jumping down some ten feet, he stood there. The proprietor gave him into custody. The next day he was taken before Mr. Knox, who committed him for a term of six weeks' imprisonment and hard labour, it being his first offence.

" Whilst he was in prison I had to part with many of my things to keep my children. On his discharge I met him at the prison gate, and saw he was worse. I did my best to cheer him up, and told him if he would not do anything of the kind again I would do all I could for him. On his reaching home I said that I had been compelled to part with some of our things, and that, therefore, he must go to work at once. The same day I went to one of our employers, a master tailor in Maddox Street, and asked for some work. A dress coat was given me to make up. My husband went to work at it, but he did it so badly that when he took it to the shop the master refused to pay him, and gave it him back again. During the

conversation my poor husband took off a pair of black
dress trousers from a hook, and put them under his
arm. He had not long left the shop when it was
discovered, and one of the shopmen, running after
him, caught him with the property. He was again
given into custody, and taken before Mr. Knox, who
committed him for trial. At his trial at Clerkenwell
Sessions shortly after, he was found guilty, and
evidence of a previous conviction having been given,
he was sentenced to six months' imprisonment and
hard labour. That his time was up yesterday
morning, that she had met him at the prison gate,
and seeing that he was much worse she had brought
him straight to the Workhouse, so that he might be
kept out of further mischief." She followed it up by
saying (with a burst of tears), "You are the only
gentleman who has ever said that he was not right in
his head, but I have known of it for months past."

I stood utterly astonished that so gross a mis-
carriage of justice should have been perpetrated; that
a man evidently so bereft of the knowledge of right
and wrong should have been punished as a criminal.
After inquiring where she lived, and also for some
references, I told her if my inquiries bore out what
she had stated, I would publicly expose the treatment
her husband had been subjected to. I made inquiry

the same afternoon, and found that both the husband
and wife had borne a most excellent character up to
the time of his first arrest. The next morning, so
soon as my official duties were over, I went to Great
Marlborough Street Police Court, and asked to see
Mr. Knox. I related the story to the magistrate.
When I had finished it he was very much affected,
and expressed his regret that such a dreadful thing
should have occurred. He also went on to state that
they had so many people brought before them, and it
was all done in such a hurried way, that without
special attention was drawn to a case, and if the facts
were not disputed, and if no one appeared for a
prisoner, a decision was come to at once. He further
said, "I remember the poor fellow being brought
before me perfectly. I do not think that it is
desirable that this story should be made public; it
can do no good. Send the wife to me and I will
give her a present from the poor-box."

When leaving the court the jailor followed me,
and said, "I am pleased you have been here. I saw
that poor fellow was out of his mind on each occasion
when he was brought before the magistrate." On
reaching the street I met Mr. W. J. Fraser,
Guardian, and now the Chairman of the Board, to
whom I told the circumstances. Mr. Fraser was

very much shocked at the treatment this poor lunatic had received, and that Mr. Knox had desired that no publicity should be given to the case, and replied, "Give it every publicity you can." That same evening I wrote to the editor of *The Times* the particulars of the case, and, as the poor husband's condition was irremediable, I pleaded that monies should be sent me to enable me to put the wife into some way of earning her livelihood. The letter duly appeared, and caused a great deal of sensation, many subsequent letters from gentlemen interested in the question of lunacy being published. As a result the sum of £85 was subscribed for the wife, and was sent to me.

It was a puzzle to me to know what to do with the money, which was not enough to buy a chandler's shop and stock it. I decided to set the woman up in business as a laundress at Battersea. I went there, took a suitable cottage, and guaranteed the rent for six months. Then I went to a firm in Holborn and purchased the laundry plant, which, under the special circumstances of the case, was sold to me at a reduced rate. I got a forewoman whom I borrowed from one of my patients in a large way of business as a laundress, and started her by inducing people to patronize her. I could do all this, but I

could not make the poor *woman a laundress, and
after a few months' trial she came and asked me to
let her dispose of the business and plant that she
might go to her friends in the country. I assented,
for I had discovered that she was a business failure.
She sold off everything, went away, and I have never
heard of her since. Her poor husband did not long
survive, and without doubt his death was hastened
by prison life and the treatment he had received
there. He died at Hanwell of general paralysis of
the insane.

It would prove instructive if it could be ascertained how many poor creatures have been similarly
taken into custody, convicted, imprisoned, and after
spending more or less time in prison discharged with
their mental condition hopelessly shattered from the
treatment received. Some years since I went over
the Naval Hospital at Yarmouth, for those who had
become insane whilst in the service. There were
several men of magnificent physique, who were
stricken with the same kind of mental infirmity as
that which had caused the death of my unfortunate
patient. I inquired of the courteous medical superintendent whether he had any history of these men.
He said yes. I asked whether the first evidence of
their mental ailment was not the exhibition of some

departure from discipline or of theft, or some other action which was totally at variance with their previous conduct. He informed me that their records showed that such was the case.

Woful results have followed the action of judges and police magistrates in dealing with numbers of their fellow-creatures as criminals when they rather required a nurse and skilful attention than the rough services of a prison warder. But then this deplorable condition of things will continue so long as such scant consideration is shown to the actions of the poor, who, being without means, cannot command the services either of barristers or solicitors.

It was during the reign of the Chairman of the Board who subsequently died in Cleveland Street Asylum, that one of the most extraordinary cases of lunacy I ever witnessed came under notice—extraordinary in one sense only, viz., in the manifest determination of certain officials to prevent me from sending to the asylum one of the most artful and yet hopeless lunatics I ever encountered.

Originally she had been admitted as a woman of unsound mind. I examined her at the time, and at once filled in a certificate that she was a case for removal to an asylum. She was not, however, sent away, as the clerk intervened, and at the next meeting of the Board he showed that the woman was the wife of the parish broker, who was a man of means and quite able to keep his wife in a private asylum, whereupon it was ordered that the husband should take her out. After her return home her husband asked me to see her; he could not live with her, her conduct was in every way so objectionable. I saw her again, certified that she was of unsound mind, and she was sent to St. Luke's, and her husband paid £1 a week for her maintenance therein. Getting tired of this, for he was a most penurious person, he took her out. Sometime after he was taken ill and died, leaving upwards of £4,000. Dying intestate, his property was divided beetween two brothers and the widow, her share, the third, being upwards of £1,500. The solicitor who wound up the estate, recognizing her mental condition, tried to induce her to let him invest the money in some security, but she refused. She would have her money paid over to her absolutely. This was in November. By the middle of the following August the money was all gone. She had squandered it all away; and having by her habits, which were to the last degree objectionable, caused her ejection from one lodging after another, the relieving officer was again called in, and removed this wretched woman

to the Workhouse insane ward. She brought with
her a large amount of property which was not
convertible into cash. Now, it may be asked, How
was the large sum of £1,500 got rid of in but little
over eight months? The explanation is a sad one.
The first thing this poor woman did was to buy some
£24 worth of plants in pots, which were taken to
a furnished room she had hired in Gerrard Street,
Soho. She never attempted to attend to them in
any way, and, therefore, in a very short time they
were all dead. She then sent to a well-known
drapery business in Regent Street to buy some
clothes. Before she left the shop the person in the
department she went to had induced her to buy some
£300 worth of personal clothing, which was all sent
to this single room in Gerrard Street. She also went
to a pianoforte manufacturer in Regent Street, and
purchased a sixty guinea piano, at the same time
being absolutely ignorant of music; and if any one
had taken much trouble they must have recognized
by her appearance her mental deficiency. About two
months after she first purchased at this draper's
shop, the shopwoman who had sold her £300 worth
of clothing, called on her in Gerrard Street, and,
although this room contained the dead flowers and
unopened boxes of the first purchase, she induced

her to buy £250 worth more, thus making a total of
£550 expended by a poor insane woman. The
Rector of St. Anne's, Soho, informed me that she
regularly attended the sacrament, and always put £1
in the plate in new gold. What made the conduct of
the shopkeeper of the firm in Regent Street the
more inexcusable was that at the time she called on
her the woman was in such a state, in consequence of
her dirty habits, as to be plainly insane, and this
compelled the landlady shortly afterwards to insist
on her leaving the house, as all the other lodgers
complained. When she was first admitted to the
Workhouse her habits were so repulsive that she was
an intolerable nuisance to the other inmates and
nurses, for she was alive with parasites.

I considered the treatment this poor creature had
received at the hands of the proprietors of the
drapery establishment so abominable that it merited
exposure, and with that view I called on a gentleman connected with the Press, and asked him to
take the matter up. He declined, as it was not
within the province of his journal. At the same
time he gave me an introduction to the editor of
Truth, who he said would do so. On going home
I drew up a history of the case, and sent it in a
letter marked private to the editor, enclosing the

letter of introduction, and asking that he would grant me an interview, when we might arrange for publishing my statements without my name appearing. I received no answer from the editor, but a day or two afterwards I was told that my statement had been published *in extenso* in *Truth*. A day or two after that the Chairman, who lived nearly opposite the draper's shop, called on me and stated that he was deputed by the firm to inform me that if I did not at once write to the editor of *Truth* and disavow the letter and story an action for libel would be commenced against me without delay. My answer was as follows : "Go back to this firm and say that I did not give any authority for the story to appear as it has done, but as it is all absolutely true I shall decline to withdraw or modify a single syllable." I certainly did write to the editor and complained of the way in which he had published the story, and told him of the threat which had been made of prosecuting me. The only result was that an annotation appeared in the next week's issue which, under the guise of an explanation, made the scandalous story a great deal worse. The firm did not prosecute me or the editor of *Truth.*

It would be imagined by my readers that there

would have been no difficulty in getting this poor
woman sent to an asylum, but I never had greater
trouble in my life, owing to the action of Mr.
Newton, the police magistrate at Great Marlborough
Street. Five times during the five months that she
was detained in the insane ward, where her habits
were most disgusting and highly objectionable to
the other inmates and to the nurses, I certified for
her removal. On each occasion she was sent back
by this magistrate. Hearing that he was gone for
a holiday, I, for the sixth time, filled in a certificate
and went with her and my out-door colleague to
the police office. To my surprise I found the
Chairman of the Board and two of his friends,
members of the Board, in attendance to give evidence in this woman's favour. The clerk had
found out what I was doing, and had sent word to
them. At the hearing before the magistrate they
attempted to interrupt me in my evidence, but they
were very properly put down by the magistrate. He
at once countersigned the certificate and she was
removed. But my troubles were not at an end.
The trio sent to the Commissioners in Lunacy an
intimation that I had unjustifiably sent a sane
woman to Hanwell Asylum. Upon this coming to
my knowledge I went there to see her, when the

medical superintendent of the female side informed
me that a special letter had been sent from the
Lunacy Commissioners requiring him, at the end of
three weeks, to send a detailed account of the case
to them.   He said, "I never met with such a case.
I was sure from your certificate she must be insane,
but she pulled herself together so wonderfully and
was so well conducted that I had come to the
conclusion that you must be mistaken, when suddenly she broke down, and her insanity became
apparent, and I have reported in that sense to the
Commissioners in Lunacy."   This story illustrates
the utter absurdity of the provision in the Lord
Chancellor's Bill committing the examination of
these cases to a county court judge, police magistrate, or Justice of the Peace, who cannot possibly
understand anything about the varied phases which
insanity presents.   The district medical officer who
jointly filled in the certificate with me was deprived
of his office, and a more manageable person was
elected by the Board in his stead—that person I have
before referred to in the earlier part of this narrative
as giving me so much needless trouble.

Some three years ago I had occasion to go to
Hanwell.   Whilst there I asked whether the woman
was still in the asylum.   On learning that she was

I expressed a desire to see her, when the superintendent medical officer gave directions that she
should be brought down. Immediately on seeing
me she sprung upon me, and, before I was able to
defend myself, pinioned me in her arms, at the
same time imploring that I would take her away
with me. It took three able-bodied women to release me from her grasp. Should I ever go to
Hanwell again I will keep clear of her. I have
had quite enough of her. She is a hopelessly incurable lunatic. As she gets older she will become
more and more demented, and will be eventually
removed to some imbecile establishment.

The female insane ward at the Westminster
Union was always full, and when a noisy or
dangerous lunatic was sent in, and whilst the
necessary steps were being taken to get them away,
the harmless patients had anything but a pleasant
time of it. But then the comfort of these people
was never at any time considered by those members
of the Board who considered themselves authorities
in lunacy. Fortunately they could not state that
my action arose from the desire to get a fee, as I
was never paid one, but they did say that I sent
them away as I did not want to attend to them.

We had on several occasions very amusing cases

of lunacy. One of the most so was a Welshman,
who, until he lost his reason, had been a very respectable journeyman tailor. I was asked to see
him by a member of the Vestry in whose house
he lodged, and who gave him a most excellent
character for honesty and industry. He had saved
money, and was exceptionally respectable in his
appearance and conduct. On being shown into his
room he rose and received me with much politeness.
I noticed a quantity of ladies' underclothing on the
table, and evidently intended for some small woman,
as the various things were all on the same diminu-
tive scale. On asking what it all meant he said,
"Oh, that is for the lady I am about to marry. I
have just purchased a complete set of ladies' underclothing as a present for my future bride." "Indeed," I said, "is it usual for the gentleman to
buy his future wife's underclothing?" "Well,"
he replied, "perhaps not, but I am a very particular
person, and my wife must dress as a lady." "Just
so," I said, "but how have you managed to get all
these things so exactly arranged as to size?" To
which he replied, "You see, I am accustomed to
measure people, and I have taken my dear little girl's
size exactly." I then took up a pair of some two dozen
of kid gloves, with the remark, "You have bought

her some good gloves, at any rate." "Do you think so?" he said. "Do oblige me by taking a pair away with you; they may suit one of your daughters." As his insanity was undoubted, I suggested his removal to the insane ward. This was carried out. On seeing me next day in the House he spoke rapturously of the ward he was in, and of his companions, all of whom he had invited to his wedding. They would have been sorry-looking persons to have made part of a company at a marriage-feast!

I was so amused at this poor fellow's delusions that next day I took one of my young lady relatives to see him. On my asking the attendant to bring him out into the yard, he came. At first he looked dazed, but, seeing a young lady, he ran towards her, and, peeping under her bonnet, he looked up and said, "She is devilishly like Mary Jane," this being the only name he had for his imaginary future wife. My young companion was so tickled that she burst into a hearty laugh in which the poor fellow joined. Subsequently he was sent to Hanwell. On visiting the asylum some months afterwards I asked to see him, when he was sent for. On entering the room he recognized me instantly, and expressed his gratification at my calling to see him. His delusions

12

were as marked as ever. As I had gone there on other business I resumed my conversation with Dr. Raynor, and forgot our Welsh friend altogether. Presently we both went out into the yard, when, to our astonishment, we found that he had gone out, and would have escaped altogether if he had not luckily been observed and taken back to his ward. Poor fellow! Some time after he was removed to Wales, where he was settled, and he ultimately died of general paralysis, and so the contemplated wedding was adjourned *sine die*. The underclothing, gloves, silk stockings, &c., were all sold to help pay for his maintenance. I never saw such a genial and absolutely happy lunatic. He lived in the company of his imaginary Mary Jane. It must not, however, be imagined that all are so light-hearted as this Welshman. I have encountered homicidal lunatics, and have personally experienced what some are capable of, having sometimes sustained severe assaults from incautiously going too near them.

Early in 1872 the present Chairman of the Westminster Union, W. J. Fraser, Esq., solicitor, asked me to visit the Rev. H. Watson, ex-master of Stockwell Grammar School, who was then located in Horsemonger Lane Gaol on the charge of killing his wife. I did so, and after an interview which

lasted an hour, came away and wrote a report that
in my judgment he was of unsound mind. I formed
that opinion from the levity of his manner, his
self-exaltation, his total indifference to his fate, the
absence of all regret for what he had done, and the
absolute want of any feeling on the subject. He
was lost in the belief that his services in the
education of youth precluded the possibility of any
punishment for his deed. At the Old Bailey, as I
was about being called upon to give evidence, the
counsel who defended him, the late Sergeant Parry,
called me over to tell me that they had decided not
to call me as a witness, but only just to support the
views of the others. He said, " We think you
may be a dangerous witness." After asking me a
few questions he said, " You can stand down."
But I was not to stand down, for the prosecuting
counsel, Mr. Poland, immediately proceeded to
severely cross-examine me. But to all his questions
I had my reply ready, and after some half hour's
trial of questions and answers I managed to get out
all the points on which I relied to prove Watson's
mental unsoundness. When I got down Dr. Bland-
ford said, " You have done well ; you have convinced the judge;" which was shown in his summing
up and in his after action at the Home Office.

Whilst under cross-examination I spoke of his enormous self-exaltation, &c., giving instances, whereupon Mr. Poland said, in a professional tone of voice, " Oh, you consider that is a sign of insanity, do you ? " " Well," I said, " seeing he was only a schoolmaster, I do." Whereupon Watson, who was listening attentively to my evidence, wrote on a piece of paper and gave it to Mr. Fraser for presentation to his counsel. He had written, " What does this d——d fellow mean by calling me 'only a schoolmaster ' ? " After his conviction and sentence he was removed to Horsemonger Lane Gaol. When Mr. Fraser went to see him next day the only thing he complained of was my having spoken of him as only a schoolmaster. He had nothing to say about his conviction and fate ; as regards that he was absolutely indifferent. There was a terrible row in the Press about this man, and the doctors were all condemned for their efforts to prove that his mind was unhinged. It was therefore some comfort to me when, in going down the street in which I then lived some few days after, I saw Lord Elliot, the son of the Earl of St. Germains. On meeting me he crossed over the road, came up to me, and holding out his hand and taking mine he said, "I see you have been figuring at the Old Bailey." " Yes, my lord,"

I replied; "I hope, however, you do not think
I have done wrong in giving the evidence I did?"
"Oh no," he said; "I have just come from the
Home Office, and have met there the Lord Chief
Justice (Cockburn) and Mr. Justice Byles, who have
both advised the Home Secretary that they consider
that the plea of insanity was, in their judgment, fully
sustained: at any rate, he will not be hanged."
His sentence was commuted to penal servitude for
life. Poor old Watson was sent to Parkhurst Prison.
Some years after the governor and surgeon informed
me that he preserved the same callous and indifferent
manner which I had described at his trial. His only
complaint was that he could not get the particular
copy of the Greek Testament he wanted, and he never
to the last referred to or expressed any regret for the
act he had committed.*

* The attacks upon me were so scurrilous for the evidence
I had given that I wrote as follows to the editor of *The
Lancet,* the staff there being divided in opinion whether I
should be supported or condemned—

"REGINA *v.* WATSON.

" To the Editor of *The Lancet.*

" Sir,—As I have been made to occupy, through the exceptionally severe and not over-courteous cross-examination
at the Old Bailey, a more conspicuous position than I had
desired before the public, perhaps you will permit me to give

After I had been at the Workhouse some two years
I was requested by the Board to go down and take
temporary charge of the Union school at Wands-

the reasons why I held, and do hold, that the prisoner in the
above case was, and is, of unsound mind ; and, subsequently,
to briefly comment on each head.

" 1st. There were the evidences of pre-existent melan-
cholia.

" 2nd. The ferocity with which the deed was committed.

" 3rd. The total absence of criminal motive.

" 4th. The calmness and indifference of the prisoner's
manner after the deed was done.

" 5th. His justification of suicide, and the expression of
his belief that God would forgive the homicide under the
circumstances.

" First, as regards the proofs of mental disease prior to the
act—they were deposed to by the Rev. Folliott Baugh and
his wife as existing a month before the murder ; by Mr. H.
Rogers on the preceding day ; whilst further evidence on
this head, not available for the defence owing to the sickness
of the deponent, has since been forwarded to the Home
Secretary, the statement being that some months before he
was in communication with the prisoner for the purpose of
employing him in his school, but on an interview he found
his mental condition to be such that he at once broke off the
engagement : the evidences of aging and altered aspect deposed to by the secretary of the school a short while after
his dismissal. And mark, that to him was no ordinary
event : at sixty-seven he found himself suddenly without
employment, without any realized money, absolute penury
in the not distant prospective, whilst, during the nine months
he had been thus thrown in upon himself, every attempt to
add to his means or to obtain an engagement, whether
literary or scholastic, had entirely failed.

worth Common. It would appear that there had
been a quarrel between the superintendent matron
and the medical officer, and an official inquiry

" Second. Passing to my next point, the ferocity of the act,
it was argued by the prosecution that it was done in a fit of
rage ; but, for the credit of our common human nature, I
would ask, Is it conceivable that mere anger would so trans-
form a mild, quiet old gentleman, as he was shown to be,
into such a brutal criminal, so that, not content with slaying
his victim, he should go on battering her head and body
long after passion alone would have been exhausted ? It is,
I contend, explicable only as the act of a homicidal melan-
cholic, not otherwise.

" Third. The senseless character of the deed. If done con-
sciously and by premeditation, as the verdict would suppose,
I would ask, Where could be the gain ? Here, again, I argue
that the act itself, done without reasonable motive, could
only be the product of reason overthrown.

" Fourth. The indifference, &c. Here I would submit—can
a parallel be produced from criminal records in any place
(Broadmoor excepted) for the remarkable calmness (self-
possession Mr. Gibson, of Newgate, phrases it) Mr. Watson
maintains whenever the act is referred to, such as to lead his
old friend, the Rev. J. Wallis, to state that he seemed perfectly void of shame and remorse ; nay, asserting that he was
an injured person by being put in prison ' ?

" Fifth. His justification of suicide, &c. I may here be met
by the remark that he is probably an unbeliever in the
Christianity he professed. To this I make reply that there is
not a tittle of evidence to show that such is the case. Until
the act was done, a regular attendant at church, a constant
communicant, his whole moral nature must have become
utterly changed and corrupt ere such a consummation could
be arrived at, standing out, as it does, in direct antagonism

having been held by a Poor Law Inspector he
had reported that he could not decide which was in
the wrong; he would advise the Board to call on all
three to resign at the end of the following Midsummer quarter.

The medical officer, Dr. Noel, who, strange to say,
had been a schoolfellow of mine nearly fifty years
before, at once sent in his resignation. I took over
the duty at the end of April, and had charge of the
schools nine weeks. It was a very pleasant excuse
for an outing, and as the Common at that time was
not much built upon and the gorse was in full bloom,
it made for me a very agreeable change. At the
Midsummer quarter a new medical officer was appointed, and my temporary appointment came to an
end. There was extremely little sickness during the
time I had charge of the establishment, and I there-

to his previous life, as portrayed by one who knew him
well and gives his opinion of his old friend in this day's
Times.

"I pass over the subsequent blundering attempts to
hide the act, as similar things have been done by others
whose insanity has not been questioned. And as I have
occupied much of your space, I subscribe myself,

" Yours obediently,
" Jos. ROGERS.

"DEAN STREET, SOHO,
   "*January* 15, 1872. "

fore came to the conclusion that the only possible explanation of the quarrelling was because they had so very little to do. My successor was appointed on the distinct understanding that in the event of any serious illness occurring he was to send for me. His neglect to do this led, some five years afterwards, to his being called on to resign, and to my being put again in control of the schools and retention of the office for eight months. The occasion for my being sent down the second time was a serious outbreak of ophthalmia which had taken place, one-half of the school, about sixty children, being more or less affected with it. I could not afford the time or undergo the fatigue to go there every day, so on my return home I made a report to the Board that on condition that the Board gave me full powers to act as I thought best I would root out the epidemic. This was assented to, whereupon I brought back forty-eight of the worst cases to the Workhouse, and isolated them in the large wards at the top of the main building. I also brought with me the nurse and assistant school-mistress. I told the Board that some of the cases were so very bad that I must be allowed to call in an ophthalmic surgeon to aid me in my treatment. This was also assented to. I also arranged that the children should go for a run in the

park every day, weather permitting. I considered the
dietary of the children, and, finding it to be wholly
insufficient, I amended it. I adopted a similar
course at the school. Fortunately for the children
the Chairman of the Board, a medical man, supported
me in all I advised and did. I had the children's
hospital at the school whitewashed and painted green
and varnished, the walls stopped and covered with
neatly-framed engravings kindly sent me by the proprietors of *The Graphic*. At the end of eight
months I gave up the appointment, leaving the children perfectly well, except in a few cases where
irretrievable mischief had taken place ere I was called
in. Much of my success was due to the Chairman of
the Board, the late Mr. Henry Cooper, of Soho, who
throughout gave me the most generous and unfalter-
ing support. Many of these poor children would
have hopelessly gone blind if it had not happened
that at the period of the epidemic the Board fortunately possessed an intelligent and public-spirited
Chairman. Not a very long time afterwards he was
taken ill, and after lingering some time died, to be
succeeded by another person who, most unluckily
for the welfare of the House, had again been returned
as a member of the Board and elected the Chairman.

About some two years after my appointment a

woman, extremely ill, was brought from Vine Street
Police Station. She was an unfortunate, as it is
called, who had been taken ill in the cell. Repeated
requests from her for attendance met with no attention. At last, her condition appearing desperate
even to the constables, the divisional surgeon was sent
for, who directed that she should at once be removed to the Workhouse. She was brought in on a
stretcher, and I was summoned to attend her without
delay. I found that she was dying, and not a long
while afterwards she succumbed. A coroner's inquiry
taking place I made a post mortem, when I found that
she had died from the rupture on an aneurism of the
abdominal aorta, which, giving way in the loins, had
slowly infiltrated the tissues until, a vent being found,
the whole thing gave way. There is no doubt that
this rupture had been precipitated by the violence
attending her arrest. The verdict, under the direction of the coroner, led to a censure of the police for
their inhumanity and indifference. The ultimate
result was to immensely add to my troubles, as will
hereafter be shown.

Just at this time the old and sagacious surgeon of
the division died, and his place was sought after by
several medical men living in the neighbourhood of
the two police stations in St. James's, some of whom

were men of acknowledged position. The gift of
the appointment was vested in the Chief Surgeon of
Police, Mr. Timothy Holmes, of St. George's Hospital. He gave the office to one of his old pupils who
at the time was non-resident, but who at once took a
house in Jermyn Street. It was not very long before I
experienced the result of the change. Case after case
was sent into the House from the two stations with
certificates that the persons were ill when they were
undeniably and plainly drunk. At first I complained
of this to the inspectors, but it led to no result. I
then wrote to the Commissioners of Police, complaining of the annoyance. I got only an official reply.
At last the nuisance became so great, for we were
always called to these police cases sent in from the
station in the small hours of the morning, that I
again wrote to the Commissioners and requested an
interview. This was granted. I took with me my
assistant who had been principally called out of bed
to attend to these cases, sometimes only to dress a
wound which the police surgeon was too indolent to
do himself although he was paid a fee for each visit.
On arrival we stated our complaint, but, although the
Commissioners listened to us attentively, not much
benefit accrued. It is true they stated that an inquiry should be made and instructions given and that

more care should be exhibited. Some time after this I happened to be at the gate when a constable brought a perfectly drunken woman, who, he said, had fallen down in a fit. I said, " Why, she is only drunk and incapable ; take her away to the station ; " and turning to the master I said, " Do not admit her." An entertainment was being held that evening which I had assisted to get up, and I went on into the dining-hall. About an hour afterwards the master came to me and said, " They have brought that woman back with a certificate from the doctor that she is dangerously ill." I went to see her. She was only a shade more under the influence of liquor than she was before, but, not caring to contest the subject any further, I directed that she should be sent to the re- ceiving ward and put to bed. The next morning on seeing her she had got over the drunkenness, and she owned to me that she had been only drunk the night before. On going to my room I directed that a special messenger should take a letter from me to the station, telling the inspector on duty that the woman that had been sent in the night before alleged to be ill, had confessed to having been only drunk, and re- questing him to send a constable and take her away. The constable came. In the after-part of the day, a constable of that division called at my house and said that Mr. Newton requested that I should attend the police court the next morning. I went, when I found the woman there and the divisional surgeon. The magistrate, before hearing a word from me, proceeded to inveigh against me for my action in the matter, and peremptorily ordered me to admit the woman at once. The divisional surgeon also jumped up and protested against my refusal to admit the woman, and stated, to my astonishment, that she had heart disease, and that she was a confirmed epileptic. I mildly replied that she was suffering under nothing of the kind, but Mr. Newton told me to leave the court. The woman did not come into the Workhouse until the evening, and she was then under the influence of drink.

On my return to the Workhouse I told the master what had occurred, and also asked him if he knew where she came from. "Oh," he said, "the receiving wards woman informs me that she belongs to Whitechapel Union, whose clothes she is wearing." I then asked him to write to the master of the Whitechapel Union and ask him what he knew of her. In less than twenty-four hours the reply came. It was to the effect that she was one of the most abandoned characters ever in their House ; that she did not suffer from fits, though she often assumed to have one ; that she never went out except to return drunk; that she had no heart disease, but was a hale, hearty woman ; that on the day she went out, wearing the House clothes, it was after three months' detention, she having returned on the last occasion drunk and disorderly.

Having received this report, I sent it to Mr. Newton. At the same time I protested against his having sent for me to attend his court, and for the remarks he had made to me on the faith of the opinion expressed by a person of very little experience, and further informed him that I should continue to protest against the use of the wards of the Workhouse as a receptacle for merely drunken men and women, and should advise the master accordingly.

The annoyance still continuing, I made a point of sending for the police each morning after every drunken admission. Then a new antagonistic element was imported in the shape of a letter to the Local Government Board from Mr. Timothy Holmes, containing a complaint against me for the trouble I was giving the police authorities in objecting to the reception of sick people from the station to the Workhouse. The letter having been sent to me to answer, I forwarded to the Local Government Board the names of some sixty persons brought in by the police under the certificate of the divisional surgeon, and showed that two-thirds of the entire number were proved to be only drunk and incapable, and that the rest were, in the majority of instances, very trivial cases of illness.   The nuisance after this was very much diminished.

It may be asked, What are the police to do with persons who allege that they are ill?   Are these complaints to be disregarded?   Certainly not.   But I contend that reasonable care should be taken by police surgeons, before they send cases of alleged illness to a workhouse infirmary; for it must be remembered that they are paid a fee for each visit and examination.   To go, therefore, to the station, make a cursory examination, and then write a certificate that the person is seriously ill and must be removed without delay, or in the case of a simply cut head send it at once away to the infirmary for the workhouse surgeon to get out of bed and dress it, is, in my judgment, an entirely unsatisfactory procedure, especially as the latter is paid no special fee, be his trouble ever so great.   There was nothing in all my duty as a workhouse medical officer, which irritated me more than these police cases.   I remember on one occasion a superintendent of police said to me, " I hold that if after our surgeon makes these mistakes he were to forfeit his fee, which should be paid to you, you would not have many then."

Sometimes the police brought cases of interest. On one occasion two Italian children were admitted. One was a boy of nine, clean and well nourished, the other was a little fellow of about five, wonderfully emaciated, and bearing about his little lean body evidence of recent ill-usage. The parents, who were Italian Jews, had been taken into custody for maltreating this child, and had been remanded. He was dreadfully dirty. I had him weighed and found that he was much lighter than he should have been, regard being had to his age. He was ravenous; but he had to be fed with care so as to prevent mischief. His parents had been remanded for a week, and a good-natured constable of the C Division who had intervened and got the parents arrested came and asked me to attend at the re-examination. Before taking the child to the court I again weighed him, and found he had gained three pounds. After some four remands at each of which I was enabled to show he had gained in weight, the parents were committed for trial. I attended as a witness at the Old Bailey when the trial came on, and the parents were convicted and sentenced to eighteen months' imprisonment with hard labour. The poor little fellow was

13

brought back to our House, whilst the elder brother was sent to the school.

Foreseeing what was probably in store for this unhappy child, if he ever passed into the hands of his unnatural parents, I wrote to *The Times* paper, and pointed out what would be the inevitable fate of this boy when his parents came out of prison and claimed possession of him, and pointed out that, as the Italian Consul had found counsel for the defence of the parents at the trial, I trusted that they would find some means whereby the child might be secured against further ill-treatment. On the same day that the letter appeared, I received a letter from the Consul asking me to call on him, which I did, when he told me that he would bring the case under the attention of the King of Italy. Some three weeks after I received a communication stating that the King had resolved to take the child, and bring him up at the cost of the State, as a ward of the Italian Government. Some ten days afterwards a tailor came and measured him for clothing, and a messenger from the Italian Consul having given an undertaking to the Board, he was taken away and I saw him no more. If alive he must be now some eighteen years old. I write "if alive," for the poor little fellow had a singular deformity. He had no abdominal muscles; what did

duty for them was a dull, parchment-like-looking
structure, stretched across the abdomen. One could
make out without much difficulty the various abdominal organs. I had never seen anything like it
before. Strange to relate, just at this time a young
lady from Natal was sent over to me with a request
from her parents that I would ask some expert to see
her. On her arrival I found that she had exactly the
same infirmity. The late Dr. Alfred Meadows, who
saw her with me, would not believe my statement at
all until he had himself seen and examined her.
Her mother was very anxious to know whether she
might be permitted to marry the gentleman to whom
she was engaged. We gave a guarded opinion on
the subject, and she returned to Natal, and was
married, and has two or three children. I therefore
trust that the little Jew Italian boy has also survived.
I have never heard anything of him since he left the
Poland Street Workhouse.

One morning in 1877, shortly after I had left the
House, the attendant came round to my residence,
and informed me of the almost sudden death of the
master, who was at my official visit half an hour
before apparently in good health. He had never
been partial to me, as my system of management
clashed considerably with the stereotyped arrange-

ments that had prevailed in the House prior to my
appointment, and I very much question whether he
ever approved of my having caused almost everything
consumed in the House to be supplied under contract. He did not openly quarrel with me, but contented himself with passive resistance; and if I
complained of any order not being carried out, he
always excused himself by saying, Did you give an
order for this, that, and the other? all the time
knowing full well, that I had given the order. A
striking instance of this obstructiveness occurred in
the first autumn and winter after I took office. I
had asked the Board's permission that some jackets
should be supplied for the sick men and some shawls
for the women, which they might wear when sitting
up in bed to keep their chests and shoulders warm.
This application was made to the Board of Guardians
early in October, and was at once acceded to. Week
after week went by, and in spite of repeated requests
made by me, either to the master or matron, no
notice was taken beyond the same answer which was
always given when the one or the other thought fit to
reply at all, " Oh, I have given the order for the
material and for the shawls, but the contractor is so
negligent, he has not sent us in the goods."

In the early part of January I received a letter from

Dr. Mouatt, Poor Law Inspector, stating that he had been instructed by the Local Government Board to go over the House and see how many persons could be described as fit to be sent away to the Sick Asylum, and, as he wished me to accompany him, he desired to know what day would suit me best. In reply I fixed the next Sunday, and as I did not wish the master to accompany us, for I knew he would report all that took place to the Board, I wrote in that sense to Dr. Mouatt. Dr. Mouatt came on the following Sunday morning. I had told the master he was coming, and, just as I expected, he stayed away from chapel, in order to go with us. Dr. Mouatt promptly said, " As this is a purely medical visit, master, we can dispense with your company." He coloured up and looked very much put out, but he had to comply. As I went through the wards I told the Inspector that I had asked the Board three months before to let me have some shawls for the women and jackets for the men, that the Board had given an order for them, but neither the master nor matron had supplied them, and that I felt satisfied they did not intend to do so, to which he quietly said, " I will soon alter that." At the same time I urged on him the necessity of so referring to the subject, as not to make them think I had said anything about it, but that the necessity for them had occurred to him, "For," I said, "if you do, they will make it the subject of an open quarrel." It was humbling to do this, but I knew what these people would do.

At the conclusion of our examination, which lasted nearly three hours, we returned to my room, where the master promptly joined us. On seeing him Dr. Mouatt asked that the matron should be sent for. On her arrival he addressed them both as follows : "I have been over the sick wards and have seen all the sick that should be sent away and taken the number ; this I shall report to the Local Government Board. I see that your House is kept clean and in good order, but there is one thing I notice which must at once be altered, and that is, the large number of patients sitting up in bed without anything over their shoulders. I have called Dr. Rogers' attention to it, and he tells me that the Board gave an order three months ago for jackets and shawls to be provided, but that they have never been supplied." Both imme-diately began to throw the blame on the contractor, but he cut them short by stating, "That excuse, master and matron, will not do for me ; you know as well as I do you could have got them if you had chosen. I shall report the omission to supply them to the Board of Guardians and also to the Local Government Board." On hearing this they were dreadfully put out, and expressed an earnest hope that, as it was not their fault, he would not be so severe. "Well," he said, "I shall request the medical officer to report to me when they are supplied, and if every person needing them is not furnished with them before the end of the week, I shall carry out what I have said." By the following Wednesday all my patients were provided with them. At his death the master left some £4,000, notwithstanding he had a large and expensive family. After his decease I learned that he had signed a quantity of blank orders for my attendance, and had given them to the porter with the instructions that if any person was admitted who either looked ill or complained of being so, he was at once to send for me. His death led to the diminution of second calls by at least two-thirds. He was nearly always out in the after-part of the day. For several weeks after his death the duties of master were performed by the labour master. At last the Board advertised for a master and matron, the appointment of matron having come to an end when the late master died. As the Guardians were fully alive to the bad discipline which had prevailed for so many years, they resolved to appoint two officers who should more strictly exercise their authority. The

choice of the Board fell upon Mr. John Bliss, a
corporal-major of the Life Guards, and a Miss
Heatley, lately assistant matron of the Manchester
Workhouse. Both of these officers were strict dis-
ciplinarians, and something besides, as the sequel
will show. For the first two or three years, indeed,
during the whole Chairmanship of Mr. Cooper, the
surgeon, they were kept in their places and behaved
fairly well, but unfortunately for them, for the inmates, and the Board, Mr. Cooper was taken ill and
died, and another Chairman being elected, serious
results soon followed, for this Chairman was always in
the House, and when so was constantly closeted with
the master and matron in their rooms. Speedily
after that the master began to dispute my orders,
and the matron did the same, and as the Chairman
again began to obstruct my sending the acutely sick
inmates away to the Sick Asylum, the House became
fu of sick people, who were detained in it through
the restrictions put in my way. At last the obstruction to the performance of my duty, by both master
and matron, became almost unbearable, especially as
Mr. Bliss thought fit to accompany his refusals by
telling me to go to h—l, and sundry other coarse
and blasphemous expressions ; and to such an extent
was it carried, that I felt I could not put up with it.

To complain to the Board would have been perfectly
futile, the majority would most assuredly have gone
against me. At last the loud-mouthed, coarse, and outrageous blasphemy of the master quite appalled me ;
and this, coupled with his refusal to obey my orders
and his general interference with me in my treatment
of the sick, by deriding my judgment and by openly
stating that I did not know my profession, caused me
to speak to Mr. Fraser, a Guardian, in reference to
the annoyance I was being daily subjected to. He
advised that I should go to the Local Government
Board and confer with the Poor Law Inspector. I
did so, but got very little encouragement by my
action. Some time after, in a letter to the Department, I did not hesitate to refer to it, and state as
much. One result, however, accrued from this visit,
which I foresaw was in the near future imminent,
and I accordingly took steps forthwith to get some
influence in the House of Commons so as to secure
a proper inquiry. On my return I again saw Mr.
Fraser, and told him of the way I had been treated.
Just about this time this Guardian came into
collision with Mr. Bliss. It happened in this way :
there was a lady living on Wandsworth Common, the
wife of the chaplain of a public institution, and, being
very benevolent, she had constantly visited the Union

school, and had interested herself in the future welfare of the girls. A girl she was much interested in had gone to a situation some months before, and, not being kindly treated, had left and returned to the Workhouse, when she wrote to this lady, who at once came up to the House to see her and some other girl. The master refused to allow her to do so, whereupon she went round to Soho Square and saw Mr. Fraser, whom she had known as a Guardian, and told how she had been treated, whereupon he wrote to the master, stating who the lady was, and asking him to allow her to see the girls. The master read the letter and replied, with a coarse oath, "I have already told you you shall not see the girls, and you shall not." On reporting this conduct to Mr. Fraser, he was much incensed, and at the next meeting of the Board brought the master's behaviour before the Guardians. To his astonishment, the majority of the Guardians absolutely howled him down. Mr. Fraser then formulated a series of charges against Mr. Bliss, among them his constant refusal to obey my orders, his swearing and generally violent treatment of the inmates, and moved that these charges should be sent to the Local Government Board, and an inquiry into the master's conduct asked for. This proposition was rejected, but, at the suggestion of

the Chairman, it was resolved that the Board would
conduct an inquiry themselves. This was done
evidently with the intention that the whole matter
as against the master should be quashed. The
inquiry was held, and I was ordered by the Board
to attend. At the inquiry by the Guardians the
Chairman presided, and proceeded to ask questions ;
but finding he was no match for the solicitor, Baron
H. de Worms, an *ex-officio* guardian, put in an appearance and conducted the inquiry for them, and
as I declined to recognize his or the Board's right
to put questions to me, the Baron threatened to
report my behaviour to the Local Government Board.
I said to him, however, that if it were a regular
legal inquiry, conducted by a properly constituted
authority, I would answer on oath, and prove all
the charges I had ever made against the master and
matron. One of my charges was that I had discovered that my Medical Relief Book had been
tampered with, and that entries for wines and
spirits, neither ordered by me or given to the
sick, had been placed against certain names. When
this was gone into by the Baron the master's clerk
was sent for and insolently denied the allegation.

The Guardians completely exonerated the master
and matron, his clerk, and all concerned with them ;

but the matter did not end there. During the progress of this so-called inquiry the matron brought before the Guardians eight of the very worst characters in the House, in order to depose to her and the master's continuous kindness and consideration to all the inmates, and that Mr. Bliss never swore at all. After they had given their evidence they were entertained by the matron in the store-room, a hot supper and brandy-and-water being provided. As she knew I was keeping a sharp look-out on my books to prevent any additional frauds, the next morning she was at her wits' end to make up the deficiency in the brandy, but at last she managed it by adding some water; but in her hurry she forgot to add clean water. She put what she wanted to increase the quantity into a jug which had contained milk, and so gave a cloudy appearance to the whole of it. On my arrival at the House I was informed of the entertainment that had been given to these witnesses to character, and on going into the women's sick ward, the head nurse showed me the brandy which had been tampered with, and I was further told by her that the brandy given out on the male side had the same appearance—indeed, that the nurse on that side had just called her attention to it. I directed that she should

carry it down into my room. On going through
to the male side, I requested the nurse to show
me her brandy. At first she objected to do so,
but on my insisting she reluctantly did so, when
I took it away. On reaching my room I sent for
a large bottle and mixed it all together and sealed
down the cork. I then wrote to the contractors,
Messrs. Hedges and Butler, of Regent Street, and
asked them to examine it and write me word whether
the brandy sent was the same as that supplied by
them under the contract. It was taken by one of
the officers. In the course of an hour he came
back with the brandy and a statement from the
firm proving that it had been lowered by the
addition of so much water, and that the water that
had been used was not clean. I then wrote to the
Board giving the history now related, and enclosed
Messrs. Hedges and Butler's certificate. I wrapped
all up together in a piece of brown paper and
addressed it to the Board of Guardians. I called
the clerk into my room and having in his presence
sealed up the parcel, I requested him to take charge
of it and not to let it go out of his hands until
the Board met. I then ordered a fresh supply for
my sick. I had hardly left the House when the
Chairman came, and, going to the clerk, demanded

to see the parcel. The clerk gave it to him, when he immediately broke it open and read my letter and the spirit-merchant's certificate. Of course his supporters passed over this abominable transaction when the subject was brought before the Board, and the matron was not even censured; at least, so I was told.

There was, however, a Nemesis. Just as they were rejoicing at the success of their proceedings a letter was on its way to the clerk from the Local Government Board, stating that, in consequence of certain information having been sent to the Department, an official inquiry into the master's management of the House had been determined on, and that Mr. Robert Hedley had been directed to hold it. I immediately went down to the House of Commons, saw some Members, and begged that they would see Sir Charles Dilke, who was then the President, and ask him to send some other Inspector instead. A day or so afterwards I heard that as his name had been mentioned it could not be changed, but that another Inspector, Mr. Taylor, a barrister-at-law, would be appointed with him in the inquiry.

In due course the inquiry took place, Mr. Robert Hedley presiding, Mr. Taylor sitting on his right,

Mr. Fraser, the solicitor, one of the Guardians, on the left. Mr. Fraser conducted the proceedings against the master, who was defended by Mr. Ricketts. The proceedings lasted several days. During the progress of the inquiry Mr. Hedley rendered no assistance whatever, and if it had not been for the conscientious conduct of Mr. Taylor, not one-half of the evidence which was given would have been brought out. Nearly all the evidence which was tendered was voluntary—that is, inmates and officers came forward to testify to Mr. Bliss's continual refusal to comply with my orders, to his swearing at me and the inmates, and his general harshness and positive cruelty to many of them. When the master's clerk was examined, he swore that he had never made false enteries in my Medical Relief Book; but when my attendant, who had assisted in making up the book, gave evidence and stated that he had seen him make them, his tone altered, and eventually he confessed to sixty-three fraudulent entries of wines and spirits, amounting in the whole to a very considerable quantity of stimulants, presumably supplied to my sick but in reality consumed by other people. When called as a witness, I deposed to the continued refusal of Mr. Bliss to comply with my orders, as to his swearing at me and at others, and to the fact that he derided my judgment, and had intimated to the sick inmates under my charge his disbelief in my knowledge of my profession, &c.

When Bliss was called on for his defence he contented himself with giving a general denial to everything that had been given in evidence against him. At last Mr. Hedley said that he should close the inquiry. I do not know whether at that time he had communicated to Mr. Bliss that he intended to report in his favour, but I had a suspicion of it, as no one could possibly be in better spirits than Mr. Bliss was that day, and it was clear from Mr. Hedley's manner and Mr. Bliss's familiarity with the Inspector what his decision would be.

I was therefore not surprised on going down to the House some three weeks after to make some inquiries that certain Members, whose names I am precluded even now from mentioning, informed me confidentially that it had oozed out that Mr. Hedley and the other Inspector had recommended to the President that Mr. Bliss should be allowed to remain as master. On my expressing my astonishment at such a monstrous decision, I was informed that, to a great extent, the President was powerless in such matters—that, having appointed an Inspector to conduct an inquiry, he was by the rules of the Department bound by his decision, and that if he made a report in favour of the individual into whose management he was deputed to inquire, and reported favourably or the reverse of that, the President was compelled to accept it, however much he felt that the evidence did not support the view taken by the Inspectors.

I lay stress upon this assumption that Inspectors cannot by any possibility err in their judgment, or be guilty of favouritism in their conduct of such inquiries, because ere long, if we are to have County Government Boards, the obligations of these Inspectors will be largely increased, and if the official inquiries of the future are to be conducted by men such as I have had experience of, Heaven help the unfortunate officials whose actions are being inquired into, unless there are some special reasons why they should be officially befriended, such as evidently held good in Mr. John Bliss's case.

Having regard to the fate that always attends crooked courses, I am very much disposed to think that a different line would have been followed could it have been foreseen that Mr. Bliss would have acted as he did three weeks after the inquiry was ended, when a woman was brought in a cab so very

14

ill that I decided to send her away forthwith to the
Asylum Hospital; but, as she was blue in the face
from difficulty of breathing and from general exhaustion, I told the receiving wards woman to come
into my room, and then gave her a written order for
some brandy and beef-tea to be given to the woman
before she went away. I addressed the order to the
matron. Shortly afterwards the nurse came back
and told me that this woman had refused to supply
what I had ordered. I then said, "Take the order
to the master." After a minute or so she returned,
telling me that the master would see me d——d
before the woman should have it. I then left the
House, and on the next day heard that, exhausted
as she was, the woman was taken to Cleveland Street
without anything being given to her. That morning
I wrote to the medical superintendent of the Sick
Asylum, and asked him to let me have a copy of
any remarks he had made on her admission (of
course, stating the refusal of both master and matron
to give her anything at all before she left the Westminster Workhouse). His reply bore out the view
I had formed of her condition, and he further said
that if I had not written to him he should have
made a special report to the managers showing her
exhausted condition when admitted. A copy of this

letter and a formal complaint against the matron
and Bliss for their refusal to give the poor woman
anything, was sent to the Board of Guardians, who
simply ignored it. I also sent a similar statement
to the Local Government Board, but no acknowledgment of its ever having been received was sent
to me. Knowing what I do, from many years'
experience, what this Department is, I very much
regret that I did not send this complaint under
cover (privately) to Sir Charles Dilke. It is a
curious fact that, although the suppression of my
statement at the Local Government Board, and the
refusal of the Chairman and his party to make any
inquiry into my complaint caused Mr. Bliss to
keep his appointment a twelvemonth longer, yet
this refusal, having been subsequently conclusively
proved, ultimately led to his being called on to
resign his appointment, as will be shown hereafter,
after the Chairman had in the interval been ejected
from office by an overwhelming vote of the indignant
ratepayers.

No report of the inquiry having been forwarded
to the Board, the Chairman, after the lapse of
about three months, caused a letter to be written
to the Local Government Board asking that the
result of the inquiry should be forwarded. The

President sent a copy of the evidence given on oath
to the Guardians, thinking that after the Board had
read it through they would surely concur with him
in thinking that Mr. Bliss was not a fit person to
remain as master. But he reckoned wrongly. Sir
Charles Dilke did not know the Chairman. This man
simply induced his dozen followers to utterly ignore
all the evidence, and to assert that it proved nothing.

Meeting one of these Guardians in the House two
or three mornings after, he came up to me, and, in
a loud tone of voice, he said, "I have been reading
your disgraceful evidence against our master." To
which I quietly replied, "It was given on oath, and
every word of it is true;" when, in a towering passion,
he said, "You have disgraced yourself, I tell you;
you have disgraced yourself;" and then, before I
could reply to this outburst of vulgar vituperation,
he went on to say, "I see the Local Government
Board have directed us to pay you five guineas for
your attending to give evidence : I am the Chairman
of the Board, and not one penny shall you ever
be paid for your disgraceful evidence." Had this
outburst been indulged in some few years before
I cannot answer for the form which my resentment
would have taken ; but I kept my temper, as I
knew no credit could accrue from any squabble

with this man. The cheque was subsequently paid. The Chairman was far too wise to enter into a struggle with the Local Government Board over such a matter.

At the next meeting of the Board of Guardians he, or one of his followers, moved that a letter be written to the Local Government Board, stating that they had considered the evidence and were of opinion that it in no way affected the character of their master, and requesting that the Board should forthwith send its opinion of the evidence and what charges they considered proved, whereupon there was forwarded to them a list of thirteen charges which the Local Government Board held had been proved against Bliss. It is probable that if the Chairman and the majority had remained quiet, these serious charges against the master would never have seen the light. As it happened, the publication of them gave the opponents of Mr. Bliss the opportunity of conclusively showing up the action of the Board. The letter of the Local Government Board, containing particulars of the charges proved, was as follows—

"Local Government Board,
"Whitehall,
"*August* 28, 1883.
"Sir,—I am directed by the Local Government

Board to acknowledge the receipt of your letter of the 10th inst. respecting the decision communicated to the Guardians of the Westminster Union in the letter which we addressed to them by the Board on the 18th ult. upon the charges preferred against Mr. Bliss, the master of the Workhouse, and recently investigated by their Inspectors, Mr. Hedley and Mr. Taylor.

" The Board direct me to state, in reply, that the charges to which they referred in that letter were the following—

" That Mr. Bliss twice threw water from a bucket over an inmate named Ellen Coleman.

" That he kicked a woman named Ann Lane on the back of the thigh [she was sixty-eight years old], the bruise caused thereby was about four inches across.

" That he kicked a boy named James Daley twice on the back [he was about thirteen years old, and was a very good boy].

" That he was in the habit of swearing, and of using expressions of an objectionable character when irritated.

" That he had exercised no supervision as regards the entries in his portion of the Workhouse Medical Relief Book.

" That he had not entered in the Provision Accounts

as absent inmates who were in fact absent on leave from the Workhouse.

"That he had contravened the Board's regulations by placing Caroline Barber, aged sixty-four years, upon bread and water.

"That there had been undue delay in the registration of four births in the Workhouse.

"That in the cases of two females, named Caroline Clegg and Elizabeth Jacob, who died in the Workhouse, he did not take sufficient care to give notice of their decease to their respective relatives.

"That through want of due care, a mistake was made as to a body sent for burial.

"That he allowed Elizabeth Farquharson to leave the Workhouse for four days to go to work, and that he charged in his accounts rations for her during that period.

"That his behaviour towards Mrs. Casher, on her visiting the Workhouse to see two girls in whom she was interested, was discourteous; and that he used very improper language to Emily Brown on her visiting the Workhouse to see her husband, an inmate [who was on his deathbed].

"I am, Sir,

"Your obedient servant,

"(*Signed*)   C. N. DALTON,

"*Assistant Secretary.*"

I have been informed that the reading of the above letter was received by the Chairman and his followers with much exasperation, which exhibited itself in threats of vengeance against all those, whether inmates or officers, who had given evidence against the master. One of the first to feel the wrath of the Chairman was Thomas Bailey, a man seventy years of age, who was discharged from his employment in aiding me and the master in keeping the Medical Officer's Relief Book, which he had done for nearly twenty years, because of his wickedness in bringing under my notice the fraudulent entries made in my portion of the Medical Book by the master's clerk at the instance of the matron, an irregularity which it is reasonable to suppose could only have been condoned by the majority of the Board on the supposition that some of them had helped to get rid of what had been falsely entered against the names of my sick patients.

Although this fraud had been clearly proved, no attention had been drawn to it in the report, but a mere misty reference was made to the subject in the fifth charge proved.

Here let me observe that I believe this˜ inquiry would have been absolutely nugatory of any beneficial results if it had been conducted without an

assessor being present, and, considering the bearing
and physique of the two Inspectors, it seems to me
that the assessor modified his own judgment, which
would have been entirely adverse to Mr. Bliss, in
deference to the manifest wish of the Inspector to
screen an old soldier from the proved charges of
blasphemy and unmanly violence to an aged woman
and a small boy, for which two latter offences Mr.
Bliss would have been taken before a magistrate and
severely punished if the miserable victims had had
the necessary means.

The Chairman thought, in flouting the Local
Government Board by his protection of his friend
the master, that he would triumph; but at that time
he was wholly unaware of what was in store for him
and the party he had so long led.

The Inspector was not, indeed, an acceptable person
to all Boards of Guardians, as the following letter
from the Holborn Board indicates—

" *February* 28, 1884.
" *Re* STANTON.   Official Inquiry.
" MY LORDS AND GENTLEMEN,—I am directed by
the Guardians of the Poor of the Holborn Union to
acknowledge the receipt of your letter of the 26th
inst., stating that you have instructed your Inspector,

Mr. Hedley, to hold an inquiry into the charges preferred against Mr. Stanton, and that Mr. Hedley
will give the Guardians due notice of the time and
place in which he intends holding the inquiry, and to
inform you that the following Resolution was passed
upon your communication being submitted to the
Guardians, viz.—

   " ' That the clerk write to the Local Government
Board and inform them that the Guardians are of
opinion that an official should be appointed to conduct the inquiry who has not already expressed an
opinion on the subject, which Mr. Hedley has publicly
done, and that if the Local Government Board
adhere to the appointment of Mr. Hedley to hold the
inquiry, the Guardians must decline to take part
therein.'

   " I am further directed to inform you that this
Resolution was carried with only one dissentient at
the Board last evening.

        " I have the honour to be,
            " My Lords and Gentlemen,
                " Your obedient servant,
                    " JAMES W. HILL, *Clerk.*
   " THE LOCAL GOVERNMENT BOARD."

   I do not know whether it was at the meeting of

the Board when the decision of the Department was
first read, or on the occasion when the Guardians
heard their clerk read out the list of charges which
the Department considered were proved against Mr.
Bliss, but it is certain that the Chairman rose in
his seat and moved that I be called on to resign my
appointment forthwith. Of course it was carried,
and the clerk was directed to forward me a copy of
the resolution. I briefly acknowledged its receipt.
I understood that at this time this person was much
put out at my not at once complying with his request,
and threatened all sorts of vengeance on me. He was
so ignorant that, in his rage, he forgot that he could
not so summarily get rid of me, and therefore I waited
patiently for his next move; indeed, I applied for and
took my usual autumn holiday. At this time there
appeared in *The Standard* daily newspaper an article
commenting on the evidence given at the official
inquiry, on the charges found to be proved, and
the conduct of the Chairman and his docile followers.

It was republished and sent to every ratepayer in
both parishes. And here I may be allowed to call
attention to the fact, that in the reforms which
I have tried to secure, I have had the assistance
of papers of all parties. The article was as follows—

" Westminster Union. The Local Government
Board, the Guardians of the Poor, and
J. D. Bliss, Master of the Workhouse,
Poland Street.

" Defend the poor and fatherless ; see that such as are in
need and necessity have right."—Psalm lxxxii. 3.

" The Local Government Board, in an official
communication to the Guardians of the Westminster
Union, say they have ' entertained very great doubt
whether, consistently with their public duty,' they
could ' properly allow' the present master of the Poland
Street Workhouse to retain his post. It is likely
that the public will go all the way with the Local
Government Board, and even a little further. The
Board, having instituted a long and searching inquiry
into sundry charges brought against the master, have
arrived at the conclusion that several of the accusa-
tions have been established. They told the Guardians
so much as this some little time back ; but these
authorities wished to know more precisely what were
the charges considered to be proved. It is fortunate
that these gentlemen were so far disposed to chal-
lenge the conclusions arrived at by the central power,
for the answer they received puts the public in
possession of some notable facts which otherwise

might have remained in obscurity. We now learn that the demonstrated delinquencies of this Workhouse master include such peccadilloes as twice emptying a bucket of water over an inmate named Ellen Coleman, and kicking a woman named Ann Lane, as well as a boy named James Daley, the latter twice. He also contravened the Board's regulations by placing an old woman upon bread and water. There might be some economy in this, but it was more than counterbalanced by an awkward habit in which the master indulged, of charging rations for paupers absent on leave. Another irregularity consisted in a 'mistake as to a body sent for burial,' coupled with which we hear of 'undue delay in the registration of four births.' Then there was confusion in the Medical Relief Books, and a neglect to give notice when people were dead. To all this must be added a 'habit of swearing and using expressions of an objectionable character when irritated.' This model master of a Workhouse is further proved to have been discourteous to the wife of a clergyman, and to have 'used very improper language to Emily Brown,' a poor woman who came to see her husband. For all this he is master of the Workhouse still, and, as he retains 'the confidence of the Guardians,' the Local Government Board 'refrain from adopting the extreme course of requiring his resignation.' But, at the same time, this redoubtable official is warned that if any further complaints are substantiated against him he will be most certainly asked, with all due politeness, to relinquish his responsible office. There is, for the moment, nothing more to be done, except, perhaps, for the Guardians to present him with a testimonial."—*Extracted from "The Standard,"* September 14, 1883.

(It should be clearly understood that this inquiry was instituted by a minority of the Board, who have steadily voted for Mr. Bliss's resignation.)

On my return to town I found that the Board generally had also gone away, but the Chairman had given notice that when the Guardians met in September he should move that I be suspended from my office; which in due course he did, and, having a passive majority, carried it. This did not alarm me at all. It was not then as it was some years ago. There was a new Secretary at the Local Government Board, who was the worthy successor of a most estimable father, the late Hugh Owen. Added to this I had several friends in the House of Commons, and most assuredly Sir Charles Dilke was not prejudiced against me. Besides this, the Chairman could not get up a case against me. So, being aware that it would take some weeks before any decision could be come to, as the head officials at the Central Department would be certainly out of town, and that it was a task beyond the intelligence of the Chairman to draft an indictment, I again went into the country.

So soon as it became known that this Chairman had moved my suspension simply for having resented the conduct of Bliss in cursing and swearing at me, and disobeying my orders for the sick, numerous friends wrote to me, and the medical journals vied with each other in denouncing the conduct of this Board, and called on my professional brethren to rally round me as I had been called on to resign, and was now suspended for interfering with Bliss in his treatment of my sick poor. The action of the Chairman and his supporters turned to my advantage, and eventually led to his and their complete and signal expulsion from office.

Among other annotations and leading articles which appeared at this date, I will here insert one from *The Lancet,* bearing date October 27, 1883—

"THE SUSPENSION OF DR. ROGERS.

"The suspension of Dr. Rogers from his duties by the Guardians of the Westminster Union because

of his honest testimony in an inquiry into the conduct of the master, is an event of very great consequence. It is impossible that the Local Government
Board can sanction the action of the Board, or disregard the memorial signed by fifty-four of the most
respectable inhabitants of St. Anne's, including the
rector, the Catholic priest, &c. ; and another, signed
by ninety-four of the ratepayers of St. James's. Dr.
Rogers is a representative man. He represents not
only the Poor Law medical service, but the inde-
pendence of the members of that service, and no
greater misfortune can befall the poor or the ratepayers than that he should be persecuted by the
Guardians of Westminster for doing his duty. We
cannot believe that Sir Charles Dilke will allow such
a misfortune to happen. The Local Government
Board have acted with a strange inconsistency in
retaining the master of the Workhouse. It is
inconceivable that they will play into his hands, and
those of the Guardians who assist him, by sanction-
ing the dismissal of Dr. Rogers. But the profession
and the members of the Poor Law service, should
lose no time in organizing a proper movement for
vindicating Dr. Rogers' claims and position."

After my suspension I went to Bournemouth, and

whilst there heard of the above movement in my support, and also saw that my friends in the profession were organizing a testimonial in my favour, subscriptions to which came from all parts of the kingdom. So that, instead of injuring me, the action of the Guardians secured me three months' holiday, a testimonial worth £200, and gave me that leisure which enabled me to work up a party that some six months after drove the Chairman and his followers from office.

On my return from Bournemouth I set to work to get up a list of candidates for Guardians for the ensuing year. It was necessary to get thirteen, as I had only five supporters. It is true that they were the most respectable men on the Board. I was not very long in getting three respectable ratepayers to stand for St. Anne's; but the great difficulty was in St. James's, where ten were required; and if it had not have happened that the Rev. Henry Sheringham, Vicar of St. Peter's, Great Windmill Street, exerted himself most earnestly, we could not have succeeded at all. He not only came forward himself, but he induced a colleague, the Vicar of St. John's, Great Marlborough Street, and four very wealthy and well-known gentlemen in St. James's to do likewise. The obtaining of four others ceased to be a matter

15

of difficulty. The Rev. H. Sheringham took the greatest interest in the election, and it was through his help that the Bishop of London, the Marquis of Waterford, and a large number of the nobility and gentry, bankers, and others who were ratepayers in St. James's, and up to that date had never voted in any election of Guardians, were, on this occasion, secured.

Mr. Sheringham was the incumbent of the poorest district in St. James's, and consequently he was constantly brought into contact with those who had either been inmates, or had friends in the House, and for a long time he had been cognisant of Mr. Bliss's management, and of the Chairman's support of the master. When I was suspended, Mr. Sheringham showed his feeling by going round to some of the leading people in St. James's and getting them to sign the testimonial in my favour, and at the election in the following April he worked hard all day long to get rid of the Chairman and his party.

It may be thought by those who have followed this narrative of Poor Law management in 1883, that I had not sufficiently referred to the action of Mr. W. J. Fraser, solicitor, of Soho Square, and of 191, Clapham Road, but it does not arise from want of

gratitude to this gentleman, who has known me for
many years, who asked me to see poor Watson in
1872, who induced me to become a candidate for
the office the same year, and whose worthy father used
to take an honest pride in bringing him to my house
nearly thirty years before, to show me how he had
got on during his half-year's schooling. If it had
not been for the high sense of conscientiousness, and
his invariable hatred of such wrong-doing as was
implied in the support of such a person as J. Bliss,
as a young solicitor he could not have made so great
a sacrifice of time, of labour, and of money.

The fact of Mr. Bliss being no longer master
of the Westminster Workhouse, and his chief
supporter no longer in power as the Chairman of
the Westminster Union, with all its possible
advantages, is owing almost entirely to Mr. W. J.
Fraser, who, recognizing the wrong-doing of both,
exerted himself untiringly to get rid of both,
which he achieved with singularly complete success.

It was not until just before Christmas that one of
the Guardians who was friendly to me, told me that
a letter had just been received from the Local Government Board, directing me to resume my duties, thereby removing my suspension ; at the same time saying
there was an oblique reference to me at the end of

the letter.   " Oh," I replied, "I understand all
about that; but I can afford to let that pass so long
as the President supports me."

I returned to my duties, but had it not been for
the fact that my nurses (one woman excepted, who
was Bliss's confidant, and whom I would have got rid
of months before for incompetence and worse qualities) welcomed me back, as did the sick inmates,
whose friend I had tried to be, I really should have
hesitated to continue in my office, for every form of
petty obstructiveness was exhibited by the master,
matron, the master's clerk, the Chairman, and his
followers.   The only retaliation in my power was to
draft questions and get them put in the House.   This
process made the names and doings of the majority of
the Westminster Board of Guardians come out rather
awkwardly before the public and the ratepayers of
the Union ; the extraordinary circumstance being
that both parties, or rather I may state all parties, in
the House assisted me in getting these questions put
to Ministers.

At last the election took place.   I feel pretty well
convinced that when the Chairman saw our list of
candidates and who were the nominators, consisting
as they did of most of the nobility, gentry, bankers,
clergy, and leading ratepayers in both parishes, he

felt that his reign was over, but he did not think, even then, that his defeat could have been so complete and overwhelming, for not only was he left in an absurd minority, but his twelve followers were left also.

Subjoined is a copy of the address sent to the ratepayers of both parishes.

" ELECTION OF GUARDIANS.

" To the Ratepayers of the Parish of St. James, Piccadilly, and St. Anne, Soho.

" MY LORDS, LADIES, AND GENTLEMEN,—Having been nominated to be Guardians to represent St. James's Parish as well as that of St. Anne's, Soho, at the Westminster Union, by many of the nobility, clergy, gentry, and leading tradesmen and large rate-payers of both parishes, we confidently solicit your votes and support at the approaching election.

" We wish it to be understood that, in offering ourselves as candidates, we are actuated by no personal motives or considerations whatever, but solely by a desire to secure the faithful, humane, and economical administration of the laws relating to the relief of the poor in the Westminster Union.

" Public attention has, during the past year, been frequently drawn to serious complaints respecting the

treatment of inmates, subordinate officials and others
in, and visitors to, the Poland Street Workhouse,
and it is very widely felt that a searching and careful
investigation should be instituted without delay into
matters vitally affecting the comfort, happiness, and
welfare of a large body of poor and helpless people,
such as inhabit our workhouses.

" We beg to draw your attention to the accompanying copies of two letters addressed by the Local
Government Board to the late Guardians; and also
to the enclosed copy of an article which appeared in
The Standard newspaper.

" Many of the ratepayers will learn with surprise
that, notwithstanding the serious and grave charges
substantiated against the master of the Workhouse,
at the Local Government Board inquiry, held by
two of their Inspectors, a large majority of the late
Guardians felt themselves able formally to record
their confidence in the master.

" It should be clearly understood that this inquiry
was demanded by a small minority of the Guardians,
who found themselves powerless to bring to light or
redress in any other way the flagrant abuses of which
they had been informed. And at the same time it
should be known that those Guardians upon whom
devolved the duty of conducting the inquiry, were

denied, both by the majority of the Board, who were opposed to any action being taken, and also by the master, both before and at the time of the inquiry, all access to inmates and resident officers, whose evidence was essential to establish the charges alleged. It was, therefore, only with the greatest difficulty that the necessary evidence could be collected.

" We have further to state that, after the decision of the Local Government Board was communicated to the Guardians, and when all the facts of the case were fully before them, the Chairman and the majority of the Board presented to Mr. Bliss, in the Board-room of the Poland Street Workhouse, a testimonial, in the form of a sum of money, ostensibly for the purpose of defraying the expenses of his professional adviser in conducting his defence during the inquiry into his conduct.

" It may be added that the Chairman, when compelled to admonish Mr. Bliss, in accordance with the directions of the Local Government Board, did so with reluctance, entertaining, it would seem, the belief that the master was not guilty of all or any of the charges proved against him ; and, when so admonished, the master himself expressed no regret that the charges set forth in the Local Government Board's letter should have been held to be established against him, and gave no assurance whatever that he would comport himself differently in future.

" Thus the official inquiry was rendered practically abortive, owing, as we believe, to the action of the majority of the Guardians in virtually upholding the master, in the face of such overwhelming evidence of misconduct.

" Various complaints have since been made both by inmates and officers respecting their treatment, and, notwithstanding the recent inquiry, the internal condition of the Workhouse remains up to the present time unaltered and unimproved.

" It is for these reasons that we feel it our duty to offer ourselves as candidates at the present election, believing that the ratepayers of St. James's and of St. Anne's, Soho, will no longer be able to place confidence in the Board as lately constituted, and that they will demand a searching inquiry into the whole system of the management of the Poland Street Workhouse.

" If, therefore, it be your pleasure to elect us as your representatives on the Board, we shall address ourselves, without fear or favour, promptly and impartially to the consideration of every matter requiring attention ; and with the co-operation of the Local

Government Board, which we doubt not will readily be given, we shall make it our chief aim and endeavour to remove all legitimate grievances, and to secure humane and kindly treatment for the many aged sick and helpless inmates of our Workhouse.

" We have the honour to remain,

" Your most obedient servants,

" ———."

As the election had mainly turned on the conduct of Mr. Bliss, one of the first things done by the new Board when it met was to suspend Mr. Bliss from his office, which being done, shortly afterwards a committee of the Board met and drew up an indictment against him; but as the Department had condoned the whole of the thirteen charges which were considered proved, they could not raise any of these again ; but as Mr. Fraser was aware that the complaints I had made subsequent to the inquiry had been ignored by the late Chairman and his friends, and that the duplicate copy had never been acknowledged by the Department, I, and the nurse of the receiving wards, and the head nurse on the female side, were called to prove the order given by me, the refusal of the matron and the master to comply with it, the woman's condition when admitted, her state

on her arrival at Cleveland Street Asylum, the remarks as to her exhausted condition when carried by
the porter in his arms, she being too ill to walk ; all
these facts were shown to be absolutely true, and
were completely borne out by evidence. Other
matters against Mr. Bliss were also gone into and
forwarded to the Local Government Board, and with
it an intimation that it was the desire of the new
Board that he should not be permitted to return to
his duties. Whilst away in Belfast, where I went in
the month of August to deliver my customary annual
address on Poor Law Medical Relief, I received a
telegram that Sir Charles Dilke had called on Mr. J.
Bliss to resign.

When the master was suspended I can hardly
describe the relief I experienced, it was so great.
No longer did I dread loud-mouthed expressions
of dissent from me in my treatment of the sick,
no longer did I fear that he would stalk, unan-
nounced, through the female sick wards when I
was examining the poor women ; but instead of it
there was respectful quiet and orderly behaviour.
The matron, who ought to have been sent away
also, kept out of my way and was obsequiously
obliging when I gave a necessary order. One person
only did I at once bring to book—it was the head

nurse on the male side. After the formation of
the new Board, I immediately drew up and sent
in a list of charges against her, comprising refusal
to obey my orders, complicity in and support of
certain malingerers who she falsely informed me
were ill. One of these I had discovered some
months before to be an impostor, and ordered his
discharge, but the nurse got her friend Bliss to
direct his return, thus flouting my authority. She
did not stop to meet my charges, but sent in
her resignation, and, it being accepted, these complaints were not investigated. I speedily got rid
of the malingerer also, and during the remainder
of the time I held office the man remained out
of the sick ward. What was the tie between the
nurse and this malingerer I was never able to divine.

During the latter part of April, the whole of May,
and the first part of June, 1884, there had been an
outbreak of fever at the Union schools on Wandsworth Common, and it appeared that the medical
officer of the schools, the Visiting Committee, and
the Poor Law Medical Inspector, could throw no
light on the causes of it, when it was suggested
at the Board that I should be sent down to examine
into the matter and report to the Board thereon.
I wrote to the medical officer informing him of the

Board's wish, and asked him to arrange a time to meet me and we would go into the subject together. He was not sufficiently courteous even to acknowledge my letter. I then asked a member of the Board (a builder) to accompany me, which he did.

On my arrival at the schools I requested the attendance of the superintendent and matron, as I wished to state the object of my visit and to obtain from them certain information as regards the commencement of the outbreak, the symptoms presented by the sick, &c. I also elicited from them that the medical officer had said that he would not meet me—an act of discourtesy to the Board, whose joint officers we were.

I speedily ascertained that the outbreak commenced amongst the girls, and had been almost entirely limited to the female side of the House, and of these girls those mainly who were employed in the laundry. But as I wanted to make a complete examination of all the water supply, I asked the Guardian to pioneer the way in our general survey. With this object I got out upon the roof of the main building and peered into all the cisterns. I did not discover anything vastly amiss in these, and nothing wrong at all on the male side. I then proceeded with my examination of the cistern supply in the laundry and kitchen, and that on the roof which furnished the kitchen and part of the laundry supply, when I came upon the source of the mischief; for, on lifting the lid of a large cistern there containing many gallons of water, my sense of smell was assailed by one of the most horrible odours I had ever encountered, and I saw a large mass of thick scum floating there which was evolving offensive gases and in constant motion from the activity of innumerable forms of the lowest type of animal life. I asked my friend to hand me up a stick, and with it I took out a large piece of it and spread it out upon the roof of the building. I also requested the Guardian to come up and judge for himself. I did this because I knew that any statement I might make would most assuredly be denied by the parties who are responsible for looking into and examining the condition of the cisterns and keeping them cleansed, a circumstance which, as I expected, did subsequently occur, but which could not be controverted by them as I had the gentleman in question as my witness.

Before leaving I left a written instruction that every cistern throughout the building should be emptied and disinfected, additional care to be taken with the offending one.

On my return home I drew up and forwarded
to the Board my opinion as to the cause of the
outbreak, and the orders I had given to the superintendent. As no other cases of fever occurred
after my visit, it was clear I had discovered the
cause and the remedy. The Board wrote me,
through their clerk, a handsome acknowledgment
of my success, and voted me five guineas for my
visit, and informed me that they had directed the
clerk to send a copy of my report and the results
that had followed it to the Local Government Board.
This was somewhat of a rebuke to those permanent
officials who had placed that addendum to the letter
directing me to resign my duties some six months
before, as I had discovered and stopped the outbreak,
the cause of which they had utterly failed to ascertain ; but then these aforesaid permanent officials
never throw any heart or intelligence into the work
they are so handsomely paid to do.

In the early part of June the honorary secretary
of the fund, Mr. J. W. Barnes, F.R.C.S., wrote to
me, stating that it was decided to present a testimonial to me at a meeting of the subscribers, at
the rooms of the Medical Society of London, in
Chandos Street, Cavendish Square, in June, 1884,
and that Mr. J. A. Shaw Stewart had arranged to

take the chair. On the day mentioned the presentation took place, and subjoined is a condensed report of the proceedings extracted from *The British Medical Journal*, June 28, 1884. The assemblage was a very large one, and certainly was a striking manifestation of good feeling towards me from many of my old friends and fellow-workers in the cause of Sanitary and Poor Law Medical Reform.

RECOGNITION.

DR. JOSEPH ROGERS.

"To THE EDITOR OF *The Lancet*.

"SIR,—Since writing my letter to you last week I am rejoiced to see that a movement has commenced for giving shape to the esteem in which Dr. Joseph Rogers is held by his professional brethren and others who know his work. I hope a large sum will be raised, which cannot fail to be the case if all whom his labours have benefited give a little. And surely the time could not be more opportune than when in a battle with his persecutors: he wants to the full the encouragement of his friends. Only one suggestion I cannot agree with—viz., that the subscription list should be limited to Poor Law medical officers. Why? Truly, he has been a great benefactor to them; but not to them only. His public work has been much wider in aim and usefulness than simply to touch the pockets of a few Poor Law surgeons.

Many years ago he was a leader in the movement that ended in stopping burials within towns. I believe I am right in saying that to his influence is largely due the establishment of mortuaries. It was he who succeeded in getting expensive medicines—which it was hopeless to expect the Poor Law officers to supply out of their slender salaries —supplied by Boards of Guardians : an improvement directly benefiting the poor, and indirectly the ratepayers. The Metropolitan Poor Act of 1867 was largely brought about by his untiring zeal. From that what good has not flowed? The supply of not expensive medicines only, but all medicines, by the Guardians. The dispensary system, leading to a very large increase, probably not less than £15,000 a year to the Metropolitan medical officers. Then that great boon, the Superannuation Act, is another monument of Dr. Rogers' energy. I do not wish to undervalue the labours of Dr. Brady, and our other friends in and out of the House of Commons; but Dr. Brady himself would be the foremost to admit that he never would have been able to carry the point had it not been for Dr. Rogers' assistance. 'Instant in season, out of season,' delivering addresses from town to town; giving advice and assistance to persecuted

16

public servants all over the country; strengthening
the hands of the weaker brethren in public and
private, he has been for fourteen years a tower
of strength to an important section of the community whose power for good has been enhanced
by his agency, which has again reacted on the whole
nation. In short, Dr. Rogers has been, and is,
a great social reformer, and of his work all classes
reap the fruit. But as a great American philosopher
says, when the flat stone of a fine old abuse is
overturned, there is a great squirming of the flat-
patterned animals that have thriven in the darkness.
Dr. Rogers has been turning over these stones for
many years, and has been attacked by the squirming
animals, as is usually the case. It is for those who
have been cast in a different mould and can appre-
ciate his valuable, arduous, and often thankless
labours, to show their appreciation now.

"I am, Sir, yours respectfully,

"JAMES MILWARD, M.D.

"CARDIFF,

"*October* 22, 1883."

"TO THE EDITOR OF *The Lancet.*

"SIR,—For a long series of years one man in
the medical profession has boldly stood forward in

maintaining the rights and in endeavouring by every legitimate means to redress the wrongs of the Poor Law medical officers of this country. As one unconnected entirely with Poor Law medical practice, I have, no doubt in common with a multitude of others, admired the courage and honesty with which this man, almost single-handed, has fought the battles of its medical officers. Had any one of them a real grievance or hardship to complain of, Dr. Rogers at once came to the front and became his champion. Now that he is, in his own person, the subject of an injustice, and a very serious one (for he is threatened with dismissal from his post as medical officer of the Westminster Union for doing that which in all honesty he felt compelled to do), it behoves the whole profession to give him all the moral support in its power. It cannot be possible that the Local Government Board will ever sanction such manifest injustice. But this is not purely a question between the Westminster Guardians and Dr. Rogers ; but one which aims a blow at professional honour and rectitude, and if settled in the way in which the Guardians would have it, it may be the means of preventing some members of our body, however right-minded they may be, from giving evidence of wrong-doing, or performing other

necessary duties not falling strictly within the scope
of their ordinary work ; because forsooth they may,
if they do, find themselves stranded and deprived
of their appointments.

"Let the profession, then, as a body, and not
merely the Poor Law medical officers, rally round
Dr. Rogers, and, whilst recognizing the benefits
derived from his unselfish public labours in their
behalf, labours which may have brought upon him
much obliquy, and perhaps have had something to
do with his present trial, present him with such
a testimonial as shall effectually demonstrate to the
Local Government Board its approval of his conduct
and its disapprobation of the ungenerous treatment
to which he has been subjected by the Westminster
Guardians.

"'He's true to God who's true to man wherever wrong is
    done,
To the humblest or the weakest 'neath the all-beholding sun.
That wrong is also done to us, and they are slaves most
    base,
Whose love of right is for themselves and not for all the
    race.'

"I am, Sir, your obedient servant,
    "WILLIAM WEBB, M.D., F.R.C.S.
"WIRKSWORTH,
    "*October* 24, 1883."

"To the Editor of *The Lancet.*

" Sir,—Will you permit me to draw the attention
of your readers to a movement which has been set
on foot with the view of presenting to Dr.
Joseph Rogers, the President of the Poor Law Medical
Officers' Association, a testimonial, as a mark of
the esteem in which he is held by Poor Law
medical officers, and as a recognition of his unwearied
advocacy of their claims, his fearless exposure of
injustice done to them, and the able assistance and
advice which he has freely given to such of them
as have been unfortunate enough to be at variance
with their Boards.

" The unjust treatment Dr. Rogers has received
at the hands of the Westminster Guardians, will,
I hope, shortly be brought before the Local Government Board. But I venture to suggest that no
better time than the present could be chosen for
his fellow-officers to express their sympathy with
him, and that such an expression from a large
number would show that they have appreciated his
labours on their behalf ; that in a good cause they
are capable of acting in concert, and that they
respect themselves and their office in manifesting
respect for one who has fearlessly done his duty,

although for doing it he has received the usual punishment accorded by Guardians to parochial medical officers.

"The following gentlemen have kindly promised to receive subscriptions, viz. :—Ernest Hart, Esq., Editor of *The British Medical Journal;* C. Frost, Esq. (Treasurer of the Poor Law Medical Officers' Association), 47, Ladbroke Square, Notting Hill, London ; J. Wickham Barnes, Esq. (Secretary of the Poor Law Medical Officers' Association), 3, Bolt Court, Fleet Street, London.

"I am, Sir, yours faithfully,

"FRANCIS WHITWELL.

"SHREWSBURY,

"*October* 23, 1883."

TESTIMONIAL TO DR. JOSEPH ROGERS.

THE presentation of a handsome testimonial to Dr. Joseph Rogers, Chairman of the Poor Law Medical Officers' Association, took place on Tuesday last at the rooms of the Medical Society, Chandos Street, in the presence of a numerous gathering of ladies and gentlemen. Mr. John A. Shaw Stewart, presided.

Mr. J. Wickham Barnes (honorary secretary of the fund) spoke of the cordial reception with which the proposition to do honour to Dr. Rogers had been received, and the support which had been given to it by the medical journals, the editors of which had been among the most liberal contributors to the fund.

The Chairman, in his opening remarks, spoke of Dr. Rogers' work and worth, which were so well known that little further need be said on those points; but, on an occasion like the present, they should not forget that Dr. Rogers was a sanitary

reformer and advocate of sanitation of about forty
years' standing, and that matters which were now
accepted as facts were then subjects of the fiercest
controversy. Dr. Rogers, in conjunction with Mr.
George Alfred Walker and others, was the first who
successfully advocated the closing of the burial-
grounds in cities, and had succeeded in establishing
the first public mortuary in London. Those facts
alone testified to his energy and ability. Those who
were older than the speaker could remember the
time when the light of heaven was taxed; and Dr.
Rogers, with the late Lord Duncan, was one who
worked hard to abolish the window-tax, a more
unjust tax than which it was impossible to conceive.
He was appointed medical officer of the Strand
Union in 1856, at a time when there were no paid
nurses and when the Poor Law officer had to pay
out of his small salary for all medicines. Dr.
Rogers, with Dr. Anstie, and Mr. Ernest Hart, was
among the stoutest advocates for the improvement
of the workhouse infirmaries; and, aided by the
full force of the Medical Press, the great work was
commenced. The first time he (the Chairman) had
had the pleasure of working with ladies was in
Mr. Ernest Hart's house; he was thankful that
now, in all useful social work, ladies came to the

front. Dr. Rogers' work led up to Mr. Gathorne Hardy's Act, and his force and determination prevailed so far that the more expensive medicines were henceforth to be paid for by the Guardians, but for a long time the bulk of the drugs supplied was still left as a charge upon the ill-paid medical officer. Dr. Rogers' great and difficult work had been in connection with Poor Law administration. He believed one of the greatest political economists of the day, whom he saw present, would bear him out that political economy and philanthropy went hand in hand when they were employed in energetic and persistent endeavours to arrest disease in its earliest stages. No one could go much about our general hospitals without seeing how much of the misery and distress of this world were caused by disease. We were subject to a variety of diseases—and diseases meant loss of health, and ultimate loss of life, to the bread-winner, and his widow and children to be cast on the world. Dr. Rogers was subsequently very instrumental in the carrying of the Bill for the superannuation of Poor Law medical officers. Since then he had visited almost every large town in England, Scotland, and Ireland, with the view of prevailing upon the authorities to carry out improvements lately talked of in the metropolis. Dr.

Rogers was a real, true specimen of the best sort of Englishmen, a man of tenacity, a hard hitter, a staunch friend, and a pertinacious foe.

Mr. G. W. Fraser, Chairman of the Westminster Board of Guardians, said he had long known Dr. Rogers, and it afforded him very great pleasure to find that he was so much respected by those who had had an opportunity of appreciating his valuable work, and the many reforms he had been instrumental in effecting in the Poor Law of this country. He was very much respected by the Board of Guardians of the Westminster Union as at present constituted, and before, until he had to draw the attention of the Guardians to matters affecting the internal welfare of the Workhouse, which action resulted in his being suspended from his duties. All he could say was, there was no logical ground for the course that had been taken. It was a great satisfaction to find that that apparent evil had resulted in some good, for Mr. Wickham Barnes had told them that the treatment which Dr. Rogers then received was instrumental in bringing about the crowning result to be achieved in the presentation of the testimonial that day. Dr. Rogers had, on several occasions, rendered very valuable services to him (Mr. Fraser) and his colleagues, and he trusted that he might long be spared to fulfil the duties he had hitherto so long and so satisfactorily discharged.

Professor L. E. Thorold Rogers, M.P., said it was a matter of great gratification to him to be present on an occasion when the merits of his brother's labours were being recognized with so much unanimity, and in so practical a form, by the profession to which he belonged, and which, he ventured to say, he had always adorned.

Mr. Samuel Bonsor, as an old Westminster Guardian, spoke of the pleasure it was to him that he had lived long enough to see Dr. Rogers' efforts recognized as they had been.

Dr. Farquharson, M.P., said he knew that Dr. Rogers had been a great sanitary reformer, but he was astonished to find that he had been a reformer of so many years' standing. Guardians were apt to go for a hard and fast rule, while medical men, on the other hand, held more towards the sympathetic side; and it was by carrying out their duties in a sympathetic and liberal spirit that medical men often got into great disputes, and great difficulty and trouble. Until recently, these gentlemen, who were often treated cruelly, had no organization or means by which they could make their

grievances known, or obtain any redress whatever.
The action of Dr. Rogers, and the Association which
he had been instrumental in forming, had been the
means of often bringing to light cases of oppression
and of obtaining redress for those who had been
oppressed. He was sure they might all congratulate
Dr. Rogers on being present, not only from the
fact that he was going to receive a substantial token
of the affection and respect in which he was held
by all who knew him, but on the expressions of
admiration and esteem which poured in from all
directions on that occasion. He hoped Dr. Rogers
would long be spared to give them the benefit of
the shrewdness, his tenacity, and his tact.

Canon Wade (Rector of St. Anne's, Soho), said
he had known Dr. Rogers for some years as a man
of war. The first thing which drew forth his kindly
feeling towards Dr. Rogers was observing the tender
and faithful manner in which he supported the case
of the sick poor in their workhouses.

The Rev. W. Benham said he thought he had
known Dr. Rogers and his family longer than any
one else in the room, excepting his brother, and if
he was a man of war, as had been stated, it was because no man in the world had a more kindly heart.

The Chairman, in making the presentation to Dr.

Rogers of three handsome pieces of silver plate in
a case, together with a cheque for £150, said he
really ought to have the assistance of a lady now,
for she would so much more gracefully, in their
name, present that testimonial to Dr. Rogers. The
inscription ran : " Presented to Dr. Joseph Rogers,
in recognition of his continuous effort in the cause
of sanitary and Poor Law medical reform, for nearly
forty years. June 24, 1884." The date reminded
them that Dr. Rogers' voice had not been that of
one crying in the wilderness ; his voice had been
most usefully and beneficially exercised in the
metropolis. With the pieces of plate there was a
substantial lining. They hoped that Dr. and Mrs.
Rogers would long be spared to enjoy very many
blessings. They had met together there with one
heart and one mind, to show their appreciation of
his excellent qualities both as a public and as a
private man. The estimate of his good deeds, he
(the Chairman) fully believed, would never be known
till that last day, when the record of his life would
be unrolled. They had met to do honour to a
good man ; let each in his own capacity strive to
follow so noble an example, that when that great
day came they might have more to record of work
done for others and less for themselves.

Dr. Rogers, who spoke with some emotion, said
he felt much difficulty in giving expression to the
feelings that actuated him on that occasion ; all he
would state was that, in his progress through life,
if he had recognized an evil, he had done his best
to relieve it ; and if in the doing of it, he had
occasionally—and doubtless he had—confronted the
prejudices of some and aroused the antagonism of
others, it was the inevitable fate of all who attempted
to deal determinedly with wrong-doing, wherever it
might exist. He happened to be, as it were, a child
of the new Poor Law, because he remembered well
when the Bill became law, and his father expressed
to him his sense of deep disappointment and dis-
satisfaction, as a Christian man, with the way in
which the Bill was framed, in regard to its harsh
and bitter spirit. They must recognize the fact that
the poor would be with us always; and that it was
best to deal with them in a spirit of conciliation,
moderation, and kindness, and especially in that
particular branch of the management of the poor
with which it had been his lot for many years to be
associated, namely, as medical officer of a large
metropolitan workhouse. He was perfectly satisfied
of one thing, and that was that a judicious administration of Poor Law relief meant economy. He

had studied this question most minutely. He
pointed out, twenty-three years ago, to Mr. Charles
Villiers, who presided over a committee on poor
relief in 1861, that a more liberal administration
of poor relief meant true economy to the ratepayers,
because if they cut short the sickness of the poor, and
if they diminished the amount of deaths that took
place among the bread-winners, they would, as the
ultimate result, economize expenditure and out-
relief. As regarded other subjects that had been
referred to, it was to him a matter of immense
gratification that he had been associated in those
labours that took place about forty-four years ago,
initiated by Mr. George Alfred Walker, of Drury
Lane, and which eventually germinated in the
abolition of the most horrible system that ever
took place in a Christian kingdom. He could tell
them many things, terribly showing the horrible
evils that arose from keeping the bodies of the dead
in the single rooms of the living. He had many
times seen the widowed mother and the children
dining off the coffin of the dead father, and other
scenes which were indescribable in a gathering like
that before him. This it was which had prompted
his action in the formation of a mortuary at St.
Anne's. Dr. Rogers concluded by offering his

sincere thanks for the great honour they had conferred on him, and to Mr. Shaw Stewart in coming and speaking so kindly of him as he had done.

Mr. Wickham Barnes proposed a vote of thanks to the Chairman, which was seconded by Mr. James Hogg, and to which the Chairman briefly replied.

CONCLUSION.

THOUGH there were several persons of both sexes who were very advanced in years, when one takes into account the difference in the numbers that were to be found in the Strand and Westminster Workhouses, yet in this latter House I did not see so many interesting old people as were to be found in the former. About ten years ago, however, there was an admission from St. Anne's, Soho, of an extremely aged woman. She claimed then to be one hundred years old. She must have been extremely good-looking in her youth, as she still retained evidences of personal beauty. Like my old friend in the Strand, she had a bright blue eye and a fair complexion ; she was in possession of all her faculties, and talked and laughed by the half-hour together when I was in the humour to sit and chat with her. She knew the younger Pitt intimately, Charles James Fox, the Prince Regent, Edmund Burke, and several of the politicians of the latter part of the last century. She also told me she knew

17

Wellington and Nelson. At last I discovered what she had been. Her constant references to Sheridan in her conversations with me induced me one day to ask her if she knew him. Drawing herself up in a sprightly sort of fashion, "I rather think I did," said she. Eventually it came out that she had been under the protection of the box-keeper of Drury Lane Theatre. On putting the question which brought out the somewhat equivocal relation in which she had lived during the latter part of the last century, she blushed up to her eyes—the only thing of the kind I ever witnessed in a lady of such advanced years, so much so that I felt sorry I had elicited the confession from her. She was a very interesting old woman, and her remarks about the appearance of the celebrities of the latter end of the last century and beginning of this, unmistakably showed that she had associated on familiar terms with many of the celebrated persons who lived and moved and produced a sensation nearly a hundred years ago. She used to sing some very good songs; they were chiefly Scotch, and when singing them she would work herself up into a great state of excitement. She was very fond of talking to me, and I suppose this arose from the circumstance of my taking interest in her conversation. She was a very well-behaved old

woman, and therefore a great favourite with the inmates and nurses, who were highly amused whenever
they could get her to sing one of her Scotch songs.
At the latter end of the last century and the beginning of the present, she had accompanied her
male friend through Portugal and Spain prior to the
war; at the same time she knew Lord Nelson and
Wellington before their names had become famous.
When she had reached 104, she rather suddenly lost
her vivacity, became childish, and insensibly passed
from time into eternity.

We had, during the portion of the time I was at
the Westminster Union, quite a little community of
aged and, so far as I could ascertain, religious women,
at any rate they struck me as being such, and I kept
them together until the harmony of their daily life
was rudely interfered with by the master and matron,
Mr. John Bliss and Miss Heatley, neither of whom
had any sympathy with, or kindly feeling for, decently
conducted pauper women. Indeed they rendered the
lives of these people so wretched by harsh interference, as to compel me to distribute them among
other wards; some of them I even sent away to the
sick asylum hospitals, so as to get them out of their
way. It was a wonder to me that Miss Heatley, after
all that was proved against her on the official inquiry,

should ever have been allowed to continue matron of
the Workhouse; but though spared by man's power,
she was destined to perish by one of the most fearful
diseases that can afflict any woman, being destined to
die of cancer of a certain internal organ, and I have
been told her sufferings were of the acutest possible
character.   It is very remarkable that, having had
very large opportunities of witnessing the deaths of
my fellow-creatures, I have constantly observed that
some untimely fate has overtaken those who, exer-
cising power in a workhouse, have exhibited a cruel
use of that power; and of one thing I am absolutely
certain from personal observation, repeated over and
over again, that, " Blessed is he who considereth the
poor and needy, the Lord shall deliver him in the
time of trouble." It has often been asserted that the
inmates of a workhouse are generally worthless
people, but I demur to that conclusion entirely.   Of
this I am certain, that many a person who has died
in the infirmary of the sick ward of a workhouse
has gone as straight to Abraham's bosom as has ever
passed from a bishop's palace, or the death-chamber
of a king or queen, or however highly placed.   During
the thirty years that I was engaged in waiting on the
sick poor, I never lost sight of the fact that they were
my fellow-creatures who were accidentally placed in a

humbler social position than myself. Though, in accordance with the custom adopted in the institution, they were stigmatized as paupers, I never allowed myself to make them feel I thought them such. After the departure of Mr. John Bliss and the disappearance (through illness) of Miss Heatley, the Guardians appointed as master and matron, Mr. and Mrs. Minter. I found them to be exceedingly respectable people, kind to the old and afflicted, and fair and kind to the general population of an urban workhouse. The sick poor were quietly attended to, whilst loud-mouthed swearing and blasphemy were banished from the place. Unfortunately, however, I began to break in health. Mounting up staircases day after day, which had gone on for nearly forty years, told upon me, aggravated as it was by repeated attacks of bronchitis. Then a heart affection, followed by its usual concomitants, proved too much for me, and I was compelled to resign the work I had done for so many years. What made the blow the greater to me was this, that in all other respects my professional life was a happy one. I had nothing to ask for from the Board of Guardians, as all my legitimate requirements were at once courteously met and complied with; a different atmosphere pervaded the establishment, and therefore it was a pleasure to me to meet my fellow-officers and to work with them. Looking back upon the change which had taken place from the day I. first entered upon my duties in January, 1856, in the Old Strand Workhouse, till I finally left the Westminster Union in 1886, a period of thirty years, the change that occurred was enormous. Then there was hardly a paid nurse in any workhouse in London, the duties being performed by more or less infirm, drunken, and generally profligate inmates of the House. It was a miracle to find an honest one among them; they were a chance medley of Sairey Gamps and Betsy Prigs, who were selected at the will of master and matron, and who obeyed the orders of the medical officer just as much as, and no more than, their fancy led them. The scenes of untold misery which might have been witnessed by the Guardians of the Poor will never be fully exposed until the grave record of all things is opened to universal gaze. Fortunately, a change has come over the spirit of these things : in the present day the sick poor are housed in buildings which were never dreamed of twenty years ago ; pauper nursing is now entirely a thing of the past; Lazarus now meets with careful, Christian consideration, and if it be possible to restore him to health, an opportunity is afforded him of resuming a position in society, useful, though it may be humble.

My readers will therefore fully understand with what great regret I took my pen and wrote the resignation of my office, especially when I recall to mind my having been twice suspended from my duties for the efforts I had made in bringing about the changes which I have above referred to, and that at last, when I was no longer able to do my work, I was constrained to sever my connection with the Board who had come to look upon me as one solely actuated by a sense of duty.

The day after the receipt of my resignation, I received the following—

"WESTMINSTER UNION,

"POLAND STREET,

"*September* 27, 1886.

"DEAR SIR,—I am directed to forward you the annexed copy of a Resolution adopted by the Guardians at their meeting held on Friday last, when your resignation of the offices of Workhouse Medical Officer and Public Vaccinator of the Union was accepted.

"I am, dear Sir, yours faithfully,

"FRED J. LAMPARD,

"*Assistant Clerk of the Guardians.*

"J. ROGERS, ESQ., M.D.,

"Montagu Place, Russell Square."

(Copy Resolution.)

" That this Board has received with much regret
the letter just read from Dr. Joseph Rogers, resigning
the office of Workhouse Medical Officer and Public
Vaccinator for the Union, on account of his continued
ill-health, and while now accepting such resignation,
the Guardians desire to convey to him their deep
sympathy that he should thus be compelled to sever
his connection with the Board after many years of
faithful service, and to record their high sense of the
zealous and efficient manner in which he has discharged the duties of his office, and for the warm
interest he has at all times taken in questions
affecting the proper treatment of the sick and infirm
poor."

After the resolution had been submitted to the
vote and adopted unanimously, Mr. Samuel Bonsor
rose in his seat and gave notice that that day month
superannuation allowance should be accorded to Dr.
Joseph Rogers. Coming from this gentleman it was
indeed an honourable recognition of lengthened
public services. Mr. Bonsor had been in various
offices of the parish of St. Anne's, Soho, since
the introduction of the new Poor Law Bill in
1834. He had filled all the usual parochial offices,

even the highest, up to the time when I first made
his acquaintance, which was in the autumn of 1846,
on the occasion when I brought before the Vestry of
St. Anne's, Soho, the terrible condition of the burial-
ground of that parish. After hearing my indictment
he at once concurred in the appointment of a committee from the Vestry, of the inhabitants, to take
the condition of the ground into consideration, and
to devise such remedies as might appear desirable.
Mr. Bonsor attended several of our meetings, and
entirely agreed as to the dreadful state into which the
graveyard had fallen, owing to the frequent funerals
and the enormous overcrowding. It was that Vestry
meeting that first made me a sanitary reformer, and
caused me to advocate extra-mural interment as well
as many other social reforms, in all of which I had
the hearty support of Mr. Bonsor. I question
whether a finer representative of a middle-class
tradesman could be found in this kingdom; for more
than half a century he has devoted more than ordinary
ability to the interests of his fellow-parishioners. I
never upon one single occasion heard, or was it ever
hinted by any enemy (if he ever made one, which I
doubt), that his actions were ever influenced by a
single act of self-seeking; indeed, he has passed
through an unusually prolonged life amidst the

18

respect and regard of all who have come in contact
with him. A very short time ago he brought me a
circular letter, issued by the Poor Law Commissioners,
proposing the Board of Guardians in London should
issue a similar letter to their respective bodies, so as
to more effectually deal with casuals. Laying it down
before me, he said, " This is a return to what they did
between forty and fifty years ago, for I was a member
of the special Board which was appointed under this
letter ; but," said he, " I suppose they have forgotten
all about it." And so they had, no doubt.

Before bringing my remarks to a close, I should
like to briefly describe the various changes that have
taken place since the Poor Law Commission was
appointed in 1832. One of the original Commissioners was the Right Hon. C. P. Villiers, M.P. for
Wolverhampton, who has told me in the course of
various conversations I have had with him, that
although a variety of subjects was referred to them in
connection with the administration of the Poor Laws,
yet that the question of sickness, as a factor in the
production of pauperism was not referred to them,
and if it had not been for the pertinacity of Dr. G.
Wallis and some others, that this important subject
would have been passed over altogether. It need not,
therefore, be a matter of surprise that there has been

a continual protest going on, on the part of those
who have accepted Poor Law medical appointments
against the way in which they have been treated by
the Board of Guardians, and a reference to the Poor
Law Commissioners resulting in the various changes
that have taken place in the composition of the central authority up to the Local Government Board of
the present day. Until 1864 the central authority
was an extremely weak body, as continuous efforts
were made throughout the country by Boards of
Guardians and others to wipe the Poor Law Board
out of existence altogether, and had it not have
happened that the investigations and deliberations of
the Select Committee on Poor Relief, presided over by
the Right Hon. C. P. Villiers, had reported in favour
of the maintenance of the Poor Law Board—not
Local Government Board—such a disastrous thing
would have happened. Let it here be fully understood that although I have taken a most determined
antagonism to many of the acts of the Board,
whether as Commissioners or as the Poor Law
Board, yet that antagonism has been due to the fact
that the administration has often been seriously
faulty in detail. The office of a Poor Law Inspector
is one which needs much judgment and tact. I trust
this will be borne in mind by those who will draft

the contemplated County Government Board. There
is one point on which, feeling most strongly the
existing mockery of so-called Poor Law inquiries, I
do trust a change will be insisted upon, and that is,
that those deputed to make the inquiry shall possess
at least a modicum of legal intelligence. Finally, I
have to express the hope that no Inspector, whether
metropolitan or otherwise, will be vested with the
sole power of deciding what shall be the evidence
that shall be taken when the inquiry shall close, nor
that he shall be the sole judge of the value of such
evidence.

UNWIN BROTHERS, THE GRESHAM PRESS, CHILWORTH AND LONDON.

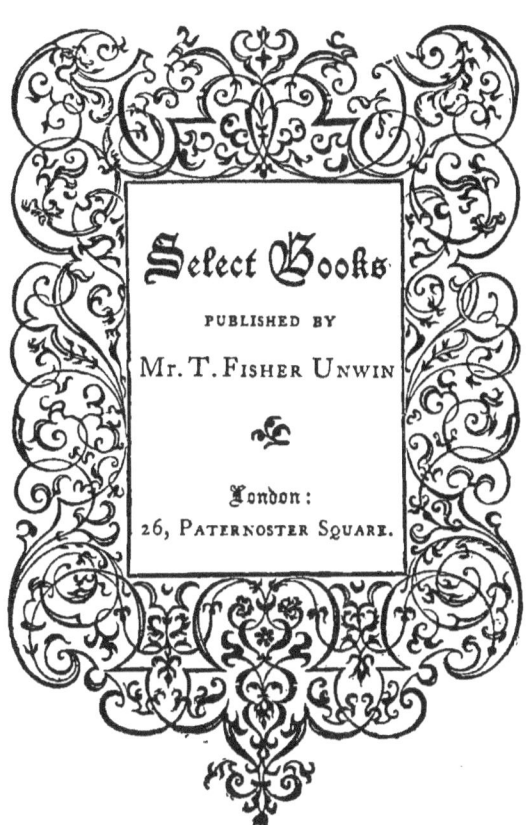

Select Books

PUBLISHED BY

Mr. T. Fisher Unwin

London:
26, Paternoster Square.

Mr. UNWIN has pleasure in sending herewith his Catalogue of Select Books.

Book Buyers are requested to order any Books they may require from their local Bookseller.

Catalogue of Select Books in Belles Lettres,
History, Biography, Theology, Travel,
Miscellaneous, and Books for Children.

Belles Lettres.

Englishᵉ Wayfaring Life in the Middle
Ages (XIVth Century). By J. J. JUSSERAND. Translated
from the French by LUCY A. TOULMIN SMITH. Illustrated.
Demy 8vo., cloth, 21s.

The Author has supervised the translation, and has added fresh matter, so
that the volume differs in some degree from "*La Vie Nomade.*" Many of the
illustrations are taken from illuminated manuscripts, and have never been
published before.

Old Chelsea.
A Summer-Day's Stroll. By Dr. BENJAMIN
ELLIS MARTIN. Illustrated by JOSEPH
PENNELL. Crown 8vo., cloth, 7s. 6d.

The stroll described in these pages may be imagined to be taken during the
summer of 1888; all the dates, descriptions, and references herein having been
brought down to the present day.

The Twilight of the Gods.
"The Purple Head,"
"Madame Lucifer,"
"The Demon Pope," "The City of Philosophers," "The
Cup-bearer," "Ananda the Miracle-Worker," "The Bell of
St. Euschemon," and other Stories. By RICHARD GARNETT.
Crown 8vo., cloth, 6s.

The Coming of the Friars,
And other Mediæval
Sketches. By the Rev.
AUGUSTUS JESSOPP, D.D., Author of "Arcady: For Better,
For Worse," &c. Crown 8vo., cloth, 7s. 6d.

Contents.—I. The Coming of the Friars.—II. Village Life in Norfolk Six
Hundred Years ago.—III. Daily Life in a Mediæval Monastery.—IV. and V.
The Black Death in East Anglia.—VI. The Building-up of a University.—VII.
The Prophet of Walnut-tree Walk.

4

Arcady : For Better, For Worse. By AUGUSTUS JESSOPP, D.D.,
Author of " One Generation of a Norfolk House."
Portrait. Popular Edition. Crown 8vo., cloth, 3s. 6d.
" A volume which is, to our minds, one of the most delightful ever published
English."—*Spectator.*
" A capital book, abounding in true wisdom and humour. . . . Excellent and
amusing."—*Melbourne Argus.*

The Romance of a Shop.
By AMY LEVY, Author
of " The New School
of American Fiction," &c. Crown 8vo., cloth, 6s.

'The Paradox Club.
By EDWARD GARNETT. With
Portrait of Nina Lindon. Crown
8vo., cloth, 6s.
" Mr. Garnett's dialogue is often quite as good as his description, and in
description he is singularly happy. The mystery of London streets by night is
powerfully suggested, and the realistic force of his night-pieces is enhanced by the
vague and Schumann-like sentiment that pervades them."—*Saturday Review.*

Euphorion : Studies of the Antique and the Mediæval in the
Renaissance. By VERNON LEE. Cheap Edition,
in one volume. Demy 8vo., cloth, 7s. 6d.
" It is the fruit, as every page testifies, of singularly wide reading and independent thought, and the style combines with much picturesqueness a certain largeness
of volume, that reminds us more of our earlier writers than those of our own time."
Contemporary Review.

Studies of the Eighteenth Century in
Italy. By VERNON LEE. Demy 8vo., cloth, 7s. 6d.
" These studies show a wide range of knowledge of the subject, precise investigation, abundant power of illustration, and hearty enthusiasm. . . . The style
of writing is cultivated, neatly adjusted, and markedly clever."—*Saturday Review.*

Belcaro : Being Essays on Sundry Æsthetical Questions. By
VERNON LEE, Author of " Euphorion," " Baldwin,"
&c. Crown 8vo., cloth, 5s.
" This way of conveying ideas is very fascinating, and has an effect of creating
activity in the reader's mind which no other mode can equal. From first to last
here is a continuous and delightful stimulation of thought."—*Academy.*

Juvenilia : A Second Series of Essays on Sundry Æsthetical
Questions. By VERNON LEE. Two vols. Small
crown 8vo., cloth, 12s.
" To discuss it properly would require more space than a single number of ' The
Academy ' could afford. —*Academy.*
" Est agréable à lire et fait penser."—*Revue des deux Mondes.*

Baldwin : Dialogues on Views and Aspirations. By VERNON LEE. Demy 8vo., cloth, 12s.

" The dialogues are written with . . . . an intellectual courage which shrinks from no logical conclusion."—*Scotsman.*

Ottilie : An Eighteenth Century Idyl. By VERNON LEE. Square 8vo., cloth extra, 3s. 6d.

" A graceful little sketch. . . . Drawn with full insight into the period described."—*Spectator.*

The Fleet : Its River, Prison, and Marriages. By JOHN ASHTON, Author of " Social Life in the Reign of Queen Anne," &c. With 70 Drawings by the Author from Original Pictures. Demy 8vo., cloth elegant, 21s. Cheaper Edition, 7s. 6d.

Romances of Chivalry : Told and Illustrated in Fac-simile by JOHN ASHTON. Forty-six Illustrations. Demy 8vo., cloth elegant, gilt tops, 18s.

" The result (of the reproduction of the wood blocks) is as creditable to his artistic, as the text is to his literary, ability."—*Guardian.*

The Dawn of the Nineteenth Century in

England : A Social Sketch of the Times. By JOHN ASHTON. Cheaper Edition, in one vol. Illustrated. Large crown 8vo., 10s. 6d.

" The book is one continued source of pleasure and interest, and opens up a wide field for speculation and comment, and many of us will look upon it as an important contribution to contemporary history, not easily available to others than close students."—*Antiquary.*

Legends and Popular Tales of the Basque

People. By MARIANA MONTEIRO. With Illustrations by HAROLD COPPING. Popular Edition. Crown 8vo., cloth, gilt edges, 6s.

" In every respect this comely volume is a notable addition to the shelf devoted to folk-lore . . . . and the pictures in photogravure nobly interpret the text."—*Critic.*

Heroic Tales. Retold from Firdusi the Persian. By HELEN ZIMMERN. With Etchings by L. ALMA TADEMA. Popular Edition. Crown 8vo., cloth extra, 5s.

" Charming from beginning to end. . . . Miss Zimmern deserves all credit for her courage in attempting the task, and for her marvellous success in carrying it out."—*Saturday Review.*

Pilgrim Sorrow. By CARMEN SYLVA (The Queen of Roumania). Translated by HELEN ZIMMERN. Portrait-etching by LALAUZE. Square crown 8vo., cloth extra, 5s.

"A strain of sadness runs through the delicate thought and fancy of the Queen of Roumania. Her popularity as an author is already great in Germany, and this little work will win her a place in many English hearts."—*Standard.*

The Poison Tree : A Tale of Hindu Life in Bengal. By B. CHANDRA CHATTERJEE. Introduction by Sir EDWIN ARNOLD, M.A., K.C.S.I. Crown 8vo., cloth, 6s.

"This is a work of real genius. . . . As a picture of the social life of the Hindus it cannot but be regarded as masterly."—*British Quarterly Review.*

The Touchstone of Peril : A Tale of the Indian Mutiny. By DUDLEY HARDRESS THOMAS. Second edition. Crown 8vo., cloth, 6s.

"'The Touchstone of Peril' is the best Anglo-Indian novel that has appeared for some years."—*Times of India.*

The Amazon : An Art Novel. By CARL VOSMAER. Preface by Prof. GEORG EBERS, and Frontispiece specially drawn by L. ALMA TADEMA, R.A. Crown 8vo., cloth, 6s.

"It is a work full of deep, suggestive thought."—*Academy.*

The Temple : Sacred Poems and Private Ejaculations. By Mr. GEORGE HERBERT. New and fourth edition, with Introductory Essay by J. HENRY SHORTHOUSE. Small crown, sheep, 5s.

A fac-simile reprint of the Original Edition of 1633.
"This charming reprint has a fresh value added to it by the Introductory Essay of the Author of 'John Inglesant.'"—*Academy.*

Songs, Ballads, and A Garden Play. By A. MARY F. ROBINSON, Author of "An Italian Garden." With Frontispiece of Dürer's "Melencolia." Small crown 8vo., half bound, vellum, 5s.

"The romantic ballads have grace, movement, passion and strength."—*Spectator.*
"Marked by sweetness of melody and truth of colour."—*Academy.*

An Italian Garden : A Book of Songs. By A. MARY F. ROBINSON. Fcap. 8vo., parchment, 3s. 6d.

"They are most of them exquisite in form."—*Pall Mall Gazette.*
"Full of elegance and even tenderness."—*Spectator.*

The Sentence : A Drama. By AUGUSTA WEBSTER, Author of "In a Day," &c. Small crown 8vo., cloth, 4s. 6d.

" The working-out of this tragical theme is nothing less than masterly."
Pall Mall Gazette.

The Lazy Minstrel. By J. ASHBY-STERRY, Author of " Boudoir Ballads." Fourth and Popular Edition. Frontispiece by E. A. ABBEY. Fcap. 8vo., cloth, 2s. 6d.

"One of the lightest and brightest writers of vers de société."
St. James's Gazette.

The New Purgatory, and other Poems. By ELIZABETH RACHEL CHAPMAN, Author of "A Comtist Lover," &c. Square imperial 16mo., cloth, 4s. 6d.

"There is not one of the poems that does not bear the sign manual of genius."
Inquirer

Introductory Studies in Greek Art. Delivered in the British Museum by JANE E. HARRISON. With Illustrations. Square imperial 16mo., 7s. 6d.

"The best work of its kind in English."—*Oxford Magazine.*

Jewish Portraits. By LADY MAGNUS. With Frontispiece by HARRY FURNISS. Small crown 8vo., cloth, 5s.

" We owe much gratitude to the author for a very delightful book."
Manchester Examiner.

Gladys Fane. By T. WEMYSS REID. Fifth edition. (Unwin's Novel Series.) Small crown 8vo., 2s.

" The author of the delightful monograph on ' Charlotte Brontë' has given us in this volume a story as beautiful as life and as sad as death."—*Standard.*

Mrs. Keith's Crime. By Mrs. W. KINGDON CLIFFORD. (Unwin's Novel Series.) Second edition. Small crown 8vo., 2s.

Concerning Oliver Knox. By G. COLMORE. (Unwin's Novel Series.) Small crown 8vo., 2s.

History.

The End of the Middle Ages : Essays and Questions
in History. By A. MARY F. ROBINSON (Madame Darmesteter). Demy 8vo., cloth, 10s. 6d.

A Series of Essays on chapters in French and Italian History—"The Claim of the House of Orleans," "Valentine Visconti," "The Convent of Helfta," "The Schism," "The French in Italy," "The Attraction of the Abyss," and other Studies.

The Federalist : A Commentary in the Form of Essays on the United States Constitution.
By ALEXANDER HAMILTON, and others. Edited by HENRY CABOT LODGE. Demy 8vo., Roxburgh binding, 10s. 6d.

"The importance of the Essays can hardly be exaggerated. . . . They are undoubtedly a great work upon the general subject of political federation ; and the education of no student of politics in our own country can be considered complete who has not mastered the treatise of Alexander Hamilton."—*Glasgow Mail.*

The Government Year Book : A Record of the Forms and
Methods of Government in Great Britain, her Colonies, and Foreign Countries, 1889. Crown 8vo., cloth, 6s.

"Mr. Lewis Sergeant has most admirably performed his task."—*Athenæum.*
"The book fills a gap which has been frequently noticed by every politician, journalist, and economist."—*Journal des Debats.*

The Making of the Great West, 1512-1853. By SAMUEL
ADAMS DRAKE. One hundred and forty-five Illustrations. Large crown 8vo., 9s.

The Making of New England, 1580-1643. By SAMUEL
ADAMS DRAKE. Illustrated. Crown 8vo., cloth, 5s.

"It is clearly and pleasantly written, and copiously illustrated."
Pall Mall Budget.

The Story of the Nations.

Crown 8vo., Illustrated, and furnished with Maps and Indexes, each 5s.

"L'interessante serie l'Histoire des Nations formera . . . un cours d'histoire universelle d'une très grande valeur."—*Journal des Debats.*
"The remarkable series."—*New York Critic.*
"That useful series."—*The Times.*
"An admirable series."—*Spectator.*
"That excellent series."—*Guardian.*
"The series is likely to be found indispensable in every school library."
"This valuable series."—*Nonconformist.* *Pall Mall Gazette.*
"Admirable series of historical monographs."—*Echo.*

Rome. By ARTHUR GILMAN, M.A., Author of "A History of the American People," &c. Third edition.
"The author succeeds admirably in reproducing the 'Grandeur that was Rome.'"—*Sydney Morning Herald.*

The Jews. In Ancient, Mediæval, and Modern Times. By Prof. J. K. HOSMER. Second edition.
"The book possesses much of the interest, the suggestiveness, and the charm of romance."—*Saturday Review.*

Germany. By Rev. S. BARING-GOULD, Author of "Curious Myths of the Middle Ages," &c. Second edition.
"Mr. Baring-Gould tells his stirring tale with knowledge and perspicuity. He is a thorough master of his subject."—*Globe.*

Carthage. By Prof. ALFRED J. CHURCH, Author of "Stories from the Classics," &c. Second edition.
"A masterly outline with vigorous touches in detail here and there."—*Guardian.*

Alexander's Empire. By Prof. J. P. MAHAFFY, Author of "Social Life in Greece." Second edition.
"A wonderful success."—*Spectator.*

The Moors in Spain. By STANLEY LANE-POOLE, Author of "Studies in a Mosque." Second edition.
"The best, the fullest, the most accurate, and most readable history of the Moors in Spain for general readers."—*St. James's Gazette.*

Ancient Egypt. By Prof. GEO. RAWLINSON, Author of "The Five Great Monarchies of the World." Second edition.
"The story is told of the land, people and rulers, with vivid colouring and consummate literary skill."—*New York Critic.*

B 2

Hungary. By Prof. ARMINIUS VAMBÉRY, Author of "Travels in Central Asia." Second edition.

"The volume which he has contributed to 'The Story of the Nations' will be generally considered one of the most interesting and picturesque of that useful series."—*Times.*

The Saracens: From the Earliest Times to the Fall of Bagdad. By ARTHUR GILMAN, M.A., Author of "Rome," &c.

"Le livre de M. Gilman est destiné à être lu avidement par un grand nombre de gens pour lesquels l'étude des nombreux ouvrages déjà parus serait impossible." *Journal des Debats.*

Ireland. By the Hon. EMILY LAWLESS, Author of "Hurrish." Second edition.

"We owe thanks to Miss Emily for this admirable volume, in some respects the very best of 'The Story of the Nations' series as yet published."—*Nonconformist.*

Chaldea. By Z. A. RAGOZIN, Author of "Assyria," &c.

"One of the most interesting numbers of the series in which it appears." *Scotsman.*

The Goths. By HENRY BRADLEY.

"Seems to us to be as accurate as it is undoubtedly clear, strong, and simple; and it will give to the reader an excellent idea of the varied fortunes of the two great branches of the Gothic nation."—THOMAS HODGKIN *in The Academy.*

Assyria: From the Rise of the Empire to the Fall of Nineveh. By ZÉNAÏDE A. RAGOZIN, Author of "Chaldea," &c.

"Madame Ragozin has performed her task in it as admirably as she has done in her earlier volume on 'Chaldea.' She has spared no pains in collecting the latest and best information on the subject."—*Extract from Letter from* PROF. SAYCE.

Turkey. By STANLEY LANE-POOLE, Author of "The Moors in Spain," &c.

"All the events of the strange and adventurous history are sketched in vigorous boldness of outline, and with fine force of style."—*Scotsman.*

Holland. By Professor THOROLD ROGERS.

"It was a happy thought to entrust the telling of the story of 'Holland' to so great an industrial enthusiast as Prof. Thorold Rogers."—*Literary World.*

Mediæval France. By GUSTAVE MASSON.

Persia. By S. G. W. BENJAMIN.

Phœnicia. By CANON RAWLINSON.

𝕭iography.

Life & Times of Girolamo Savonarola.
By Pasquale Villari. Translated by Linda Villari. Portraits and Illusts. Two vols. Demy 8vo., cloth, 32s. This new translation of Villari's "Savonarola" by Madame Villari contains much additional matter, and is fuller and completer than the last published Italian edition. The biography is illustrated with many portraits of famous men of the times.

Francis Bacon (Lord Verulam): A Critical Review of
his Life and Character, with Selections from his Writings. By B. G. Lovejoy, A.M., LL.B. Crown 8vo., half-bound cloth, gilt top, 6s.
"Is, perhaps, the most readable and incisive sketch of Lord Bacon's career and character that has yet been written."—*Christian Leader.*

Anne Gilchrist: Her Life and Writings. Edited by Herbert Harlakenden Gilchrist.
Prefatory Notice by William Michael Rossetti. Second edition. Twelve Illustrations. Demy 8vo., cloth, 16s.
" Here we find a kind, friendly, and humorous, if splenetic Carlyle ; a helpful and merry Mrs. Carlyle ; and a friendly and unaffected Dante Gabriel Rossetti. These characteristics, so unlike the Carlyle of the too copious memoirs, so unlike the Mrs. Carlyle, the *femme incomprise*, so unlike the Rossetti of myth, are extremely welcome."—*Daily News* (Leader).

Charles Dickens as I knew Him: The Story of the
Reading Tours in Great Britain and America (1866-1870). By George Dolby. New and cheaper edition. Crown 8vo., 3s. 6d.
" It will be welcome to all lovers of Dickens for Dickens' own sake."—*Athenæum.*

Charles Whitehead: A Critical Monograph. By H. T. Mackenzie Bell. Cheap
and Popular edition. Crown 8vo., cloth, 5s.
"Mr. Mackenzie Bell has done a good service in introducing to us a man of true genius, whose works have sunk into mysteriously swift and complete oblivion."
Contemporary Review.

Ole Bull : A Memoir. By SARA C. BULL. With Ole Bull's "Violin Notes" and Dr. A. B. Crosby's "Anatomy of the Violinist." Portraits. Second edition. Crown 8vo., cloth, 7s. 6d.

" A fresh, delightful, and charming book."—*Graphic.*

Johannes Brahms : A Biographical Sketch. By Dr. HERMAN DEITERS. Translated, with additions, by ROSA NEWMARCH. Edited, with a Preface, by J. A. FULLER MAITLAND. Portrait. Small crown 8vo., cloth, 6s.

" An original and excellent little study of the composer."—*Saturday Review.*

The Lives of Robert and Mary Moffat.
By their Son, JOHN SMITH MOFFAT. Sixth edition. Portraits, Illustrations, and Maps. Crown 8vo., cloth, 7s. 6d. ; Presentation Edition, full gilt elegant, bevelled boards, gilt edges, in box, 10s. 6d. ; Popular Edition, crown 8vo., 3s. 6d.

" An inspiring record of calm, brave, wise work, and will find a place of value on the honoured shelf of missionary biography. The biographer has done his work with reverent care, and in a straightforward, unaffected style."
Contemporary Review.

The German Emperor and Empress :
The Late Frederick III. and Victoria. The Story of their Lives. (Being the Sixth and Popular Edition of "Two Royal Lives," 7s. 6d.) By DOROTHEA ROBERTS. Portraits. Crown 8vo., cloth, 2s. 6d.

" A book sure to be popular in domestic circles."—*The Graphic.*

Arminius Vamb´ry : His Life and Adventures. Written by Himself. With Portrait and Fourteen Illustrations. Fifth and Popular Edition. Square Imperial 16mo., cloth extra, 6s.

" The work is written in a most captivating manner."—*Novoe Vremya, Moscow.*

Henry Irving : In England and America, 1838-1884. By FREDERIC DALY. Vignette Portrait by AD. LALAUZE. Second Thousand. Crown 8vo., cloth extra, 5s.

" A very interesting account of the career of the great actor."
British Quarterly Review.

Theology and Philosophy.

The House and Its Builder, with Other Discourses :
A Book for the Doubtful. By Dr. SAMUEL COX.
Small crown 8vo., paper, 2s. 6d. ; cloth, 3s.

" Expositions." By the same Author. First Series. Third Thousand. Demy 8vo., cloth, 7s. 6d.

"We have said enough to show our high opinion of Dr. Cox's volume. It is indeed full of suggestion. . . . A valuable volume."—*The Spectator.*

" Expositions." By the same Author. Second Series. Second Thousand. Demy 8vo., cloth, 7s. 6d.

"Here, too, we have the clear exegetical insight, the lucid expository style, the chastened but effective eloquence, the high ethical standpoint, which secured for the earlier series a well-nigh unanimous award of commendation."—*Academy.*

" Expositions." By the same Author. Third Series. Second edition. Demy 8vo., cloth, 7s. 6d.

"When we say that the volume possesses all the intellectual, moral, and spiritual characteristics which have won for its author so distinguished a place among the religious teachers of our time . . . what further recommendation can be necessary ?"—*Nonconformist.*

" Expositions." By the same Author. Fourth Series (completing the Set). Demy 8vo., cloth, 7s. 6d.

"The volume is one of the most interesting and valuable that we have received from Dr. Cox. It contains some of the strongest analytical character-sketching he has ever produced."—*Glasgow Mail.*

Present-Day Questions in Theology and

Religion. By the Rev. J. GUINNESS ROGERS, B.A. Cloth, 3s. 6d.

Contents.—I. The "Down Grade" Controversy.—II. Congregationalism and its Critics.—III. Modern Thought.—IV. Broad Evangelicals.—V. Progressive Theology.—VI. Jesus the Christ.—VII. Creed and Conduct.—VIII. Evangelical Preaching.—IX. The Church and the World.—X. Congregationalism of To-day.

The Risen Christ : The King of Men. By the late Rev. J. BALDWIN BROWN, M.A.,

Author of "The Home Life," &c. Crown 8vo., cloth, 7s. 6d.

"We have again felt in reading these nervous, spiritual, and eloquent sermons, how great a preacher has passed away."—*Nonconformist.*

Christian Facts and Forces. By the Rev. NEWMAN SMYTH, Author of

"The Reality of Faith." New edition. Crown 8vo., cloth, 4s. 6d.

"An able and suggestive series of discourses."—*Nonconformist.*
"These sermons abound in noble and beautiful teaching clearly and eloquently expressed."—*Christian.*

Inspiration and the Bible : An Inquiry. By ROBERT HORTON,

M.A., formerly Fellow of New College, Oxford. Second and Cheaper Edition. Crown 8vo., cloth, 3s. 6d.

"The work displays much earnest thought, and a sincere belief in, and love of the Bible."—*Morning Post.*
"It will be found to be a good summary, written in no iconoclastic spirit, but with perfect candour and fairness, of some of the more important results of recent Biblical criticism."—*Scotsman.*

Faint, yet Pursuing. By the Rev. E. J. HARDY, Author of "How to be Happy

though Married." Sq. imp. 16mo., cloth, 6s. Cheaper Edition, 3s. 6d.

"One of the most practical and readable volumes of sermons ever published. They must have been eminently hearable."—*British Weekly.*

The Meditations and Maxims of Koheleth.

A Practical Exposition of the Book of Ecclesiastes. By Rev. T. CAMPBELL FINLAYSON. Crown 8vo., 6s.

"A thoughtful and practical commentary on a book of Holy Scripture which needs much spiritual wisdom for its exposition. . . . Sound and judicious handling."—*Rock*

The Pharaohs of the Bondage and the

Exodus. Lectures by CHARLES S. ROBINSON, D.D., LL.D.
Second edition. Large crown 8vo., cloth, 5s.

"Both lectures are conceived in a very earnest spirit, and are developed with much dignity and force. We have the greatest satisfaction in commending it to the attention of Biblical students and Christian ministers."—*Literary World*.

A Short Introduction to the History of

Ancient Israel. By the Rev. A. W. OXFORD, M.A., Vicar of St. Luke's, Berwick Street, Soho, Editor of "The Berwick Hymnal," &c. Crown 8vo., cloth, 3s. 6d.

" We can testify to the great amount of labour it represents."—*Literary World*.

The Reality of Religion. By HENRY J. VAN DYKE, Junr., D.D., of the

Brick Church, N.Y. Second edition. Crown 8vo., cloth, 4s. 6d.

" An able and eloquent review of the considerations on which the writer rests his belief in Christianity, and an impassioned statement of the strength of this belief."
Scotsman.

The Reality of Faith. By the Rev. NEWMAN SMYTH, D.D., Author of " Old Faiths

in New Light." Fourth and cheaper edition. Crown 8vo., cloth, 4s. 6d.

" They are fresh and beautiful expositions of those deep things, those foundation truths, which underlie Christian faith and spiritual life in their varied manifestations."—*Christian Age*.

A Layman's Study of the English Bible

Considered in its Literary and Secular Aspects. By FRANCIS BOWEN, LL.D. Crown 8vo., cloth, 4s. 6d.

" Most heartily do we recommend this little volume to the careful study, not only of those whose faith is not yet fixed and settled, but of those whose love for it and reliance on it grows with their growing years."—*Nonconformist*.

The Parousia. A Critical Inquiry into the New Testament Doctrine of Our Lord's

Second Coming. By the Rev. J. S. RUSSELL, M.A. New and cheaper edition. Demy 8vo., cloth, 7s. 6d.

" Critical, in the best sense of the word. Unlike many treatises on the subject, this is a sober and reverent investigation, and abounds in a careful and instructive exegesis of every passage bearing upon it."—*Nonconformist*.

The Ethic of Freethought : A Selection of Essays and Lectures. By

KARL PEARSON, M.A., formerly Fellow of King's College, Cambridge. Demy 8vo., cloth, 12s.

"Are characterised by much learning, much keen and forcible thinking, and a fearlessness of denunciation and exposition."—*Scotsman.*

Descartes and His School. By KUNO FISCHER. Translated from the

Third and Revised German Edition by J. P. GORDY, Ph.D. Edited by NOAH PORTER, D.D., LL.D. Demy 8vo., cloth, 16s.

"A valuable addition to the literature of Philosophy."—*Scotsman.*
"No greater service could be done to English and American students than to give them a trustworthy rendering of Kuno Fischer's brilliant expositions."—*Mind.*

Socrates : A Translation of the Apology, Crito, and Parts of the Phædo of Plato. 12mo., cloth, 3s. 6d.

"The translation is clear and elegant."—*Morning Post.*

A Day in Athens with Socrates : Translations from the

Protagoras and the Republic of Plato. 12mo., cloth, 3s. 6d.

"We can commend these volumes to the English reader, as giving him what he wants—the Socratic . . . philosophy at first hand, with a sufficiency of explanatory and illustrative comment."—*Pall Mall Gazette.*

Talks with Socrates about Life : Translations from the

Gorgias and the Republic of Plato. 12mo., cloth, 3s. 6d.

"A real service is rendered to the general reader who has no Greek, and to whom the two ancient philosophers are only names, by the publication of these three inviting little volumes. . . . Every young man who is forming a library ought to add them to his collection."—*Christian Leader.*

Natural Causation. An Essay in Four Parts. By C. E. PLUMPTRE, Author of "General

Sketch of the History of Pantheism," &c. Demy 8vo., cloth, 7s. 6d.

"While many will find in this volume much from which they will dissent, there is in it a great deal that is deserving of careful consideration, and a great deal that is calculated to stimulate thought."—*Scotsman.*

Proverbs, Maxims, and Phrases of all Ages.

Classified subjectively and arranged alphabetically. By ROBERT CHRISTY. Two vols. Large crown 8vo., Roxburgh, gilt tops, 21s.

Travel.

R anch Life and the Hunting Trail.

By THEODORE ROOSEVELT, Author of "Hunting Trips of a Ranchman." Profusely Illustrated. Small 4to., cloth elegant, 21s.

The contents consist of the articles on Ranch Life in the Far West, which have been appearing in *The Century Magazine*, combined with much additional matter which the author has prepared for the book, rounding it out (especially in the chapters on hunting) and making it complete as a record of the ranchman's life in the cattle country, and on the hunting trail. The illustrations are the work of a ranchman, and are true to life.

Rides and Studies in the Canary Isles.

By CHARLES EDWARDES. With many Illustrations and Maps. Crown 8vo., cloth, 10s. 6d.

Guatemala : The Land of the Quetzal. By WILLIAM· T. BRIGHAM. Twenty-six full-page and Seventy-nine smaller Illustrations. Five Maps. Demy 8vo., cloth, £1 1s.

"A book of laborious research, keen observation, and accurate information concerning a region about which previously scarcely anything was known."
Leeds Mercury.

A Summer's Cruise in the Waters of

Greece, Turkey, and Russia. By ALFRED COLBECK. Frontispiece. Crown 8vo., cloth, 10s. 6d.

The Decline of British Prestige in the

East. By SELIM FARIS, Editor of the Arabic "El-Jawaïb" of Constantinople. Crown 8vo., cloth, 5s.

"A perusal of his book must do the English reader good."
Asiatic Quarterly Review.

Daily Life in India. By the Rev. W. J. WILKINS. Illustrated. Crown 8vo., cloth, 5s.

"A very able book."—*Guardian.*

Modern Hinduism : An Account of the Religion and Life of the Hindus in Northern India. By Rev. W. J. WILKINS. Demy 8vo., cloth, 16s.

"A solid addition to our literature."— *Westminster Review.*
"A valuable contribution to knowledge."—*Scotsman.*
"A valuable contribution to the study of a very difficult subject."—*Madras Mail.*

Central Asian Questions : Essays on Afghanistan, China, and Central Asia. By DEMETRIUS C. BOULGER. With Portrait and Three Maps. Demy 8vo., cloth, 18s.

"A mine of valuable information."—*Times.*   [*Mail.*
"A mine of information on all 'Central Asian Questions.'"—*Allen's Indian*
"A very valuable contribution to our literature on subjects of vast and increasing interest.' —*Collum's United Service Magazine.*

The Balkan Peninsula. By EMILE DE LAVELEYE. Translated by Mrs. THORPE. Edited and Revised for the English Public by the Author. Map. Demy 8vo., cloth, 16s.

"A lucid and impartial view of the situation in the East."—*St. James's Gazette .*
"Likely to be very useful at the present time, as it is one of the best books on the subject."—*Saturday Review.*

Tuscan Studies and Sketches. By LEADER SCOTT, Author of " A Nook in the Apennines," " Messer Agnolo's Household," &c. Many Full-page and smaller Illustrations. Sq. imp. 16mo., cloth, 10s. 6d.

"The sketches are of that happy kind which appeal to the learned through their style, and to the simple through their subjects."—*Truth.*

Letters from Italy. By EMILE DE LAVELEYE. Translated by Mrs. THORPE. Revised by the Author. Portrait of the Author. Crown 8vo., 6s.

"A most delightful volume."—*Nonconformist.*
"Every page is pleasantly and brightly written."—*Times.*

Miscellaneous.

Industrial Rivers of the United Kingdom. By various well-known Experts. With numerous Illustrations. Crown 8vo., cloth, 7s. 6d.

These Chapters are not confined to the commerce and industries which characterise the great rivers: the history of each stream is traced from the earliest times. The foundation of the trade and manufactures which distinguish the several ports and districts are noticed ; and the improvement of the rivers and harbours, and the development of the trade and commerce, up to the latest possible period, are dealt with at length.

Crime : Its Causes and Remedy. By L. GORDON RYLANDS, B.A. (Lond.) Crown 8vo., cloth, 6s.

A treatise on crime and its causes, presenting many interesting statistics and tables on its fluctuations, and suggesting remedies and a new method of meeting it.

The Five Talents of Woman. A Book for Girls and Young Women. By the Rev. E. J. HARDY, Author of "How to be Happy though Married," &c. Sq. Imperial 16mo., cloth, 6s. ; Presentation Edition, bevelled boards, gilt edges, in box, 7s. 6d.

Contents.—The Five Talents of Woman.—The Power of a Woman's Smile.—How to be a Lady.—Housewife or House-moth.—A Centre of Order.—Woman's Work : to Teach.—Between School and Marriage.—Choosing a Husband.—Helpful Wives.—The Influence of a Wife.—Pets or Pests ?—Daughterfull Houses—for what ?—How to be Happy though Single.—Nurses and Nursing.—Daughters and Sisters.—Woman's Letters.—Woman's Studies.—A Girl's Religion.—Woman's Recreations.

How to be Happy though Married. Small crown 8vo., cloth, 3s. 6d. Bridal Gift Edition, white vellum cloth, extra gilt, bev. boards, gilt edges, in box, 7s.6d.

" We strongly recommend this book as one of the best of wedding presents. It is a complete handbook to an earthly Paradise, and its author may be regarded as the Murray of Matrimony and the Baedeker of Bliss."—*Pall Mall Gazette.*

" Manners Makyth Man." By the Author of " How to be Happy though Married." Popular Edition, small crown 8vo., cloth, 3s. 6d. ; imp. 16mo., cloth, 6s. Presentation Edition, imp. 16mo., cloth, bevelled edges, in box, 7s. 6d.

The Theory of Law and Civil Society.

By Augustus Pulszky (Dr. Juris), Professor of Law at Budapest. Demy 8vo., cloth, 18s.

"The book is in our opinion a contribution of unusual importance to the theory of law and the state."—*Westminster Review.*

Representative British Orations. With Introductions, &c.,

by Chas. K. Adams. 16mo., Roxburgh, gilt tops, 3 vols., in cloth box, 15s. The volumes may also be had without box, 13s. 6d.

"The notes are extremely useful, and contribute largely to making the work one of value to students of political history."—*Pall Mall Gazette.*

Jottings from Jail. Notes and Papers on Prison Matters.

By the Rev. J. W. Horsley, M.A., Oxon., late (and last) Chaplain of H.M. Prison, Clerkenwell. Second edition. Crown 8vo., cloth, 3s. 6d.

"The jottings are full of vivacity and shrewd common sense, and their author, amid uncongenial surroundings, has preserved a keen sense of humour."—*Echo.*

Literary Landmarks of London. By Laurence Hutton.

Fourth, revised, and cheaper edition. Crown 8vo., Illustrated cover, 2s. 6d. ; cloth gilt, 7s. 6d.

"He has made himself an invaluable *valet de place* to the lover of literary London."—*Atlantic Monthly.*

About the Theatre : Essays and Studies. By William Archer. Crown 8vo., cloth,

bevelled edges, 7s. 6d.

"Theatrical subjects, from the Censorship of the Stage to the most recent phenomena of first nights, have thoroughly able and informed discussion in Mr. Archer's handsome book."—*Contemporary Review.*

English as She is Taught. Genuine Answers to Examination Questions

in our Public Schools. With a Commentary by Mark Twain. Demy 16mo., cloth, 2s. ; parchment, 1s.

Mark Twain says : "A darling literary curiosity. . . . This little book ought to set forty millions of people to thinking."

Books for Children.

Æsop's Fables for Little Readers:
Told by Mrs. ARTHUR BROOKFIELD. Twenty-five Illustrations by HENRY J. FORD. Small 4to., cloth, 3s.6d.

"In their present shape, the fables should be very popular among the inmates of the nursery, more particularly as they are illustrated with nearly thirty clever drawings by Henry Ford, which are beautifully printed in monochrome."
Scottish Leader.

Six Girls.
A Home Story. By FANNIE BELL IRVING. Illustrated by F. T. MERRILL. Crown 8vo., cloth, 5s.

"The six main characters are drawn carefully, and well differentiated. The book has many a touch of simple pathos, and many a passage of light-hearted high spirits."—*Scotsman.*

The Brownies : Their Book.
With all the Original Pictures and Poems by PALMER COX, as published in *St. Nicholas*, and with many new Pictures. Second Edition. Medium 4to., cloth, 6s.

"Never, perhaps, has a book been published better calculated to afford unlimited amusement to little people than 'The Brownies.'"—*Rock.*

New Fairy Tales from Brentano.
Told in English by KATE FREILIGRATH KROEKER, and Pictured by F. CARRUTHERS GOULD. Eight Full-page Coloured Illustrations. Square 8vo., illustrated, paper boards, cloth back, 5s. ; cloth, gilt edges, 6s.

"A really charming collection of stories."—*Pall Mall Gazette.*

Fairy Tales from Brentano. Told in English by KATE FREILIGRATH

KROEKER. Illustrated by F. CARRUTHERS GOULD. Popular Edition. Sq. imp. 16mo., 3s. 6d.

" An admirable translator in Madame Kroeker, and an inimitable illustrator in Mr. Carruthers Gould."—*Truth.*

In the Time of Roses : A Tale of Two Summers. Told and Illustrated by

FLORENCE and EDITH SCANNELL, Author and Artist of " Sylvia's Daughters." Thirty-two Full-page and other Illustrations. Sq. imp. 16mo., cloth, 5s.

" A very charming story."—*Scotsman.*
" A delightful story."—*Punch.*

Prince Peerless : A Fairy-Folk Story-Book. By the Hon. MARGARET COLLIER (Madame

Galletti di Cadilhac), Author of " Our Home by the Adriatic." Illustrated by the Hon. JOHN COLLIER. Sq. imp. 16mo., cloth, 5s.

" Delightful in style and fancy."—*Scotsman.*
" A volume of charming stories."—*Saturday Review.*

When I was a Child ; or, Left Behind. By LINDA VILLARI, Author of " On

Tuscan Hills," &c. Illustrated. Square 8vo., cloth, gilt edges, 3s. 6d.

" A finer girl's book could not be had."—*Scotsman.*

The Prince of the Hundred Soups :

A Puppet Show in Narrative. Edited, with a Preface, by VERNON LEE. Illustrated. Cheaper edition. Square 8vo., cloth, 3s. 6d.

"There is more humour in the volume than in half-a-dozen ordinary panto-mimes."—*Spectator.*

Birdsnesting and Bird-Stuffing. A Complete Description of

the Nests and Eggs of Birds which Breed in Britain. By EDWARD NEWMAN. Revised and Re-written, with Direc-tions for their Collection and Preservation ; and with a Chapter on Bird-Stuffing, by MILLER CHRISTY. Crown 8vo., 1s.

The Bird's Nest, and other Sermons for Children of all Ages. By the Rev. Samuel Cox, D.D., Author of "Expositions," &c. Second edition. Imp. 16mo., cloth, 6s.

"These beautiful discourses were addressed to children of all ages, and must have found an echo in the hearts of many youthful listeners."—*St. James's Gazette*

Spring Blossoms and Summer Fruit;

or, Sunday Talks for the Children. By the Rev. John Byles, of Ealing. Crown 8vo., cloth, 2s. 6d.

"They are of simple and instructive character."—*Dundee Advertiser.*

Arminius Vambéry: His Life and Adventures. Written by Himself. With Introductory Chapter dedicated to the Boys of England. Portrait and Seventeen Illustrations. Crown 8vo., 5s.

"We welcome it as one of the best books of travel that our boys could have possibly placed in their hands."—*Schoolmaster.*

Boys' Own Stories. By Ascott R. Hope, Author of "Stories of Young Adventurers," "Stories out of School Time," &c. Eight Illustrations. Crown 8vo., cloth, 5s.

"This is a really admirable selection of genuine narrative and history, treated with discretion and skill by the author. Mr. Hope has not gathered his stores from the highway, but has explored far afield in less-beaten tracts, as may be seen in his 'Adventures of a Ship-boy' and 'A Smith among Savages.' "—*Saturday Review.*

The Adventures of Robinson Crusoe.

Newly Edited after the Original Editions. Nineteen Illustrations. Large crown 8vo., cloth extra, 5s.

The Century Magazine

For 1888-9 *will include :—*

The Century Gallery of Italian Masters,

from the Byzantines to Tintoretto—engraved by TIMOTHY COLE from the original paintings, and accompanied by historical and critical papers by W. J. STILLMAN.

Notes and Studies in Japan.
By JOHN LA FARGE, illustrated with engravings from original studies by the artist.

Ireland :
Studies of its People, Customs, Landscape, Town Life, Literature and Arts.

A Series of Irish-American Stories,
both humorous and pathetic; each complete in itself, but having a connected interest.

Kennan in Siberia.
Mr. GEORGE KENNAN's Siberian articles, illustrated with sketches and photographs taken by GEORGE A. FROST, will contain, from November on, what the author believes to be the best and most striking of all his material.

Price 1s. 4d. *Monthly. Post free,* 19s. *a Year.*

St. Nicholas,

Conducted by MARY MAPES DODGE.

AN " ALL-AROUND THE WORLD" YEAR.

St. Nicholas for the coming year will tell English boys and girls of the thousands of millions of children of other countries : of French girls in their little black alpaca aprons, and German girls with their flaxen hair, and Italian boys with their dark eyes, and clever American children (the cleverest take in *St. Nicholas*), and little Chinese maidens, with their almond-eyes and long pig-tails, and woolly-headed African pickaninnies. Of the homes of all these children, of the toys of the shy Japanese, of the pine woods of the blue-eyed Norwegians, of the furs and toboganning of the Canadians, of the gum trees and kangaroos of the Australians, of the sharks and clear blue seas of the chocolate-skinned South-Sea Islanders—in fact, of nearly everything that amuses girls and interests boys, from the nursery rhymes of the Hottentot mothers to the guns and spears that the Icelandic fathers use to kill the white bears, *St. Nicholas* means to tell its readers in Great Britain and Ireland.

Price 1s. *Monthly. Post free,* 14s. *a Year.*

LONDON : T. FISHER UNWIN, 26, PATERNOSTER SQUARE.

www.ingramcontent.com/pod-product-compliance
Lightning Source LLC
Chambersburg PA
CBHW020810060726
47498CB00017B/1401